Boundaries

Boundaries

FARIDA KARODIA

PENGUIN BOOKS

PENGUIN BOOKS

Published by the Penguin Group
80 Strand, London WC2R 0RL, England
Penguin Putnam Inc, 375 Hudson Street, New York, New York 10014, USA
Penguin Books Australia Ltd, Ringwood, Victoria, Australia
Penguin Books Canada Ltd, 10 Alcorn Avenue, Toronto, Ontario,
Canada M4V 3B2
Penguin Books (NZ) Ltd, Cnr Rosedale and Airborne Roads, Albany,
Auckland, New Zealand
Penguin Books India (P) Ltd, 11 Community Centre, Panchsheel Park,
New Delhi – 110 017, India
Penguin Books (South Africa) (Pty) Ltd, 24 Sturdee Avenue, Rosebank,
Johannesburg 2196, South Africa

Penguin Books (South Africa) (Pty) Ltd, Registered Offices:
Second Floor, 90 Rivonia Road, Sandton 2196, South Africa

First published by Penguin Books (South Africa) (Pty) Ltd 2003

ISBN 0 143 02432 9

Typeset by CJH Design in 10.5 on 12.5pt Sabon
Cover painting: Boyd Brockman
Printed and bound by CTP Book Printers, Duminy Street, Parow,
Cape Town, South Africa

Boundaries is a work of fiction. Any resemblance of any character to any
person alive or dead is entirely coincidental.

I dedicate this book to my mother,
an astonishing woman.

Acknowledgements

My grateful appreciation the National Arts Council of South Africa for their assistance.

I also wish to thank A World of Words and the Hedgebrook Foundation for inviting me to Whidbey Island for three weeks of blissful residency.

To my friends who listened endlessly: Liv Beck and Diane Cherney in Canada and Ursula Alberts for her wisdom and spiritual advice. To all the friends at Hedgebrook who gave me advice and valuable criticism and especially to Lucrecia Guerrero and to Nancy Osa for her continued friendship and support. To RMP for his valuable input. To my friends in South Africa whose brains I constantly picked for information: Christine and Danny Madden, to Sandi van Niekerk for her encouragement and to Ursula Johnson whose belief is so incredibly unshakeable. To all the others who listened on the golf course – many thanks. My thanks, too, to Alison Lowry and Pam Thornley at Penguin Books in South Africa.

If one had to isolate a single event that marked the turning point in the Vlenterhoek Saga, it could have been any one of several incidents: the discovery of a body in the veld, the return of three of Vlenterhoek's former residents, the arrival of a development company, or the arrival of a film company. No one, however, could say with any certainty whether one of these, or all of these, or none of these events were responsible for catapulting this insignificant town into international headlines.

Tucked away in the ridges and folds of a hilly plateau in the northern regions of South Africa, the town of Vlenterhoek lay, like a precious stone, glistening in the sun. Off the beaten track, it was undiscovered and underpopulated.

The town had a relatively mild climate; the air was clear and exhilarating – except for six weeks in summer when it crackled like oven-breath and waves of blistering heat rose off the hot tarmac. If conditions were right, some said, you could cook an egg on the surface of the main street. As far as anyone knew, no one had tested this theory. But it was a good topic for idle speculation on those sweltering days when residents simply sat around, drained of fresh ideas.

Most of the older residents, including the one surviving

centenarian, bore the heat with remarkable stoicism, languishing indoors during the hottest hours of the day while the town's youth, in dwindling numbers, hung out on the veranda at the Glory Café.

At the entrance to the town a rusted signboard proclaimed WELCOME TO VLENTERHOEK. The main street was part of the national road. It was twelve blocks long and formed the boundary between the *whites* and the *blacks*. At one of the intersections a solitary traffic light blinked its programmed signal. The green light-cover had been smashed some years before by celebrating high school graduates and had never been replaced.

The Vlenterhoek Filling Station, Pep Store, Portuguese Buy & Save, bank, lawyer's office, post office, Cash & Carry, Glory Café, Imperial Hotel and the Dutch Reformed Church sprouted along the main street like dust-bloated cacti.

The post office, an old sandstone structure built by the first Vlenterhoek settlers, remained as a proud tribute to the town's heritage. In the absence of a breeze, the new South African flag, recently hoisted to replace the old one, hung flaccidly from the white pole. In the bar of the Imperial Hotel snide analogies were made about the white flagpole representing the Afrikaner nation and the limp flag the new South Africa.

Development in the small town had taken place only along one side of the main road. On the other side were a couple of dilapidated houses and a *sloot* separated the town from the Location, an area designated for Africans during the apartheid years. Even after the country's first democratic elections brought a black government to power, much of the town's former political and social structure remained intact. The burning issue on the minds of the more conservative residents was still the question of an independent Afrikaner territory – envisaged as some kind of loose federation of Afrikaner towns, strung like a necklace across this remote area and independently administered by an Afrikaner body, much like an Afrikaner homeland.

The Dutch Reformed Church with its steeple, bell tower, clock face and immaculate gardens, was the town's centrepiece and occupied almost an entire square block. The Town Office, a small box-like structure located in one of the side streets, was set far back off the street, out of sight of passersby. In front of the building was a magnificent old willow tree with long whispering fronds draped like a fringed shawl.

Despite the arid conditions, splashes of colour surprised travellers to the area and held their attention as they drove through town on their way to the Rustig Mines, 120 kilometres to the north.

Hydrangea and hibiscus grew in profusion. Burgundy, purple, cerise, peach and white blossoms of bougainvillaea cascaded over wire fences and trailed on to sandy pavements. The residents themselves were often flabbergasted by the abundance of flowers that seemed to grow so effortlessly. They all knew that it had to do with the Hemelslaagte Springs, which they suspected were fed by an underground lake. However, since there had never been enough money in the town coffers to hire a geologist, these suspicions were never confirmed.

While many of the Vlenterhoek residents took their good health and longevity for granted and accepted the fact that the small town was dying, the town clerk Danie Venter, an inveterate optimist, believed that the town had potential and that with good management and a little luck the economy could be stimulated to provide work for the many unemployed residents. Unfortunately he was the only one in town who held such an optimistic view. The others had long since given up hope.

Easy for him to talk, he has a job, they grumbled whenever he tried to whip up enthusiasm for his ideas. He knew that he was one of the fortunate few, and each morning as he walked the eight blocks to work, he counted his blessings. It was the best time of the day: refreshing and stimulating – a time of day when much of his creative thinking was done.

He felt enormously good about everything: about himself, his work and his life. That very morning, he'd caught a glimpse of his reflection in the plate glass windows of the Glory Café and had noted, with some satisfaction, that he was still in excellent shape. The only detraction, as revealed by the small hand-mirror which he kept in the back of his desk drawer, was his forehead. With his rapidly receding hairline, his brow was becoming more prominent and dishearteningly dome-shaped and he couldn't help wondering if it had anything to do with being married for forty years.

Danie had married Petronella, the late minister's younger daughter, on the rebound from an unrequited love. Leah Hopkins, the only woman he had ever truly loved with all his heart, and the only woman he had wanted to spend the rest of his life with, had left town on the arm of another man.

Four decades after this fact, Danie continued to feel wistful. He could still see those soft brown eyes, the long tendrils of blonde hair cascading down to her shoulders, the smell of the gardenia blossoms braided into her hair – all of it as fresh as yesterday's memory.

Although his wife Petronella had all the physical attributes of a woman capable of bearing many children, they were childless. Sex, according to Petronella and according to her interpretation of the Bible, which she read every night before going to bed, was mainly functional – for procreation only. Since she had no hope of procreating because of a medical condition, she saw no point in sharing her husband's bed or in participating in the farce of fulfilling her conjugal obligations. Instead, she focused all her talents and energies on finding ways of making money. Not that Vlenterhoek provided many opportunities, but the wily Petronella was not averse to using her privileged position as wife of the town clerk to further her ambitions.

She had noticed recently the lightness in her husband's

step and his preoccupation with his appearance, but dismissed this as yet another phase that men went through. She'd recently read a magazine article about men suffering mid-life crisis – the equivalent of female menopause – and reasoned that like most women got over menopause, he'd eventually get over it.

But in Danie's case there was another reason for the light-ness in his step. His secretary, Rena Oosthuizen, was probably the only person in the entire town who knew the truth.

Just as Petronella thought Danie was getting over his mid-life crisis, she noticed a new restlessness about him and wondered anxiously if there was another problem, one that she was not aware of. She hated problems.

To Danie, however, problems were just glitches on the radar screen of life – his analogies were always rooted in aeronautics. In another life, he might have been a pilot. Instead, there he was, clerk in a town slowly expiring while he was desperately trying to breathe new life into it.

That night as he and his wife sat watching TV and he was just about to change channels to watch the rugby, his wife stopped him. Her attention had been caught by a news insert about Rebecca Fortuin, opposition member of parliament and former Vlenterhoek resident, who had apparently created another fracas during question time in parliament. Rebecca, Petronella recalled, was an outspoken candidate who evoked strong reactions. She was the kind of woman one either loved or hated.

Despite the other woman being coloured, Petronella couldn't help admiring her. She respected women who spoke their minds, even though in this case she would not have sung her praises because of the colour issue. According to the news, the MP had apparently accused one of the ministers in the ruling party of accepting bribes from an overseas invest-ment company. Just like *them*, she thought, bristling with indignation. That's why she didn't trust any of *them*.

After the news Petronella couldn't stop thinking about

Rebecca. She and Danie had been wondering who they could contact in government to discuss their ideas for rejuvenating the town of Vlenterhoek. She wondered if Rebecca might not be the right person. At least she was honest and trust-worthy. Hadn't she proved herself by bringing political shenanigans to public attention?

The only drawback was that neither she nor Danie knew Rebecca personally. They knew *of* her because of her ties to Vlenterhoek, but she'd left when she was quite young and had never returned again, except for her mother's funeral. All they knew about her background was that she was the daughter of the coloured labourer on the Joubert farm.

It seemed that the only person outside Rebecca's family who knew her was one of the local girls, Suzette le Roux, who worked as a waitress at the Glory Café, which Petronella owned. Suzette had once told her that she and Rebecca were childhood friends who used to meet after school – Suzette from the Vlenterhoek school for whites and Rebecca from the black school in the location. This was the only mention Suzette had made of Rebecca. On the odd occasion when the other woman was in the news, Suzette merely laughed and shook her head at Rebecca's political antics.

Petronella put her knitting aside as the news ended.

'Danie, why don't you go to Cape Town to speak to that Fortuin woman?' she asked.

'About what?' he said absently as he flipped channels.

'Tourism,' Petronella said. 'Isn't that what we've been talking about the past two weeks? We've got the Hemelslaagte Springs here and everyone knows how good the air is. It's the perfect tourist destination.'

'Y . . . es,' he said, reluctant to enter the discussion because Petronella, given half a chance, was like a dog with a bone and he wasn't in the mood to listen to her endless chatter. It was his idea after all and now she'd latched on to it as though she was the first to think about it.

'I think it would be in all our interests for you to go to

Cape Town to speak to her . . . Tourism is a big thing now,' she continued. 'And you are the town clerk.'

'But she's got nothing to do with tourism,' he said irritably. 'You heard what they said – right there on the news. She's an MP for the opposition party. She has no power. No real power.'

Petronella shook her head. 'She's a very determined woman. Afraid of nothing. And most important of all, Danie, she's from here. She'll understand. I know she'll want to help if we tell her about our plans to improve the town. Besides, she'll probably know all the right people in government who can help us. She's just the person we need on our side; she's black and you know nowadays the government just wants to see black faces in business.'

'She's not black, she's coloured,' Danie corrected her. 'That's not so good, is it?'

Petronella thought about this for a few minutes. She wasn't sure either. The only coloured people she had any contact with were the two Erasmus sisters, Noelle and Sissie, who lived on the town side of the sloot. Now and then Petronella gave some of her overripe fruit to them, rather than throw it away. Other than that, neither she nor Danie knew much about race relations.

In spite of changes elsewhere in the country since the first democratic elections, and changes in the world at large – like the Berlin Wall coming down, which they had seen on television, and Nelson Mandela walking out of prison to international acclaim – transformation had not yet reached the small town. It had wound its way around the country, taking small detours, travelling some bumpy routes along the rutted tracks to lesser-known outposts.

'Black, coloured, what difference does it make,' Petronella snapped. 'Just go talk to her. That's all. And maybe while you're there, you can find out if she knows the people who wrote that letter to you.'

'What letter?' Danie asked.

7

'The letter from those people who want to make the film here.'

He looked blank for a moment.

'That letter for the film . . . Amb . . . Ambi . . . something or other.'

'Oh, yes,' said Danie. 'The film. I'd almost forgotten.'

'I wonder who the people are who wrote that letter,' she said.

He shrugged. 'I'll find out.'

'I'm sure the Fortuin woman will help us. She might even come back here. What do you think, Danie?'

'You forget, when she was living here, we didn't even know her name. Why should she want to come back here and why should she want to help us?'

'It's not our fault, Danie,' Petronella said, trying to sound reasonable. 'We didn't make the laws of that time, but we had to live by them, didn't we?'

Danie thought for a long moment, puckering his lips and absently massaging his head – little habits that tended to creep in whenever he focused on something. 'You may be right,' he said. 'But we should have a plan, don't you think?'

'That's not so hard. Write everything down on a piece of paper – everything we can think of. Rena can type it. Right?'

He nodded absently and flipped channels again.

Later that night as he lay awake reflecting on his wife's idea about consulting Rebecca Fortuin, he had to give her credit. At times her ideas were simple but astonishingly clever. What harm could there be in contacting the woman, he asked himself as he lay in the dark, staring at the ceiling. Petronella was right. His secretary Rena could make the arrangements.

Two weeks after this conversation with Petronella, Danie drove to Cape Town. He left early on a Thursday morning and arrived at Rebecca Fortuin's office around noon. Her assistant, a young black woman in a navy trouser suit, was clearly surprised when he told her who he was.

'But I telephoned you this morning to say that the meeting was cancelled,' she said. 'Miss Fortuin is expected to be out of her office all day attending a parliamentary committee meeting.'

'I didn't get the call,' Danie said, somewhat peeved. Almost a whole day's driving and for what, he thought swallowing his irritation. A film of perspiration had formed on his brow and he carefully extracted his handkerchief to dab at it. He hated it when he broke out in a sweat – and any small aggravation tended to trigger such episodes.

'Well, I spoke to someone in your office,' the assistant said, her voice taking on a harder edge when he again denied knowledge of the message. 'I made the call myself. I left the message with your secretary.'

'Must have been on my way,' Danie said, his calm tone belying the irritation he felt at having his time wasted. 'I'll wait a bit.'

He waited for almost an hour. There was no sign of Rebecca. Her assistant eventually took pity on him.

'You can wait in her office,' she said. 'Miss Fortuin will be in shortly. She has to rush back, though, so you'll only have a minute.' She showed him into a small office crammed with books and files. Danie sat in the chair across the desk from the MP's vacant seat, surveying the clutter. It was a bright office and on her desk was a vase with an arrangement of fresh flowers; a shaft of sunlight refracted through the cut glass vase, creating a rainbow on a sheet of writing paper. He did not hear her entering the room. Suddenly Rebecca Fortuin was there at his elbow. Startled, he looked up.

'I'm so sorry you had to wait,' she said. 'My assistant said she telephoned to cancel. I've been tied up for days in a meeting.' She spoke rapidly as she released her hold on an armful of papers, dropping them on to her desk.

She took his hand in a firm grip. Danie had never held the hand of a coloured woman before and wasn't sure how much pressure to put into the handshake or for how long it would be prudent to hold her hand. He didn't want to release it too quickly in case it sent the wrong message. While she greeted him, her assistant waited at the desk for her to sign a letter.

Danie was tall, the wooden chair was lower than he expected, and he sat down too quickly, relaxed his knees too soon and almost lost his balance. By the time he crossed his legs the flush, like a strawberry stain, had spread all the way from his neck to the top of his dome. He glanced up quickly to see if either of the women had noticed, but Rebecca, pen poised, was about to put her name to the letter.

Surreptitiously, while Rebecca was still busy with the letter, he studied her. She was a big woman, physically well endowed and his eyes inadvertently strayed to the expanse of her bosom. She looked up and noticed. Mortified, Danie's eyes jumped to the picture behind her.

'So, Mr . . . Mr . . .' she said, as she searched around her desk for a clue to his name.

'Venter . . .' Danie offered.

'Mr Venter . . . From Vlenterhoek, I see,' she said, without batting an eyelid.

As if she'd never heard of Vlenterhoek, Danie thought testily.

After a brief pause she became brusque and businesslike. 'So, what brings you to Cape Town and, more specifically, to my office?' she asked.

He noticed in a distracted sort of way that she had a very pleasant face, a wide brow and light brown eyes. He noticed, too, the intensity of her eyes. Her hair was drawn back off her face and braided with extensions. He sensed that she was honest and sincere. In his capacity as town clerk, he considered himself a good judge of character.

Because she was speaking English, he didn't want to appear rude and thought it would be more prudent to respond in like manner. The only problem was that sometimes he had to dig deep to find the language when he was flustered.

Composing himself, he came straight to the point. 'I have come to you for help,' he said.

'And how may I be of help?' she asked.

'It's about tourism . . .'

'Oh,' she said fixing him with a questioning look.

'Uhmm . . .' he started. 'It's like this. We have many good things . . . in our town . . . as you know . . .'

'I know . . . I know what you have in your town, Mr Venter,' said Rebecca Fortuin. 'In case you've forgotten or perhaps did not know, I am from there.'

Danie nodded, irritated by her patronising tone. An awkward pause followed and he shifted uncomfortably in his chair.

'So . . . tell me . . . how do you expect me to help? I have nothing to do with tourism and I have nothing to do with your town. Not any more . . .' she said tersely. 'I left there a long time ago.'

'I thought . . . You could . . . I just want to meet the right people,' Danie said quickly. 'To speak to,' he added. 'I have brought all the information. Right here, in my briefcase.' He swung the briefcase on to the desk and in the process almost knocked over the vase of flowers. He caught the vase with one hand before it toppled, silently cursing himself for his clumsiness. He mopped up the small puddle of water with his handkerchief.

He had to pull himself together, salvage some of his dignity.

'I really don't think . . .' She started again.

'It'll only take a minute . . .' he said. He removed a file, snapped his briefcase shut and leaned forward a little more confidently as if to engage her in conversation. He was feeling more relaxed. He'd stopped perspiring, which was a big relief. The briefcase on the desk between them was in the way and, with an apologetic grin, he swung it off the table, felt his neck jerk and out of the corner of his eye saw that the end of his tie was caught in the briefcase.

'Sorry,' he said sheepishly.

At that moment the phone on her desk rang and he was grateful for the diversion. She picked up the phone and spoke in flawless Afrikaans. Mercifully, she seemed oblivious to Danie's battle to extricate himself.

He was obliged to return the briefcase to the desk to rescue the trapped tie. It was his new tie and it was ruined; several threads had caught in the locking mechanism when he tried to pull it free. He tugged at one of the loose threads, intending to break it off. Instead, he unravelled almost two centimetres of the tie before he realised what he was doing. Giving up on it, he smiled wryly, removed the tie, folded it and put it in his jacket pocket. Rebecca never said a word, never gave any indication of her thoughts, except for the little twitch of a smile as she turned away to gather her files.

'I thought you might be willing to help,' he said, aggravated by his clumsiness and his lack of progress. Now that he knew she was an Afrikaans-speaker, he spoke Afrikaans, a little aggrieved, of course, that she had led him on by speaking English.

'I'm sorry,' she said, 'but I have to rush off again. The committee has reconvened.' She reached for the intercom on her desk.

Her assistant appeared in the doorway and in her brusque manner said, 'You're going to be late, Miss Fortuin.'

Rebecca eased herself out of the chair and picked up her files and her briefcase. Her assistant watched her with a sympathetic smile. There were times when she felt sorry for Rebecca, who had no personal life. No man to go home to. It was a price she had paid for her career. A price a lot of women these days were willing to pay.

'Will we be able to meet later?' Danie asked. 'After your meeting?'

'I'm afraid that won't be possible. This could end up being an all-night session. We're debating one of the bills,' she explained, rising. 'I'm sorry you came all the way for nothing.'

'Will you be coming to Vlenterhoek?' he asked.

'Not in the foreseeable future.'

'I thought . . .' he started. 'What about tomorrow?' he asked.

'Sorry, but I'm not in a position to make any promises.' Her tone indicated that he was being dismissed. Danie's face fell with disappointment. 'I'll leave the file with you, then,' he said.

She took the file, adding it to the pile on her desk. 'Thank you, I'll take a look at it.'

'I've left my contact number . . .'

'Good,' she said, firmly. Her attitude was businesslike once again. 'Will you please show Mr Venter out,' she said to her assistant. Danie reached for her hand, sweeping back the non-existent hair from his brow with his free hand.

'I'll be in touch, Mr Venter,' she said.

Danie remembered then that he had forgotten to bring the letter from the film company. For the life of him he could not remember the name of the company or the film they were going to shoot.

'Darn,' he thought. But there was no point wasting any more of her time.

'Thank you, Miss Fortuin.' Danie backed away – right into the assistant standing at the door. He flung his arms around her to keep himself from falling. Flustered, he apologised profusely before retreating. Resisting the impulse to flee, he paused in the corridor and, leaning against the wall to catch his breath, ran his middle and index fingers along the metal zipper of his fly to ensure that it had not come undone in the stumble. One more embarrassment would have been more than he could bear.

For Danie, it had been a day of many firsts: in one day, he had not only shaken the hand of a coloured woman, but had also inadvertently embraced a black woman.

2

Petronella and Suzette were cleaning up, getting ready to close the café. Petronella was anxious to get home to find out how Danie had fared in Cape Town. But Portia Hopkins, of all people, had stopped in for a cup of tea and had delayed the closing of the café. Petronella was surprised to see Portia out so late in the day. The Hopkins sisters, Portia and Ephemera, rarely called at the café. They were usually inseparable and seldom was one sister in town without the other.

Anxious as Petronella was to get home, she kept the café open in the spirit of good business practice. Although she didn't dare approach Portia to question her, she wondered where Ephemera was. Mercifully, Portia didn't linger too long over her tea and as soon as she had finished it she paid her bill and left.

The two Hopkins sisters, locally referred to as the Hopkins Spinsters, lived in a rambling old farmhouse on a twenty-acre plot in Vlenterhoek. The old house had a stoep that ran all the way along the front of the building. Portia, who was the eldest of the three sisters, was usually addressed by her given name Portia – a name her mother had chosen from Shakespeare's *Merchant of Venice* – with variations of

14

pronunciation by the Afrikaner residents. Her stern no-nonsense demeanour discouraged familiarity. None of the locals would have dared to corrupt her name – not to her face, anyway. The youngest sister, Ephemera, locally pronounced *Effiemeera* or abbreviated to Effie, was a derivation of *Ephemeral* and, given Ephemera's disposition, it seemed an appropriate choice. Long before she left Vlenterhoek, the middle sister had her name Cordelia shortened to Leah. Her mother had chosen her name from Shakespeare's *King Lear*, but for no particular reason, it seemed.

Their mother, a gentle, loving soul, had sailed through life on a cloud of bemusement, having burdened her daughters with an eclectic assortment of whimsical names. When it came to choosing a name for the farm, their father chose HOPKINS LANDING. His wife was disappointed; she would have preferred something more original. But having left the naming of the girls to her, her husband thought it wise to choose a simple name, one that could be remembered and pronounced by the locals.

The two sisters – the youngest and the eldest – remained in Vlenterhoek, while the middle sister Leah left the country with a new husband. Portia and Ephemera remained unmarried and it was said that they had paid their dues to society by leading exemplary lives.

It was said, too, that Portia, now seventy-three, had remained single because she considered herself too high and mighty for any of the local men – just like her sister Leah who had preferred an outsider to Danie Venter, even though he was besotted with her. The locals also blamed Portia for Ephemera's strangeness, claiming that Portia had discouraged Ephemera's potential suitors. Had she been married, they said, Ephemera would have had all her marbles today.

The truth was that Portia's focus had always been the family – to the exclusion of any kind of personal life. It was not a role she had chosen for herself but one that was thrust upon her. Her mother and Ephemera both lived in a world of their own and Ephemera, even in later years, was much too capricious and scatterbrained to be trusted with anything.

With her family responsibilities, the question of marriage had never entered Portia's mind. There had never been time in her busy schedule to indulge in the kind of frivolity that occupied the minds of her mother and Ephemera.

They were like two Southern Belles who had an imaginary army of servants waiting on them hand and foot while they indulged in their silly teas and poetry readings – just the two of them, pretending to be what they were not. It irritated Portia no end, especially since she had so much to do.

'Darling,' her mother would call to Portia from the stoep, 'if you're in the kitchen, could you put the kettle on for tea?' 'Darling, if you're coming out here, could you bring the tea?' And so it went on. 'Darling, I'm not feeling well.' Her mother would lie down around midday, with Ephemera curled up on the bed next to her.

Ephemera was extremely close to her mother and the shock of her mother's death unhinged her mind, disconnecting her from reality. She eventually retreated to a place of safety – taking refuge somewhere in her early childhood. There was no medication available at that time to reverse her condition and Portia would never have dreamed of having her institutionalised. The damage was done and Ephemera was now just an effigy of a woman. Although the flighty expansive gestures were still present, her laughter sounded empty and her blue eyes were vacant.

Occasionally a nostalgic moment crept up on Portia, especially when she was sitting out on the stoep by herself, her thoughts flitting in and out of the past. She thought about their parents and especially about Leah, and she felt a sense of relief that at least Leah was happy and doing well for herself. The last news they'd had of her was that she was now living in a smart neighbourhood in Canada, in the city of Vancouver, and that her daughter Erica was married and had moved to Toronto.

The Hopkins family – father, mother and three girls – had arrived in Vlenterhoek from England in 1945. Portia, then sixteen years old, took over responsibility for raising her two younger siblings while her mother struggled to adjust to their new life in the small town. Their father, who worked long shifts at the Rustig Mine, was hardly ever home. Twenty-five years later, in 1970, he retired from his job as foreman, but he remained restless and elusive, often disappearing for days at a time without explanation.

All Portia had left were memories. Memories which flowed into all the tiny crevices of her soul and, like warm honey, displaced the bitterness and resentment she nurtured about Leah. After all, Leah had been gone for forty years.

Living out in the veld it was easy to lose track of time. Years slipped by stealthily – each day like the next, each year like the one before – accumulating somewhere like lost baggage. And the older one got the faster the years seemed to trot by. Then in a blink of an eye it was too late: seventy-three and wondering what her life had been about. But self-pity was not a luxury Portia allowed herself. She was much too busy, especially with Ephemera becoming increasingly dependent on her.

Even though Portia never talked about Leah, not even to her younger sister, she often thought about her. That Leah had not come home when their father died and, later, when their mother died, had been like a knife plunged into her heart. When her father died, she'd sent Leah a telegram, but her sister had merely responded with a *Regret I can't come home* message. Leah was still in Zambia then and Portia didn't think it unreasonable to expect her to come home for the funeral.

After their father's death their mother had become increasingly distracted. Two years later she followed her husband to the grave. Once again, Leah had responded by telegram. That was years ago, of course.

Every now and then Ephemera would ask, 'Where is Leah?'

as though she had plucked her name out of her memory like a choice grape from a tangled vine.

'Canada,' Portia would say in her abrupt manner that usually discouraged further questions.

'Where is Canada?' her sister would ask with her charming blank smile.

'America,' Portia would reply.

And Ephemera would repeat the word slowly, saying 'America' over and over again as if she enjoyed the sound of it, savouring it, opening her mouth to expel the *Aaah* sound and puckering to bleat around the *mehh* sound.

Thousands of kilometres away in Vancouver, and not in America, Leah was living a starkly different life to the one Portia imagined. She'd often thought about Vlenterhoek, especially after her first few years in Zambia when she was lonely and missed her sisters terribly, when she longed for the closeness of the family she had so readily abandoned.

But she had left Vlenterhoek such a long time ago that she assumed most people in the small town would either have forgotten her or would never have known her.

As a young girl, Leah was thrilled at the prospect of leaving. She felt stifled in the small town. She wanted so much more out of life. For her sisters, it was different; their entire existence revolved around small-town life. It was all they knew or cared about. But not Leah.

Not even Danie Venter and Walter Potgieter, who were both infatuated with her, were of any interest. As far as she was concerned, none of the boys in Vlenterhoek could give her what she wanted. Marrying one of them, she had feared, would have sucked her so deep into Vlenterhoek that her life would have imploded, burying her under tons of Vlenterhoek debris.

Charlie Barker, who worked as an engineer at the Rustig Mines, was the best chance she had of escaping the confines of the small town. He and her father had been friends for years. They had known each other from the days when her father was a foreman at the Rustig Mines and Charlie an engineer. The two men, both originally from England, had gravitated towards each other and became good friends. Through the years Charlie had been in and out of their home. He was like one of the family – until the night Leah saw him through different eyes. When Charles Barker came to the house that fateful night and discussed his plans to transfer to the Copperbelt, in what was then Northern Rhodesia, she knew what had to be done. It was right there, right in front of her eyes, everything she dreamed of: a husband, a home, children, security and, above all, freedom. She listened to Charlie speaking and her heart warmed to him, her cheeks glowing with an inner radiance that Charlie could not resist.

Later that evening, as she and Charlie stood out on the stoep, she no longer regarded him as an old family friend but as her saviour – her White Knight in a shiny blue Oldsmobile.

The age difference between Leah and Charlie seemed inconsequential then. Every part of her, every fibre of her body was focused on one thought only – getting out of Vlenterhoek.

'Don't you be foolish now,' Portia warned sternly. 'I can see right through him. He's nothing but a swaggering middle-aged fool.'

'You're being silly, Portia,' Leah said laughing. Sour grapes, she thought.

Four months later, just before his transfer came through for the job on the Copperbelt, she and Charlie were married.

'You've made your bed. Now you have to lie in it,' her sister told her as Leah packed her bags. She and Charlie were driving to Northern Rhodesia.

Leah was too happy to pay attention to Portia's sombre warnings. She was ecstatic. Her life was just beginning.

Free at last from what she regarded as a life of servitude, she waved goodbye to her family as she and Charlie drove away, the Vlenterhoek sun glinting off the chrome on the Oldsmobile.

The mining company provided them with a furnished home in the town of Kitwe. They had packed whatever they could into the car when they left Vlenterhoek, and bought whatever other extras they needed from expatriates who had completed their contracts and were returning to the UK. Leah soon discovered that everything was handed-down – including sexual partners.

Her excitement about being in a 'foreign' country, and her expectations of finding a job there, were soon dashed. Charlie would not let her work. He provided her with a comfortable home and almost everything she wanted, in return for which she had to stay home. In the beginning this arrangement suited her but later, overcome with boredom, even house-work became an attractive alternative. But Charlie told her she was not to lift a finger, for that she had an army of ser-vants – a gardener, a cook, and a houseboy – to do her bidding.

It took years for Leah to realise how manipulative and controlling Charlie was. At first his tactics were so subtle that she hardly noticed. It started with her not being able to go anywhere without his approval, ostensibly because he knew more about the culture than she. He constantly told her what a rotten bunch the expats were and warned her to steer clear of them. Yet he was around them constantly.

The expatriate women, most of whom were English, did not seem bound by any constraints of language or morality. This was the sophisticated society she so much wanted to be part of, but it was a society that rejected her. Leah with her strange small-town South African attitudes and behaviour just did not fit in.

This was the beginning of Leah's spiral into depression, the beginning of the misery that screwed itself into their lives, tightening, twisting and turning until it had fastened itself firmly.

Bitterness surfaced. She focused her anger on those who had rejected her, who had formed a community that was as closed to outsiders as it was to newcomers.

Charlie never had this problem. He was accepted almost immediately into their midst because he was one of them – an Englishman. He was perfectly content, while she was miserable and isolated.

'It's not that bad, Girlie,' he told her. She hated it when he called her Girlie. It wasn't a term of endearment, it was a term of ridicule.

'How would you know?' she flung back at him. 'You're never there to see how they treat me.'

'I think the sun's getting to you,' he told her.

'Go to hell!' Leah spat and locked herself in the bathroom while Charlie went to the club for a beer and a game of darts. Leah remained in the bathroom; she sat on the lid of the toilet and cried for hours. The houseboy heard her sobbing and knocked on the door several times, but she would not open it.

The other expatriate women thought she was stupid and naive and that she had nothing to contribute to their society. Although they would not have known it, her wide-eyed, bewildered expression often bore a distinct resemblance to that of her mother. Some of the husbands who were into wife swapping eyed her as they did most new arrivals. With her pert nose, curly hair and child-like innocence she was quite eye-catching. Some of the wife-swapping men imagined they could teach her a thing or two. But Charlie wasn't interested in sharing his wife. He was obsessively possessive about his property, especially Leah.

She and Charlie were in Northern Rhodesia for five years before Erica was born. It was around the time of independence when Northern Rhodesia became Zambia and Kenneth Kaunda its first president. At this time many of the Europeans, fearful of integration, sent their children abroad to be educated.

Erica was their only child. For medical reasons which she never quite understood, doctors advised a hysterectomy. She had it done without question, believing that the doctors knew best. It was the end of her dream to have another child.

When Charlie's contract ended ten years later, he decided it was time to move on.

In the years that followed they moved around a lot – to South America, to Australia and then later Charlie was transferred to a nickel mine in Canada. They spent three years living in a small mining town in Manitoba.

Erica hated the small town. Like Leah, she was accustomed to the African sun and could not get used to the cold.

Three years later Charlie was injured in an accident at the mine and almost lost his leg. He was transferred to a hospital in Winnipeg for rehabilitation, but never recovered the full use of his leg again. Not only did the accident damage him physically, but it affected his mind and spirit as well.

Six months later when Charlie was retired on a disability pension, they moved to Vancouver in British Columbia.

Leah often talked about her family in South Africa. It was through her mother's anecdotes about life at Hopkins Landing that Erica, who had never met her aunts, got to know them.

Much as Leah wanted Erica to meet her family, especially when they were in Zambia, which was still close enough for a quick trip home, Charlie would not let them out of his sight – not even when her parents died.

When they moved to Canada, hopes of visiting Vlenterhoek became increasingly remote. Vlenterhoek and her family drifted out of reach. Later, when Charlie had almost driven Leah out of her mind, she often thought longingly about her family and about the simple life she might have had in Vlenterhoek. She had so many regrets about marrying Charlie. The only good thing that came out of her marriage was Erica.

Charlie might have driven Erica out of her mind too had

she not left home at the first opportunity and moved to Toronto where she enrolled in a science programme at York University. As soon as she graduated, she found herself a husband and settled in Toronto.

After that they had hardly any contact with Erica. Charlie pretended indifference, but Leah knew that he was bitterly disappointed at the way Erica had cut herself off from them. He never mentioned her. Leah missed her daughter. The fact that Erica was happy was small consolation. Charlie wouldn't give in; always arrogant and stubborn, he wielded his silence like a lethal weapon against his daughter.

The phone calls from Erica became more infrequent. Finally she called only on special occasions like birthdays or at Christmas time. They were informed, by phone, of the birth of their two grandchildren, both boys.

Charlie never acknowledged the fact that he had grand-children. He was cold and silent and grew more cantankerous with each passing day.

In the last ten years of his life he became increasingly paranoid. He hid everything from Leah. It didn't matter how insignificant or how small and non-essential the item was, if it was of benefit to her in any way, he made sure that it was out of her reach – money, food or cooking utensils – all secreted away in the most unlikely places. This was the life that none of her family in Vlenterhoek knew about. It was also one of the reasons why Leah had not written home.

She could just imagine Portia's expression and the unspoken, 'I told you so.'

'Ahhmeeheerica . . .' Ephemera sang out, over and over again, driving Portia out of her mind. She muttered a silent prayer that Ephemera would forget about America and Leah, for them to be washed out of her mind as other things were.

'Come look, Ephemera,' Portia called from the stoep. 'There goes Sissie Erasmus. Wave to her, dear.'

Ephemera rushed out on to the stoep and waved. 'Sissie,

23

Sissie,' she called.

Sissie heard her and stopped to wave back at Ephemera. 'Hello, Miss Hopkins,' she called.

'They're such nice girls, aren't they?' Portia said. 'Remember her sister Noelle? She used to help us bake.'

Ephemera nodded vigorously. America was forgotten.

3

The Erasmus sisters – Sissie and her older sister Noelle – lived
at the opposite end of town from the Hopkins sisters. They
lived on the town side of the *sloot* in one of the dilapidated
houses, a grey, nondescript, one-bedroomed building with a
zinc roof held down by rocks and at least a dozen pumpkins.
Petronella Venter grew many of the vegetables used in the
café and generally disposed of the surplus by donating it to
poor families. It was because of the glut of pumpkins the
previous year that so many of them, in various stages of
dehydration, ended up on the Erasmuses' roof.

Sissie and Noelle had always lived in the same grey concrete
house. The interior was very basic. The two metal spring
cots had been there since their mother's time. The only new
addition to the bedroom was the narrow mirror and a chest
of drawers Noelle had bought from the local Cash & Carry.
Their father had made some of the kitchen furniture, like the
table and four chairs. The wood stove still worked well. A
Primus stove, and a blue plastic basin for washing their dishes
stood on a metal stand by the window.

The house was essentially much as it was when their mother
was still alive. All Sissie knew with any certainty about her
parents was that they had moved into the house from

Helderfontein, one of the farms in the neighbouring district, that Ivan was born in the house and that their father was given a job on the Joubert farm.

A short distance from the Erasmuses' house, and also on the same side of the sloot, was the Oosthuizens' house – a squat, three-roomed structure that overlooked the location, as though the house and its white occupants had turned their back on the town and had embraced the blacks. Rena and her sister Esther lived there with their mother who was confined to a wheelchair. The older sister, Rena, who was Danie Venter's secretary, had added the ramp access after her mother's accident.

The accident that had taken the life of their father and had left their mother paralysed from the waist down had happened eight years before, when their parents were on their way home from church one night and had ploughed into a tractor owned by the wealthy farmer, Hendrik Joubert. The tractor, driven by one of his labourers, was travelling without lights. Charges against Hendrik Joubert for negligence were eventually dropped and he was exonerated of blame. Their mother, however, held Hendrik Joubert personally responsible for her disability.

'I will hound him into his grave,' was what she said when they received news of his acquittal.

Ironically, the house they lived in belonged to Hendrik Joubert and if it hadn't been for his wife interceding on behalf of the Oosthuizens, he might have evicted them because of their mother's hostility.

Eight years later, the Oosthuizens were still living in Hendrik Joubert's house and relied almost entirely on Rena's small salary. With the advent of the new government their mother's welfare benefits had been pared to the barest of bones. The only other assistance they received was from the church.

One Monday morning before school, Hendrik Joubert's

younger son Jannie was test-flying his huge red and green kite. He had to sneak out of the house because his father disapproved of his hobby. The red and green kite was a prototype of the one he and his friend Albert Fortuin were planning to build for the kite festival. The business community was sponsoring a prize of two hundred rand. The boys had an agreement that if they won the competition the money would go towards repairs on Albert's guitar, or a replacement guitar, whichever was cheaper. The neck on Albert's guitar had broken again and although he had tried to mend it with super glue, it just wasn't producing the same quality of sound.

Albert Fortuin, small and delicately built, was Rebecca's brother. She had left Vlenterhoek before he was born and he had seen her only once, when she came home for their mother's funeral, but he was too young then to have any memories of her. All he knew about his sister was what he heard from others – that she was a Member of Parliament in one of the opposition parties. His father never talked about her and wouldn't allow him to mention her name at home.

Albert was born on the Joubert farm, Tweeriviere, in the same brick and mud house that they still lived in. Albert was fifteen, a year younger than Jannie. The boys had practically grown up together and although children of different races often drifted apart as they grew older, Albert and Jannie had remained friends. They both regarded themselves as outcasts, both despised by their fathers because they were imperfect.

From the top of the ridge overlooking the town where Jannie and Albert went to fly their kites, they could see for miles in all directions. On this particular morning there were no vehicles on the roads, only three dew-covered cars parked outside the Imperial Hotel.

One of the parked cars was a dark-blue BMW with Cape Town plates.

A dog slept undisturbed in the middle of the road while the traffic light, even in the absence of traffic, continued its cycle. White. Orange. Red.

On the roof of the Imperial Hotel was a huge satellite dish that fed its signal to a big-screen television in the bar. Locals agreed that the three main attractions of the town were the big screen in the bar at the Imperial Hotel, the airfield (owned by three farmers who had their own private plane), and Herman's Rock, an enormous boulder in the veld, which, by some incredible feat of natural engineering, was balanced on a rock the size of a football.

One would have thought that the Hemelslaagte Springs might have been a feature too, but they remained basically just as they had been when a shepherd stumbled on the site decades earlier – a rudimentary hole in the ground which oozed water. This water, however, was not just your run of the mill water; it was crystal clear, health-giving and invigorating water which people collected in huge vats. Although the existence of the Springs was acknowledged by the healthy residents, they weren't something they could stand around admiring as they could with the airfield or the big-screen TV or Herman's Rock. They were thus not counted among the town's attractions.

On this morning the elderly coloured cleaner at the Imperial Hotel paused in his sweeping to light a *stompie*. He often collected discarded cigarette butts, stripped the remaining tobacco and rolled it in scraps of brown paper. Gazing into the distance, he leaned on his broom and watched as Jannie's kite dipped dangerously and then, catching a current of air, soared once again.

At street level, not a breath of air stirred.

In the restaurant of the Imperial Hotel, four guests were having breakfast before continuing on their journey to a game reserve. They had not planned to stop in Vlenterhoek. The radiator of their four-by-four had been damaged on one of the gravel roads in the area and had to be repaired. Since Vlenterhoek was the nearest town, they had made the detour and had decided to spend the night.

The four guests all worked for the same company – International Resort Holdings or IRH, a subsidiary of American Resorts Inc with headquarters in New York. Two of the guests were American – one of them an African-American, a term which residents only became familiar with later when the newspaper reports appeared. The whole concept of hyphenating people was still an unknown phenomenon in Vlenterhoek. People were either black or white.

Although their white waitress gave no indication of her thoughts, she could see no difference between the African-American sitting at the breakfast table and any of the blacks from the location on the other side of the sloot. They were the same colour, had the same features, they only spoke differently. She was having a hard time trying to understand what the black man was saying.

This black man, seated at the table and chatting comfortably to the three whites, was a rarity in Vlenterhoek. Until quite recently blacks were not served in the restaurant. But, because of the furore a couple of years before when a black diner was refused service and then turned out to be from the upper echelons of government, blacks were now served, albeit grudgingly.

Free social mixing with people of colour was something the locals still resisted.

The waitress drew closer as the black man spoke. Because of his accent, she could only catch fragments of his conversation: 'Must say I had a good sleep last night . . . Effervescent air, an ideal place for a health resort . . . tourists will come in droves, especially Americans. Think of the boom, man.'

'You've got to be kidding, Wesley,' one of the women said.

The other man, obviously South African, laughed cynically.

'Hey, man. I'm serious,' the African-American said. 'There's a lot of potential here. A lot of money to be made.'

The mention of money electrified the waitress. She had no idea who these people were, or where they came from. In that part of the world English was not a language that sat easily on the tongue or on the ear.

'You Americans are all mad,' the woman laughed.

At the mention of Americans, the accent suddenly rang a bell. The waitress recognised it as the same language spoken on soapies like *All My Children* and *The Bold and the Beautiful* – of which she had not missed a single episode in two years.

At the Imperial Hotel that morning, a lifetime away from the lives depicted in the soapies, the young Afrikaans waitress, pretending to be busy at the next table, strained to hear what was being said by the two Americans.

When they left, she accompanied them to the door to wave goodbye. They had left a very generous tip, most of which was quickly secreted into her bra. The transfer of money from table to bra had been done with a sleight of hand that would have dazzled Houdini. Neither of the two other employees in the restaurant had noticed how quickly part of the tip had disappeared off the table.

As soon as the guests had left, the waitress was on the phone to her brother-in-law. The Americans were coming, she told him. They were coming to buy up the town.

As happens in small towns, by mid-morning the entire population knew that the Americans were coming.

There was discussion everywhere: on every street corner, in front of the bank, at the post office and in front of the Imperial Hotel. In fact there was discussion wherever there were people, and there was also a great deal of outrage. It was clear to everyone that the visitors' intentions were not good. They had come for the water. There was no doubt in anyone's mind about it. Soon their God-given right to the Hemelslaagte Springs would be taken from them and they would have to pay for the water.

Why did Danie Venter, who was the town clerk, not know anything about this?

As could be expected, after a great deal of speculation,

everyone had a theory.

'Are these the same people . . . the Americans coming to make the film?' Portia asked pointedly, her question demanding an answer.

The same question about the Americans was asked on the street. No one seemed to have the answers.

With all the talk about the Americans swirling around her, Ephemera approached her sister in the kitchen one afternoon. 'Is Leah American too?' she asked Portia.

The question startled Portia. It seemed that every now and again incidents or words, like tiny pinpricks, tweaked Ephemera's memory and thoughts would swim to the surface, gliding in a ray of light and then suddenly and quite abruptly the light would go out and all would be dark again.

It took a moment for Portia to compose herself. 'No, she's South African, just like us. But why are you asking, Ephemera?'

'Because the Americans are coming,' Ephemera said as though Leah's arrival was a foregone conclusion and she couldn't understand why her sister didn't know this.

'Why would Leah be coming?' Portia asked gently.

'The Americans are coming.'

Portia looked up from the stove where she was about to slip two pans of bread dough into the oven. She recalled now how she had dismissively told her sister that Leah was in America because it was easier than having to explain Canada to her. Now it was too late to correct that mistake.

'I wish you wouldn't believe everything they tell you,' she said under her breath. 'The Americans are not coming,' she told her sister, straightening up and shutting the oven door. 'People here have nothing better to do than make up stories.'

'I know Leah's coming,' Ephemera interjected.

'Now don't be silly.' Portia was tired and not in the mood for questions. 'It's time for your nap, Ephemera.'

But Ephemera was too excited to take a nap. She was all wound up. Portia sighed, wiped her hands on her apron and turned to the sink.

Ephemera could hardly wait for Leah's arrival. She remembered her sister – remembered that she was a lot more fun than Portia. But then Leah had left them. Portia had told her a long time ago that Leah, like a shameless hussy, had run off with Charles Barker. Ephemera couldn't remember much about that event, even though she was seventeen at the time. Her memory had become moth-eaten and the holes always seemed to represent important events. None of this mattered though. As far as she was concerned, Leah was coming. She became obsessed with the notion. Portia did not have the heart to burst her bubble.

At the Town Office Danie Venter inspected the progress of the renovations. Work had finally begun on the council building – much of it in desperate need of major repairs, but they could only afford a facelift and it was taking much longer than expected. Danie was growing impatient with the clutter that had found a permanent home on the front lawn.

He was beginning to wonder if the work would ever get done. It had taken the painters two months to finish the exterior. He glanced up as he strode towards the offices. Above the entrance hung an old sign that had been painted over. Through the several coats of white paint, bought from the local Cash & Carry, the black lettering of the old 'Whites Only' sign was still visible.

The other members of the town council had considered the renovations a waste of good money. But Danie had pushed and pulled with mulish obstinacy until he'd worn them down.

Apart from the water of the Hemelslaagte Springs, the quality of air and the quality of light were two of the other magnificent features unique to the area. The theory expounded by various locals who considered themselves experts on the matter, was that the reddish colour of the earth was absorbed or reflected into the atmosphere (no one was quite sure which) and it was this that gave the sky its particular hue.

Apart from these attributes, it was also a safe place. The older residents, who had spent their lives there, knew that Vlenterhoek was a good place in which to live. Unlike the paranoia of city life, there was no need for high walls and security gates in Vlenterhoek. People still slept with their doors unlocked at night and left their garden furniture outside.

The only incident of any significance in recent times was the mysterious disappearance of a dust-covered garden gnome from the front garden of one of the town's elderly residents. Accusations flew back and forth and suspicions had focused on the inhabitants of the location.

The gnome eventually turned up in a garage belonging to the town's centenarian. More than a hundred years old and hard of hearing, the old woman had no idea how the gnome had got there.

'Too many idle minds and hands during the school holidays,' the police sergeant grumbled when he discovered it was all a prank. Of course he wanted to give the residents the impression that he was overwhelmed by criminal activity. But the truth was that since the town had hired a constable to assist him, his free time was spent visiting an attractive young widow five kilometres out of town. In his absence his constable was left to man the station, a bicycle his only mode of transportation.

The new flag and the hiring of a black constable were two of the concessions the town had felt obliged to make, mainly due to pressure from certain members of the provincial government who considered the town and its council too white. It was the town's only compromise. Despite opposition from many locals, the changes were pushed ahead by Danie, a man much more progressive in his thinking than the other members of the town council. He'd realised a long time ago that in order to survive, the town had to emerge from its Laager Mentality. Apart from this, another reason for change, and probably the most significant one of all, was the funding the Council received from the government to run the small town.

'It's time we took this town out of mothballs and showed it to the rest of the country,' Danie told his cohorts. 'There's a whole world out there. People are going to come here and they'll spend money.' The locals, however, did not care to have their lives disrupted. Danie found it easier chatting to people individually in the town offices, away from the herd, where they were much more open to his ideas. He assumed correctly that people were interested in money. It was all pretty simple, he thought. Money transcended differences of race, colour and language. It was a universal language and Danie hoped it was a language he could use to catapult his town into the twenty-first century.

'By God, I'm going to do it,' he told Rena. 'I'm going to do it even if it means I have to drag them by the hair.'

Danie's brief visit to Cape Town had inspired him. He had had no assurances of Rebecca's help, but believed she'd come around to his thinking.

His thinking was that renovating and cleaning up the town would be an added benefit in the event that there was some truth to the stories about the Americans coming to town. There was, of course, also the possibility of the film company arriving. He hadn't heard from them since that first letter of enquiry. He wondered what the odds were of the film company being American, as someone had suggested. Perhaps the breakfast group was an advance group sent by the film company. It was a thought worth considering.

Danie had no idea whether the film company was American or local. There had been no indication in the letter he had received from Safari Films. They had merely mentioned that they might be sending someone to visit the town in order to assess its suitability for the purposes of 'shooting some film'.

Danie wished he'd taken the letter to Cape Town to show

34

Rebecca Fortuin. He studied it, analysed every word in it, perplexed about the phrase: shooting some film. What did they mean, he wondered.

Did they plan to shoot the entire film there, or were they shooting a portion of it? How much was some? How much time would it take? Were they going to be there for weeks or days?

No answers. They'd have to wait to see what happened.

The man coming to visit the town was referred to in the letter as a 'location scout'.

Danie, who had picked up some of the film jargon from the letter, bandied it about in the office. Since it sounded as if it had something to do with the blacks in the location, he avoided the word 'location', referring to the 'scout', which increased local confusion and led to stories about American scouts coming to town. It was all becoming too tiresome and Danie stopped giving explanations. By this time there were so many rumours that one didn't know what to think any more.

Danie had responded to the letter from the film company, and had included a copy of the article that had appeared in the Rustig Mining Gazette about the centenarian Mrs Roussouw, with the photograph of her smiling into the camera on the occasion of her one hundredth birthday. But there had been no further word from them. No one had been to look at the town, and no deals had been struck.

Nothing much was known about the company or the film, except that in the letter they indicated that the title of the film was *Ambiance*. Danie didn't have a clue what the word meant. Frustrated with the delay, he finally asked Rena to find the file they had opened in expectation of the burgeoning correspondence. There was still only the one letter from Safari Films.

Rena always seemed knowledgeable and so he asked her about Ambiance, sheepishly admitting that he did not know what it meant. She didn't know either. She had to look it up in her old school dictionary tucked away in the bottom drawer, behind a lot of other rubbish accumulated over the years.

But the word wasn't in her Oxford Minidictionary.

What kind of a word could this be, she wondered, as she conducted a futile search through the front pages of the dictionary.

Danie hoped that whatever *Ambiance* was, it had nothing to do with the Hemelslaagte Springs because there was already enough trouble with all the rumours about the Americans.

Rena, who continued to think about *Ambiance*, decided that Nora Naude would be their best bet. She told Danie that she would stop by Nora's place after work. It was frustrating to be stymied by a word that started with an 'A'. She muttered the word under her breath as she worked, trying to establish the correct pronunciation. Eventually she composed a little ditty around it, which she hummed around her office.

Rena had a good voice and might even have been considered for the church choir, had the story about her having an affair with Danie not got around. Arraigned by the town, she found herself isolated as the women of Vlenterhoek united against her. Petronella, with her tightly permed hair, had never been popular before, but gained stature now as the wronged wife.

No one considered that Danie's marriage might have been in trouble long before his attention strayed and that Rena might not be the other woman. It was much easier just to tack the blame on to her.

The town gossips had a field day. With pious self-righteousness, they were quick to condemn the philandering husband and the wanton mistress.

The rumours continued for months. No one bothered to ask Rena whether there might be any truth in them.

She kept her mouth shut and went about her own business. Danie, who was indeed philandering, but not with her, also decided that denial would only lend credence to the stories and so he, too, kept his mouth shut.

Despite all that was said about her, Rena maintained her silence and a strange, sad kind of dignity. She realised, with great satisfaction, that refusal to corroborate merely added to the moral torment of the upright residents of the town. She despised Petronella Venter and the other women for their false sense of morality. And knowing the identity of the 'other woman' in Danie's life gave her a sense of power.

On her way home that day, Rena went to see Nora Naude. She was the only one in town who had sided with her throughout the furore about Danie. Ever since that time Rena held Nora in high regard. She was one of the few people in town that Rena respected.

Nora explained that the word *Ambiance* was a French word for Ambience, which meant atmosphere or surroundings. The significance of this word in a film title was still not clear to Rena but Nora thought that it might have something to do with the veld and capturing a mood.

Rena nodded, thought about it and stored the information. Nora invited Rena in for a cup of tea.

'*Ag*, no thank you, Tannie Nora. I have to get home. My mother is probably waiting and wondering why I'm late.'

'You're a good girl, Rena, and so is Esther. I don't care what anyone has to say. I know what a struggle life has been for you and your sister and I admire you for sticking with your family.'

Rena lowered her head and sighed. 'What else can I do, Tannie Nora.'

'Of course,' Nora said.

She genuinely liked the girls and was particularly fond of Esther, who visited her regularly. They might be poor, Nora thought, but they had a lot more character than many people in town who were better off, and they were respectful, always addressed her as *Tannie*.

Nora walked Rena to the gate. Like Esther, Rena was tall

37

and although she didn't have Esther's beauty, there was an elegant quality about her, about the way she walked and carried herself. Nora always thought it a pity that Vlenterhoek did not have more to offer girls like Rena, Esther or even Sissie, who was just as attractive.

4

Nora Naude, the only person in Vlenterhoek who had thus far thought of opening a *bona fide* B&B, was in her own way preparing for the arrival of the Americans. Originally from Cape Town, Nora had lived in Vlenterhoek for twelve years. In the eyes of the locals, she was still a newcomer and most definitely a foreigner. Anyone not born and raised in Vlenterhoek was, as a matter of course, regarded as foreign.

The mystery of the word *Ambiance* had finally been solved and Rena told Danie about her visit to Nora's – the meaning of the mysterious word and the B&B sign on Nora's gate.

The next day Danie went to see Nora to find out what her plans were. He was keen on any ideas to promote the town and was particularly encouraging of entrepreneurial spirit. He was in a good mood. He had a feeling that things were eventually going to go his way. He and Nora had tea on her stoep.

'Tourism is good for the town.' he told Nora. '*Ja nee,*' he said, casually switching between English and Afrikaans. 'I'm still waiting to hear from Rebecca Fortuin . . .'

'One would have thought you'd have heard by now,' said Nora. She was one of the few people who did not know Rebecca, although she would later get to know her well.

He shook his head. 'They're busy, those people. Or so they say. But I'm getting on with things. Can't wait forever. Time is marching on, you know.'

'Tell me about it,' Nora replied. 'We're not getting any younger. If we don't do anything for this town, who will?'

'That's why I'm grabbing the reins now.'

'Keep at them,' was Nora's advice as she walked him to the gate where they stopped to inspect her sign. She could read the criticism in his eyes.

'It's the paint. The same paint that you've used on the signs at the town hall,' she told him. 'I think it's watered down.'

When Danie left, Nora spent time in her garden. There was so much to do, but she loved every moment of it. She didn't trust anyone but herself to do the pruning.

She was still pruning her roses when Esther Oosthuizen stopped in to have a look at the latest copy of the Afrikaans magazine *Rooi Rose* which usually arrived on Wednesdays. Nora subscribed to the magazine more for Esther's sake than her own. She watched as Esther carefully stepped over the mat of thorns along the edge of the pavement. She was a tall, gangly girl of fifteen. Barefoot, and walking on her toes, one hand holding her hair back out of her face, she made her way to the gate. She was pretty, her features accentuated by a pert nose, a wry mouth and eyes the colour of cornflowers. Nora thought that Esther had great potential as a model and since her mother, stuck in a wheelchair, had no interest in anything but venting her bile on Hendrik Joubert, she had taken it upon herself to groom the young girl.

The path was littered with rose cuttings. Fearing that Esther would come to grief on the thorns, Nora edged them away with the toe of her shoe and removed her gardening gloves.

At the gate Esther paused to read the new sign – NORA'S B&B – which was painted over the Afrikaans equivalent. Nora hoped she'd have better luck with the English version –

especially since there were so many stories about the Americans and the expected arrival of the film company – English-speaking people, she assumed.

'Hello, Tannie Nora. Is this a new sign?' Esther asked, as she pushed open the gate. At first Nora had found the local practice of shortening names quite exasperating, but eventually she accepted the fact that she was no longer Leonora, but plain old, insignificant Nora.

'I can still see the old sign,' Esther said.

'Yes, I know. I've just had Danie Venter here, saying exactly the same thing. Looks like they're watering down the paint at the Cash & Carry. Esther, for goodness sake child, how many times must I tell you not to walk barefoot? Look at your feet.'

Esther, whose heels were horribly cracked, loved going barefoot. 'Has the *Rooi Rose* come yet, Tannie?' she asked, ignoring the admonishment.

'Mmm.'

Esther waited impatiently as Nora removed her dark glasses and placed them on the stoep wall with her hat and gardening gloves. Lately Nora found that she was paying meticulous attention to where she put things, since they had a tendency to become misplaced and even lost.

'*Ag*, Tannie . . .' Esther started.

'English only,' Nora said, wagging a finger, which stopped Esther in mid-breath. 'Remember, we made a deal?'

Esther took a moment to consider what Nora had said. 'Well, can I loan it then?' She asked in English.

'May I?' The correction was automatic. 'And it's not loan it's borrow.'

'What?' Esther asked, looking baffled.

'You would say – May I borrow the magazine.'

'Oh, OK,' Esther said.

Although they now studied English as a second language at school, Esther still struggled with the nuances of the language.

41

'If I'm going to turn you into a lady, you have to learn to speak English properly.'

'I don't know if I want to be a lady, Tannie,' Esther muttered. 'I'm quite happy as I am.'

'Not while you're walking barefoot, Esther. The Jouberts are a very old and respected family and they're going to be very particular about who Jannie marries one day.'

'I know,' Esther sighed. 'Why does Jannie's father hate me so? Jannie and I haven't done anything wrong.'

Esther walked to the door. Nora followed, tapping her on the shoulder and reminding her not to slouch. She had explained to Esther more than once that her height was not a handicap, that most ramp models were tall and very erect, proud of their carriage.

Esther pushed her shoulders back.

'Your hair looks very pretty today,' Nora remarked.

'Do you really think it looks pretty?'

'Of course,' Nora said. 'Come inside I'll get you a cold drink.'

Nora's compliment boosted Esther's confidence. It made her feel good about herself, especially when she had to face criticism from some of the local women.

The magazine was lying on the coffee table. Esther paused at the door and wiped her feet on the coir mat. Nora went into the kitchen while Esther settled into an armchair, the magazine on her lap.

Nora returned with a small tray bearing two glasses.

'It's cooler on the stoep,' she said. 'Let's sit out there.'

Esther followed her and sat on the bench, curling her feet up under her. She sipped her glass of lemonade.

Nora watched Esther, who so desperately wanted to get out of Vlenterhoek.

For her, however, it was the ideal place. She loved the air. Loved the colour of the sky. She had often thought of capturing its brilliance on canvas, but had never got around to it.

When her husband was still alive she used to enjoy painting. The two of them used to walk the veld together. Now the canvases were packed away in the storeroom, gathering dust. Each time she saw them, she promised herself she'd start painting again – soon. But the canvases lay forgotten and the oil paints had long since dried and crumbled. And she always had the same excuse for procrastinating – she was waiting for inspiration or waiting for the right time.

She sighed wearily. She understood Esther. Understood her problems with Jannie Joubert's family. They were much like the ones she and her late husband had. But in the end they were married, despite her family's disapproval.

When her husband died Nora chose not to return to Cape Town or the family who had disowned her. This was where she wanted to be, coaxing her roses into ever larger blooms – amazing in an area that should only have supported succulents. It was a triumph for her to see the bushes yielding their enormous, multilayered blossoms. Whenever she looked at her garden, her heart fluttered with a feeling of pride and satisfaction. She had never felt so well and so content as she did in Vlenterhoek.

It was the air and the water. The one thing everyone agreed about was that Vlenterhoek had the clearest, cleanest, sweetest water on earth – and all of it oozing from the Hemelslaagte Springs just three kilometres out of town.

She watched as Esther slid her feet off the bench, closed the magazine, stretched, yawned and then gulped down her drink. 'I've got to go,' she said.

'What's the hurry?'

'Because of Jannie's father, my mother says I must come straight home after school.'

'But you didn't go straight home, you met Jannie, didn't you?'

'You know what it's like, Tannie, the same thing happened to you.'

'Yes. But our circumstances were different. In Jannie's case,

43

his father is still twisted out of shape about Frikkie. He had high hopes for his older son and just look how things turned out. A brilliant rugby career: all of it over in a wink of an eye. Maybe Hendrik doesn't want Jannie to end up like his brother.' Nora liked Jannie. He was a gentle, sensitive boy, obviously more like his mother than his father.

'But that has nothing to do with Jannie or me, Tannie,' Esther muttered. 'Frikkie was shot. That's why he couldn't play rugby no more.'

'Yes, and it broke his father's heart that he never came home after that. One feels that way about one's children, Esther.'

'It's only because we're poor. That's why he doesn't like me. And that's not my fault,' she said petulantly.

'Of course not, child.'

Esther was silent, her attention on the sign at the gate. 'You'll have to paint that over again.'

'I'll make a new sign when I have time.' Nora said pensively. 'I always wanted to own a bed and breakfast,' she sighed. 'Perhaps . . .' and then her eyes glazed over. 'Oh, I don't know . . .' With a shrug she cast a critical glance at the exterior of the house. 'Perhaps the house needs a fresh coat of paint . . . I wonder about magenta.'

'What's that?' Esther asked.

'Blue,' Nora said.

'Blue,' Esther said, frowning her disapproval.

'I think blue might look quite lovely, especially with the colours here.'

Nora knew a lot about colour. She was still thinking about colours when Esther said: 'I think you were crazy to leave Cape Town.'

'This is a nice town, Esther. I like it. It's quiet and it's safe and I love the veld. I love the colours of the sky and the earth. You must learn to see the beauty around you, child.'

'I hate Vlenterhoek . . . I hate the people. They're horrible to my sister and me – Mrs Becker especially. I don't know what Rena and I have done to them.'

Nora went to retrieve her gloves and hat from the wall of the stoep. 'The world is full of people like Mrs Becker,' she said as she removed the hatpin and placed the hat back on her head. 'You must learn to ignore them.' She carefully pressed her hat into place and skewered the crown with the hatpin.

Esther leaned up against the wall, arms crossed, looking disgruntled.

Nora gave her arm a reassuring squeeze.

Esther smiled and seemed to shake off her petulance.

Nora watched her go, still on her toes, stepping over the pile of dead rosebush stems. She shut the gate behind her, waved and crossed the street. Nora's mind moved to some other space as she continued to gaze at an imaginary figure long after the real one had disappeared from view.

Esther was late getting home that day. Her mother was waiting in the doorway in her wheechair. Esther carefully picked her way across the rough stones, pushing her hair back behind her ears, a habit she resorted to whenever she was anxious.

'I've been waiting for you all afternoon!' her mother cried, her voice rising. 'What is wrong with you? Why can't you come straight home from school? You know you have to make supper. Talk to me, Esther! Where have you been? I hope you haven't been with Jannie again. Do you want us to end up in the street? Don't you have any shame? I don't want you anywhere near that boy. I want nothing to do with any of them. Do you hear me?'

'We're living in his father's house,' Esther muttered under her breath as she slipped past her mother who was blocking the way with her wheelchair.

'Yes, and he was here this very afternoon, telling me that he'd evict us if you don't stop seeing Jannie.'

Esther ignored her mother's tirade and hurried into the small house.

'I'm talking to you!' her mother screamed after her.

Esther reached the safety of her bedroom and slammed the door.

That night Esther was restless. She got up and went outside. She sat on the step, lit a cigarette and studied the sky. It was a brilliant night with a full moon and the stars seemed brighter than she'd ever seen them before. In Vlenterhoek the night sky was always spectacular. One of the Rustig engineers, a keen astronomer, had once proposed the area as a location for a small observatory. The Astronomical Society had never even bothered to respond to his suggestion. The observatory was eventually built elsewhere.

The next day Albert and Sissie were on the ridge with Jannie and Esther.

Esther deliberately ignored Jannie, speaking to Sissie instead, but Sissie's mind was too busy with other thoughts to pay much attention to Esther. Esther was still furious about Jannie's father coming to the house to threaten them. She was annoyed with Jannie too, not because he'd done anything, but because he was Hendrik's son.

Jannie sensed that something was amiss and sat back on his haunches, watching her. He was very sensitive to her moods and always knew when something was wrong. He couldn't see her face because she'd turned away from him, but he sensed that she'd been crying.

Finally, in an effort to get her attention, he went over to where she was sitting with Sissie and showed her the new kite.

'T-t-th-th-is is-s-ss a p-p-p-ro-to-t-t-type,' he stuttered as he held up the kite for her to see. At times his stutter seemed much worse, especially when he was agitated. The wonderful thing about being with Esther and his friends, though, was that he didn't have to say much. Esther, especially, seemed able to read his mind.

It was absolutely remarkable, how well she understood him.

'What's that?' Albert asked all agog as he gazed at the huge kite.

'A-an e-e-ex-ppp-eri-ment. I-I-I've b-b-b-een w-w-w-orking on. A m-m-m-ma-t-t-t-hem-m-matical f-f-f-ormula. With the w-w-w-ind v-v-ve-ve-locity, t-t-the w-e-e-ight of the k-k-ite and the ae-ae-ae-rodymics,' Jannie said.

'Whoa! *Wag 'n bietjie*. What does all that mean?' Albert laughed. 'Aero . . . *wat*?'

'A-a-a-e-ae-aer-o-dy-dy-namics,' Jannie said, struggling to get the word out again. He was enthusiastic, happy to explain what he had in mind.

But what they did not know was that Jannie was building a hang-glider.

He hadn't told anyone about it. Not even Albert. It was his secret, which he planned to reveal only on the day of the kite competition.

'I-I-If the w-w-w-w-ind is r-r-r-ight w-w-we c-c-an g-g-get t-his s-s-sucker r-r-ri-ght up t-t-t-t-th-ere as h-h-h-igh as it can go,' he said.

Jannie's enthusiasm was infectious and Esther smiled, resting her chin on her knees, watching as he and Albert worked on the kite.

From her kitchen door, Jannie's mother, Anna Joubert, saw Jannie's new kite in the sky and couldn't help admiring the brilliant colours of blue, coral and yellow as it dipped and soared across the skyline. She hoped that her husband hadn't seen the kite, otherwise there was bound to be trouble again.

5

The Joubert farmhouse was about five kilometres out of town.

The farm, Tweeriviere, appropriately named since it was situated at the confluence of two rivers, had belonged to the Jouberts for as long as anyone could remember, lands that were settled in 1895 by Hendrik Joubert's great-grandfather. Tweeriviere was one of the single, largest tracts of land owned by any one individual in the district, the first Joubert having settled the land in the days when springboks still roamed freely. At one time the Joubert lands had included the town of Vlenterhoek, but Jannie's great-great-grandfather had ceded much of what he owned, especially the land along the riverbanks, to a group of settlers. Eventually, in 1947, the town was incorporated and because of the ragged nature of the settlement, it was named Vlenterhoek.

It was a source of pride to Hendrik that five generations of his family had lived there. Many things had changed since then, though, and Hendrik had little hope of the farm being in the family for another generation. His sons Frikkie and Jannie were a huge disappointment to him. Even though Frikkie had made rugby history, it seemed such a hollow triumph when he had to give up the sport because of the shooting.

He would have preferred to have both his sons with him – the two of them running the farm with him, side by side. Father and sons. But all hopes he might have had of this happening were crushed by Frikkie's hasty departure. Hendrik had pleaded with him to come home, even after the shooting, but Frikkie had told him quite bluntly that he had no intention of returning to Vlenterhoek. Except for one letter, there had been no further communication from him. Now Hendrik was left with Jannie, who could barely utter a single word without making a fool of himself. He wondered what he'd done to deserve such a fate.

Hendrik viewed Jannie's stutter as retribution for a ghastly mistake he'd made as a young man. He'd wished often enough that he could turn back the clock, wipe out one night's terrible mistake that had haunted him through most of his adult life. With a shudder, Hendrik shunted the memory aside. It was something that he preferred not to dwell on.

There were business problems to occupy his mind now. Not only had the price of wool become dependent on the vagaries of the fashion industry, but production levels were also a matter of concern. He hoped prices would improve soon because of low reserves. Production was down world-wide. But his particular problem in Vlenterhoek, as he saw it, was that they had been hit by the worst drought in decades. The two rivers had literally dried up. And not only that, but the cost of labour had increased dramatically with the advent of a black government. Stock thefts, droughts and the escalating cost of fuel also had to be factored into costs. That meant only one thing – smaller profit margins.

With all these problems weighing heavily on his mind, Hendrik emerged from his office that afternoon and heard Jannie in the kitchen. Albert was waiting outside in the yard. Jannie's mother had tried to entice him in with a cold drink but the boy was terrified of Hendrik and steadfastly refused to enter the house. He would never set foot in the house when Hendrik was home. When Hendrik entered the kitchen and saw Jannie with the kite, his blood pressure soared. He was furious that Jannie would rather fly kites than get involved in the day-to-day activities of the farm. It was obvious, too, that his son was still meeting Esther in the afternoons.

Jannie's mother tried to keep the peace between father and son. But the two of them were usually so determined to lay bare their hatred of each other, that neither paid any attention to her. From the moment they set eyes on one another in her kitchen, their resentment bucked and reared like a horse with a burr under its saddle.

'You're not a child any more. You're almost a man. You've got Joubert blood in your veins. Tough blood. But look at you. Where in God's name have I gone wrong with you?' Hendrik asked furiously, hardly pausing to draw breath.

Anna winced at the way her husband took the Lord's name in vain.

'Look at you! You're a disgrace! And look at him!' Hendrik cried, spotting Albert outside. 'Another weakling. You're both useless. What kind of sissy stuff is this? He grabbed the kite out of Jannie's hands and ripped it apart. What's wrong with you?' He took a deep breath, his face scarlet with rage.

Jannie paled. The veins on the side of his neck stood out like swollen ropes. Whenever he became angry, all his freckles sprouted simultaneously, giving his skin a strange mottled appearance. 'I-I-I h-h-ha-te y-y-you. I-I-I'm n-n-not s-s-s-ca-scared o-of y-y-y-ou a-an-any-m-m-ore.' It was a struggle, but he managed to get the words out.

His mother gasped.

In two strides Hendrik was almost in Jannie's face. He raised his hand and Jannie stepped back, bracing himself. His father's flat hand caught him a glancing blow to the jaw. Slightly stunned, Jannie reeled. For a split second a fire seemed to ignite behind his eyes. It burnt brightly for a moment and then died down.

Jannie brushed past his mother.

Startled, Albert watched as Jannie hurtled from the house, his mother running after him.

'Let him go,' Hendrik called to his wife. 'It is you who is turning him into such a *papbroek*.' Hendrik always went on and on about what a weakling his son was, and his remarks merely served to increase Jannie's resentment.

Jannie fled from his father's thundering voice; from the confining atmosphere of the house; from his own anger.

'While he's under my roof, he'll do as I say!' Hendrik yelled.

His wife gazed at him in dismay. 'He's almost a man, Hendrik. Why do you insist on treating him like a child? Why must all my sons hate you? What about Suzette and my grandson? Why can't the truth come out for once, Hendrik? Why?' she sobbed. 'I don't want to go through this again. Speak to Jannie!' Her sobbing ended in a whimper when Hendrik, bent on venting his temper on his son, rushed outside after him.

'I can destroy both her and her sister just like that . . .' he shouted after Jannie, snapping his fingers.

'You should tell him. You should speak to . . . tell her you know the truth . . .' his wife continued. 'Tell her that hiding the boy by sending him to private school didn't fool me for one minute. I can tell that that boy is my grandson. No use him lying, making up stories. Now I have to suffer too because of you and Gert . . .'

But Hendrik wasn't there to hear her. He was standing in the yard, shaking his fist at Jannie.

Jannie rushed past the astonished Albert and was halfway across the yard before Albert could think of stopping him. By the time he decided to go after Jannie, the other boy was almost out of sight. Standing in the middle of the road, Albert stared helplessly after him as he disappeared into the distance.

The next morning as the sun slowly tracked a path into the sky and traffic along the main street increased, a school bus

51

arrived, followed by a bakkie, and then an assortment of vehicles. It was another school day and as uniform-clad students arrived at the school gates they veered off, some to the Vlenterhoek Primary School and others to the Vlenterhoek High School. Both schools were on the same grounds, separated only by a chain-link fence.

Despite the exodus of young people, there were still students in sufficient numbers to warrant a high school. Numbers in the primary school, however, had dwindled to the extent that three of the teachers had become redundant and had to be transferred to other centres. It had taken a few years, but there was a dawning realisation that unless utilisation of the schools increased, they might have to close. The logical solution was to make education accessible to all. Unfortunately the Vlenterhoek school officials were not renowned for their logic and, with few exceptions, the idea of universal education was still anathema to the residents.

Esther Oosthuizen was barefoot, walking on the balls of her feet like a ballerina. The only concession she made to conformity was on Sundays when she went to church wearing shoes, although they came off as soon as she was seated. Jannie Joubert, a year older and at least three inches taller, accompanied her, walking a few steps behind because of the kite he was carrying. Wound around his free hand was the tail that had been damaged a little earlier when he reeled the kite in. This was a new kite. He'd built it during the night in defiance of his father. First thing that morning, long before anyone at home had awakened, he'd been back to the ridge to fly the kite.

Esther and Jannie arrived at the school grounds just as the bell rang. Sissie was lagging behind them, sedately strolling along without a care in the world, her head gracefully balanced on her long, slender neck.

She and Albert were the only coloured students at the Vlenterhoek High School. The school authorities, by raising school fees, had managed to stem the tide of black students

52

who, they feared, were poised to migrate from the location. The few black students who had been allowed into the school to appease the provincial government authorities, tended to clique together in a form of self-imposed apartheid. Occasionally tension between the white and the black groups flared and local authorities used such incidents to justify their actions.

The four friends – Jannie, Esther, Sissie and Albert – met at the school gates. Albert, with his guitar case slung over his shoulder, urged Sissie to hurry. She was perpetually late – always lost somewhere in a world of her own. He shifted the weight of the case, spotted Esther and Jannie and called to them. Albert was anxious to find out what had happened the previous day. He hadn't seen or spoken to Jannie since the previous afternoon when Jannie had hurtled out of the house. Jannie had taken off so fast that Albert didn't even try to catch up with him.

One of the boys in the schoolyard, an oafish fellow with big ears, was lying in wait for Albert and followed him with small mincing steps. The boy's friends watched, laughing and jeering.

Another boy crept up behind Jannie, hunching his shoulders in a parody of the Hunchback of Notre Dame, a film they had recently seen in class, and mimicked Jannie's stutter at its worst. Behind Albert, Big Ears pranced, his hand raised in an exaggerated effeminate pose.

Jannie and Esther reacted instantly to this mocking behaviour. While Jannie grabbed the Hunch Back of Notre Dame and landed a solid punch to his jaw, Esther caught hold of Big Ears by his pachydermatous appendages and gave him a few good slaps to the head.

Esther, tall and intimidating, usually did most of the work of defending her friends. Albert hated fighting, and Sissie never got involved. She was an observer, always on the sidelines, watching. The physical stuff was left to Jannie and Esther.

Later that afternoon when her sister Noelle got home, it was apparent that word had got out about the scrap at school. Sissie shrugged off her sister's questions. 'You know what they're like,' she said.

Noelle was twelve years older than Sissie and worked as a domestic for Mrs Becker. She had the kind of eyes that could cut right through you. When she glared, you knew you were being glared at. Mrs Becker said she was cheeky, but Noelle didn't care what Mrs Becker thought or said. Noelle had a dead-eyed look about her, as if she'd shut down everything inside her. Sometimes Sissie wondered if her sister blamed her for all the misery in her life and for all the responsibilities that had been thrust on her at too early an age.

Noelle and Sissie were very close. She'd practically raised Sissie after their mother died. She knew that Sissie was not a troublemaker, even though this wasn't the first time that Sissie and her friends had been involved in fights at school. She knew Sissie well enough to know that she would never start a fight. It had to be Esther. That girl stood back for no one. She wished that Sissie would be more assertive. She was much too soft. Noelle often wondered if having such a soft nature had anything to do with the fact that Sissie was a twin and that she had had to watch her twin die.

Sissie's twin brother David had died at the age of six. Older by five minutes, he was an extremely sickly child who, in the end, died of rickets. Their mother, already ill with liver disease, was in labour for ten hours. No one thought she'd survive the arduous birth of twins, but she did. Sissie was the healthy baby, David was always ill. The two were never too far from each other – even as babies. Whenever they were separated, one could see one twin's eyes searching for the other. It was quite amazing.

Sissie was different in many other ways too. She was extremely intuitive. Noelle thought it might have been because Sissie was born with a caul and had emerged at birth with her head neatly packaged in a membranous wrap.

The midwife, aware of its significance, had buried the caul with the placenta and told no one about it. But as Sissie grew older, it became clear that there was something special in her quiet countenance and in the penetrating eyes that seemed to gaze right into one's soul.

Sissie realised at an early age that she had some kind of sixth sense, a heightened intuition that sensed things before they happened.

Some things Sissie didn't dare mention to anyone – like the dream she had of the death of her twin brother. Five years later, when their mother died, Sissie had dreamt of her death as well.

Noelle sensed that something was troubling Sissie.

'What is it, Sissie?'

'Nothing,' said Sissie.

But Noelle didn't believe her. She'd noticed for some time now that something was wrong with her younger sister.

Sissie wanted to tell Noelle about her dream, but didn't know how. She was afraid that if she said anything, something bad might happen again. She hadn't had these strange dreams in a long time, but for a while now she'd been dreaming about their older brother Ivan. The dreams were disturbing – more so, perhaps, because she had not known Ivan. She and David had been born several years after Ivan had left home. They were strange dreams in which her older brother was not clearly identifiable, but somehow she knew that it was him.

Lately she'd been thinking about him, and wondering why Noelle never volunteered information about him. Whenever she broached the subject Noelle simply shrugged her shoulders dismissively.

Poor Ivan. It was as though he had never existed – not in this household, anyway. It seemed tragic to Sissie that she had a brother she knew so little about.

Sissie's dreams continued for weeks and one night she

could contain herself no longer. She confronted Noelle when the two of them were in the kitchen preparing supper.

Noelle was about to light the Primus stove when Sissie took the bottle of methylated spirits and the matches from her.

Noelle recognised the signs.

'What's wrong?' she asked.

'I want to know about Ivan,' Sissie said, as she poured the methylated spirits into the Primus head and lit the flame.

'I don't remember much about him,' Noelle said as she cut two thick slices of bread.

Sissie had heard this response before. 'But you must know,' she said. 'You were here. Why won't you tell me about him?'

Her sister did not respond.

'I want to know, Noelle. I've been dreaming about him . . .'

'What have you dreamt?' Noelle asked.

'First you tell me,' Sissie said firmly.

'What do you want to know?'

'Everything . . . How old was he when he left home?' she asked.

'Fifteen,' Noelle said as she spread margarine on the bread. 'He left for the city to look for a decent job.'

'Did he find a decent job?' Sissie asked.

'I don't know. He never wrote to us.'

'How old were you when he left?'

'About eleven.'

'What did he look like, Noelle?'

Noelle grew impatient. 'How am I supposed to get supper done if you keep bothering me with questions?'

'You promised . . .'

'If you must know, he was fair,' she said. 'He looked like a white man.' Sissie waited but her sister didn't say any more.

'And?' Sissie prompted.

'He had straight hair and freckles,' Noelle said and then her expression softened. 'He looked a little like Mama. She

56

used to be so beautiful, . . . you just can't imagine . . .' She shut her lips firmly and turned away. That was all the information she was going to volunteer.

'Where is he now?' Sissie asked.

Her sister flashed her a look of exasperation. 'No one knows. Seven years ago the woman he was living with in Upington wrote to say that Ivan had disappeared. He'd left home one day and told her he was going to see his father. She didn't understand what he meant because she knew that Pa was dead. Ivan never returned and she thought he had killed himself because of what he said about going to see his father. Poor woman, she wanted to know whether we wanted any of his belongings. She had a child too. I wrote back to tell her that we didn't want any of his things.'

'Why didn't you say anything before?' Sissie asked.

Her sister shrugged and walked away. 'So what's your dream?' she asked as she picked up the bucket to go and fetch water.

'I don't know what the dream was about. But I know it was about him. I couldn't see his face. It was just a figure, really. Tall and thin. I can't remember much except that he'd come to visit me.'

'Ja, he was tall,' Noelle said as she walked to the door. 'Put the kettle on the Primus,' she said and left to fetch water from the outside tap.

Despite what Noelle told her about their mother's beauty, Sissie could not imagine her mother as a young or beautiful woman. She remembered her only as sickly yellow – the colour of death – her eyes dulled with sadness. In the last few weeks of her mother's life, her breath had been like fire: thick with the stench of rot. Some said it was the bad gas from her liver.

Sissie felt that she had never really known the others in her family: her mother, her older brother or, for that matter, her father. The only constant person in her life had been Noelle. Even her twin brother had been taken from her.

Their home might also have been taken from them after

their mother's death had Mrs Joubert not insisted that her husband allow them to stay rent-free. She had done the same for the Oosthuizens. In their case it was justified, but Sissie never quite understood why they were allowed the same privilege.

It seemed to Sissie that no matter how things might have changed in other parts of the country, life in Vlenterhoek continued the same as before. She was still the same honey colour and her hair was still frizzy and she and Noelle still lived on the boundary which separated white from black. Although under the new constitution she was guaranteed the right to education – even in a white school, if that was what she wanted – the white people of Vlenterhoek still treated her and others like her the way they had in those years when there were separate entrances for them. And yes, the *sloot* was still there and was still the boundary between the whites and the blacks.

In all the years they had lived on the banks of the sloot, only once, during the Year of The Big Rains, could Sissie remember seeing water in it. That was the year that their house was almost swept away. It was also the year that their father left and her twin brother died.

Their mother started drinking then. Sometimes Sissie and Noelle had to fetch her from her favourite spot on the pavement in front of the Imperial Hotel where she would sit and wait, hoping that one of the patrons would take pity on her and buy her a drink. Only whites were allowed in the bar, and so she sat outside waiting, whining and pleading for a drink. Sometimes she sat out there long after the bar had closed.

'You see, Sissie,' Noelle would say on the occasions when they went to fetch their mother from the hotel where she sat puking into the gutter, 'that's what happens when you've got no pride.'

Then when their mother got really sick and her condition deteriorated, Sissie had the dream. It was so clear that she awakened with a start. Because she feared her dream would become reality, she never told anyone about it. It didn't matter in the end because her mother died anyway. Sissie was terrified of her dreams. They were bad omens which had a way of coming true. She usually tried to avoid thinking about them – focusing only on the good things that happened in her life, although these were rare events.

6

Leah surveyed her small cramped basement flat in East Vancouver. She had often thought of her sisters, especially in those last few years when Charlie had become unbearably peculiar. But because of the great distance which separated them physically, she felt that the likelihood of her ever seeing them again was quite remote.

She remembered Portia's parting words: 'You've made your bed. Now you have to lie in it.' This was her world now. She felt a visceral tug as she glanced around the room.

The small suitcase under the bed contained everything she owned – all her worldly possessions tightly rolled to fit into the one piece of luggage. The rest of her baggage – both literal and figurative – had been left behind the day she walked out of the house in Point Grey. She was determined now never to look back on her life with Charlie.

During those last years with Charlie the only bright spot in her existence was Jock – a stray tomcat that had climbed into her life through the open bathroom window. One day she'd found him hiding in the linen closet in the bathroom. He was a huge cat – part Manx she guessed from the indecisive growth of his tail, and she had named him Jock after Jock of the Bushveld, even though the Jock of literary fame was a dog.

Jock stayed with them whenever he chose, wandering in and out of her life. Sometimes he spent the night in her bed. She found his soft purring and the light pressure of his body against her back comforting. She always knew when Charlie came into the room by the way the gentle ball of fur would suddenly rise on all four legs, hair on end, hissing like a steam engine. Then, with one leap, he'd bound off the bed and out of the room.

Charlie hated the cat. Sick as he was, when Leah wasn't around he'd always find the strength to aim a vicious kick at Jock's ribs.

Despite all of these aggravations, Leah had the pleasure of Jock's company for three years. Then, the day before Charlie collapsed and was rushed to hospital, Jock disappeared. The next day one of the nurses at St Paul's Hospital phoned and suggested that she come in. Charlie's condition, she said, had deteriorated. Leah got ready to go to the hospital. It was a mid-January night, cold and blustery and she negotiated the narrow steps down to the basement to find Charlie's down-filled jacket. She did not own a coat and the jacket was the only warm item of clothing in the house. She knew it would be too big and that she'd probably look ridiculous in it, but she no longer cared about the way she looked, or how others perceived her. Charlie had long since wiped the floor with her self-esteem.

When she turned on the light switch at the bottom of the basement stairs she saw Jock's bloodied body lying on the floor next to the small window. The blood had congealed. Jock had been dead for a couple of days.

She remembered then that Charlie had been in the basement the morning before his admission to hospital. She guessed that he had trapped Jock as he leaped in through the basement window and had kicked him to death.

'Charlie, you filthy bastard,' Leah muttered, as she lifted Jock's mangled body and wrapped it in a towel hanging on the door. She found Charlie's jacket and with Jock's body tucked under one arm, struggled back up the steep basement stairs.

She had endured years of abuse from Charlie and after his cancer was diagnosed she had taken care of him. After months of cleaning up blobs of brown, bloody sputum, and of boiling his sheets stained brown from episodes of incontinence or diarrhoea, there had never been a single word of appreciation from him.

Her anger and grief at Jock's death had exhausted her, but she found a spade in the shed and dug a hole near the rhododendron bush. The rain was coming down steadily, her hip ached and she was ankle deep in mud, but none of this seemed to matter as she carefully laid Jock's body to rest, covering it with clods of mud.

She returned the spade to the shed, cleaned the mud off her boots and walked to the corner to flag a cab.

By the time the cab made the U-turn and pulled up at the Burrard Street entrance to the hospital, she was too tired to get out. She wondered why on earth they'd hospitalised Charlie at this end of town instead of the Vancouver General, which was so much closer, but then she remembered that there hadn't been any beds available at the General.

She asked the driver, a Sikh in a pink turban, to wait for her. 'I won't be long,' she said, 'and it's so hard to get a cab from here.'

He nodded. 'I'll wait.'

She didn't expect her visit to Charlie would take any time at all.

Wriggling to the edge of the seat, she shimmied out, taking the driver's proffered hand. His hand was warm and soft and there was a sense of world-weariness in his eyes – a look that said he'd seen it all.

The rubber soles of her boots were worn smooth and were treacherous on the slippery sidewalks. Her foot slid over the moss along the edge of the kerb.

'Can I leave my jacket on the seat?' She asked, turning back. It was too cumbersome. She felt trapped in it.

'Yup,' the driver nodded.

Leah tossed the jacket on to the back seat and shut the door. She had worn an old sweater under the jacket and as she carefully stepped over the cracks in the sidewalk, she began to feel the cold. She walked along the pathway to the entrance, climbed the two steps and looked back. The taxi was still there, waiting.

Her long heavy grey hair had come undone. She swept a few tendrils off her brow and pushed open the door into a corridor, blindingly bright under the white fluorescent lights. Holding on to the rail along the wall, she steadied herself. Her hip was still throbbing and her heart pounded with a mixture of apprehension and rage. She saw her reflection in a glass door and paused to tidy her hair. There were splatters of mud on her face, which she tried to remove with spit. She appeared much older than she actually was – thanks to Charlie she'd aged considerably in the past few years. The pert nose was no longer as attractive as it had been when she was young, and the warm brown eyes had become hard and sceptical. She straightened her collar and fiddled with her appearance for a moment longer and then gave up with a shrug. It was too much trouble and she didn't really care what anyone thought of her. The elevator took ages to come and so she climbed the stairs to the second floor.

She stopped at the nursing station and a nurse escorted her to the ward and then discreetly left.

Charlie's eyes flickered open and snapped shut again. He looked pale and wasted. Under other circumstances she might have felt a twinge of sympathy for him, but without the slightest hesitation, Leah limped up to Charlie's bed and, leaning over him with her lips close to his ear, whispered, 'I hope you rot in hell, you bastard!'

His eyes shot open.

She turned and left the room. Outside the door of his

room was a chair and Leah, feeling that her legs would carry her no further, sat down. She must have dozed off because a while later one of the nurses gently touched her shoulder.

'Mrs Barker,' the nurse said, 'I'm afraid your husband has passed away.'

Leah let out a sigh of relief. The old curmudgeon was finally gone.

The nurse took her arm to assist her back into Charlie's room. She assumed that Leah would want to see her husband for the last time, but Leah didn't want to see Charlie again and disengaged her arm.

'Come and sit down for a while,' one of the other nurses said sympathetically and led her away to the waiting room.

'I have a taxi waiting outside,' Leah said, much more sharply than she intended.

'The taxi left,' the nurse said. 'The driver couldn't wait any longer. He left your jacket at the reception desk downstairs. Are you sure you're all right, Mrs Barker?'

'Better than I've been in years,' Leah responded.

'What about funeral arrangements?' asked one of the other nurses. 'Do you have family? Children?'

'My daughter is in Toronto. Could you please call her?' Leah's hand trembled ever so slightly as she handed the nurse a slip of paper. 'He locked our phone. I don't have change for the public phone . . .'

'I'll call,' the nurse said, taking the number from her. 'Do you want to talk to her?'

Leah shook her head. 'I'll talk to her later.'

'Do you have the name of a funeral home?' the nurse asked.

'No. You do whatever you want with him. I don't care.'

One of the nurses accompanied her to the elevator. 'If you need help, call this number,' she said, giving Leah a card with the name of a counsellor. 'And this is the name of a shelter – just in case you might need help some day.' She scribbled the address on a slip of paper. Leah took the paper

64

with a small grateful smile. Then she seemed to gather herself, drew her shoulders back, her neck slender and sinewy as her fragile frame rose out of the threadbare folds of the old sweater. With head held high, she slowly made her way to the reception desk to collect Charlie's jacket.

Now what? she wondered, as she left the hospital. She had no intention of returning to the house on Massey Place in Point Grey. She couldn't care less about what happened to it. With nothing but the money she had in her purse, she walked out of the hospital and out of her old life, firmly shutting the door on it.

Leah hailed a cab. It was raining steadily again. She climbed into the back of the cab, grateful to get out of the rain and sank back against the seat, the cold leather upholstery folding around her buttocks.

'Take me to this address,' she said to the cab driver, handing him the slip of paper on which the nurse had written the address of the shelter.

She dozed off, waking to hear the driver saying, 'Here we are.'

She gazed around, confused and disoriented.

The driver turned to look at her. 'You want me to come in with you?'

'No, thank you,' Leah shook her head. She opened the door and hesitated. 'I don't know if I have enough money to pay you,' she said handing him twenty dollars. 'Is this enough?'

'Yes.' He handed her her change. 'Good luck,' he said, smiling cheerfully.

She managed a smile for him, leaned over and squeezed his shoulder. 'Thank you. God bless you.'

She shared a room at the shelter with another unfortunate woman who never said a word. Her silence suited Leah who had no inclination to talk or to unburden herself to some curious, garrulous confidante. All she wanted was peace and quiet to sort out her life.

She phoned the hospital from a pay phone in the lobby.

One of the nurses who had been on duty the night Charlie died answered the phone.

'We spoke to your daughter, Mrs Barker. She won't be coming for the funeral. She's in hospital. She's just had a bit of surgery.'

'What kind of surgery?' Leah asked.

'She's had some ovarian cysts removed.'

'I see.'

'She's been trying to get you at home. Her husband phoned this morning. He wants you to call them. They want to know about funeral arrangements . . .'

'I'll let them know as soon as I know.'

'Will you call them?'

'Yes.'

Leah did not have a penny to her name. A counsellor suggested that she take Charlie's death certificate to the bank and ask them whether she was able to draw money from his account. But the bank told her that there was no money in Charlie's account and that a service charge of twelve dollars was owing. Leah left the bank and walked around in a daze, trying to figure out how she was going to survive without money. The house would have to be sold. She was not going back there.

Charlie's Canada Pension Plan paid for his funeral. It was just as well because she didn't have the money to bury him. The arrangements were made with the assistance of a social worker, a funeral home was selected and the body was picked up from the hospital morgue. She went to see his body once only and then told them to seal the casket.

He was buried in a cemetery in Burnaby, miles from where they lived. The car from the funeral home dropped her back at the house and Leah went through their belongings, searching for an account of Charlie's finances. She couldn't make head or tail of what he'd done with their money. She felt tired. Her legs were shaky, her blood pressure had no doubt gone through the ceiling, and her hip hurt like hell.

Dear God, Leah prayed, *forgive me. I'm not really this miserable. It's just that this man has brought out the worst in me. Let me get through the next few days and I promise I'll be a better person.*

She broke the lock on the phone and was about to call for a cab when it rang. It was Erica.

'Mum,' her daughter said tentatively.

'Erica, is that you?'

'Yes. How are you, Mum?'

'I'm fine,' she said. 'How about you? I heard you were in hospital.'

'I'm much better,' Erica said. 'They removed a cyst as big as a football. But you, Mum ... the funeral?'

'It's all over. He's been put into the ground. Life is for the living now.'

'Will you manage?'

'Of course.'

'Ron said you're not living at home. Where are you staying?'

'With friends,' Leah lied.

'Who are they?'

'You won't know them, dear ...'

'Can you give me a phone number?'

Leah hesitated briefly. 'I'll call you. You just take good care of yourself, dear.'

'Will you keep in touch, Mum?'

'Of course, dear.'

Pleasantries exchanged between mother and daughter. Empty words. Leah tried to inject some warmth into her voice, but everything inside her felt dead.

The cab arrived soon afterwards.

She did not want to spend a minute longer than necessary in the house. She'd been back a few times since Charlie's death and had found it difficult to breathe in the oppressive atmosphere of the old house, crammed to the rafters with Charlie's collectables.

Apart from the smell of mildew and of rotting wood, there were other smells too, smells she had never noticed before. Looking around her, she realised that she had never belonged there. The house had never been part of her.

There was no warmth. No fond memories. No carefully nurtured love or affection – just Charlie's icy-cold breath, which froze everything in its path.

She was quite happy to leave the house and everything in it – happy to put it all behind her and never to return.

7

Ephemera, convinced that Leah was coming home, begged
Portia to get out the family photographs. Knowing that she
would have no peace from her sister until she did, Portia got
on her knees and pulled the box out from under the bed.
There were more photographs stored in their father's old
trunk which had not been opened in years. Only once, after
her mother died, had she opened it. Lying on the top of a
neat pile of her father's clothing she'd found a pack of playing
cards. She'd realised then where their father had gone on all
those occasions when he disappeared without explanation.
The deck of cards said it all. Fearful of what else she might
find in the trunk, she'd shut the lid on her father's iniquitous
life, locked the trunk and covered it with a cloth.

Ephemera, sitting close to her sister as they sat on the bed
scrutinising each photograph, clapped her hands ecstatically
when they came across pictures of Leah.

Portia eventually grew tired of the pictures and Ephemera's
incessant questions. 'I think we should go into town now to
buy supplies,' she said.

The two women, in their frocks, hats and gloves, set off
for town to purchase supplies at the Portuguese Buy & Save.
Summer or winter, whether at home or out of the house,

Portia always wore black dresses, some of them trimmed with white. She'd started wearing black when her father died and had continued well past the period of mourning for both her parents. In her black dress and black lace-up shoes, she looked like a German *Frau*. Ephemera, more girlish than her sister, wore floral dresses with a lace trim around the collar or the cuffs. Between them they owned four hats. There was a wide-brimmed black straw hat trimmed with organdie net and a sprinkling of plastic flowers, which was Portia's church hat. For their day-to-day excursions she wore the other black hat with the brown ribbon around the brim – it was more like a bonnet than her Sunday hat. Ephemera's favourite was a beige cloche, decorated with pink net and pink and blue roses. If she had her way, she would probably have worn this hat every day of her life, but Portia insisted that she wear her good pink hat for church on Sundays.

While they were shopping Ephemera told anyone willing to listen that her sister Leah was coming home.

'We've got to go now,' Portia said, half-dragging her sister away, but even as they were leaving, Ephemera had more to say, tossing tit-bits of news, like confetti, with the same flamboyant gestures that had been such a familiar trait of their mother's.

Portia eventually frog-marched her sister out the door. The packer followed, wheeling their shopping trolley. Empty handed, Ephemera paused, clutching Portia's arm. They were halfway across the street when Ephemera came to an abrupt halt, right in the middle of the street. As the two sisters stood there immobile, a donkey-cart clipped by, deftly swerving around them.

Ephemera's eyes had glazed over. Portia gave her arm a little tug. 'Come on Ephemera, we've got everything,' she said. 'Let's go.'

Ephemera shook her head. 'Portia, could we please have tea at the café?'

The notion of having tea at the café was an echo of

Ephemera's youth when she and her mother used to visit the city and have tea and scones at a café.

'We're supposed to be baking,' Portia said irritably. But when she saw the bewildered look in her sister's eyes, her voice lost its edge. 'Come on, dear,' Portia urged. 'We've got to go now. We have to finish the baking and you can help.'

'Okay,' Ephemera said and meekly followed her sister across the street.

One of the town gossips had seen them and hurried out of the store to intercept them. Portia spotted her coming and ushered Ephemera to their vintage car. She opened the passenger door for her sister and then opened the boot for the packer to load their parcels, urging him to hurry while she kept an eye on the woman who was heading in their direction.

By the time she got into the driver's seat, the woman was at her window, her thin lips pursed into a trembling O.

'Hello Portia,' she said. Her eyes darted around the interior of the car. 'I see you've been shopping.'

Portia nodded and turned the key in the ignition. The engine jumped to life.

'Is it true that your sister's coming home?'

Portia smiled absently and, signalling with her gloved hand, sedately pulled away from the kerb, leaving the woman gaping after her.

'Leah is coming . . .' Ephemera said eagerly, the other woman's question finally penetrating the barriers of her consciousness.

'I wish you would stop telling people that Leah is coming home,' Portia said sharply. 'She's not coming. Get that into your head, Ephemera. LEAH IS NOT COMING. And whatever happens at home is *our* business. Can you remember that? Our business!'

Ephemera smiled absently. Her mind had taken off on one of its flights of fantasy – soaring way above the veld with its shrubs and succulents, reddish sand and rocks scrubbed

71

to gem-like perfection by aeons of exposure to the elements. She had dreamt once that she was a bird and the images in her dream had remained, supplanting the view from the car. In her dream she was a hawk, dipping and gliding effortlessly; below her a field mouse had darted across the veld and she had swooped after it. Ephemera leaned her head back, closed her eyes and felt herself rise from her seat, float out of the car and into the clear blue sky.

Portia passed Sissie Erasmus going in the opposite direction and waved a gloved hand at her. Sissie was on her way to meet Esther at the Glory Café and then the two of them would head for the ridge to meet Jannie and Albert.

It was an excruciatingly hot day and a heavy drowsiness had settled over the countryside. The two girls, both wearing straw hats, walked to the ridge and sat in a sliver of shade under a *koker boom*. There they waited for Albert and Jannie. Sissie leaned back, her languid gaze lazily following the flight of a bird, while Esther fished a packet of cigarettes out of her pocket.

Sissie drew her legs up and rested her head on her knees while Esther dreamily leaned back against the tree. She had a lot to think about – mostly about Jannie. 'That man is mean,' Esther muttered. 'Really mean.'

'Who?' Sissie asked.

'Jannie's father.' After a long pause she patted her pocket, looking for her lighter.

Sissie watched as Esther made several attempts to light her cigarette. She tried one more flick and a small flame leapt up at the tip of the wheel. She quickly held her cigarette to it.

'Poor Jannie, he's having such a hard time with his father,' Esther said taking a long drag on her cigarette. She exhaled and then shook her head. 'Because of me.'

'Albert gets a hiding too,' Sissie said.

'Ja, but Jannie gets smacked because of me. I wish we

could get out of here. Just get the hell out of here. But he won't go. He wants to stay here because he likes this place.' There was bitterness in her voice as she inclined her head in the direction of the ridge.

'I like it too,' Sissie said. 'I don't want to go anywhere either.'

'I can't see myself sitting here for the rest of my days,' Esther said. 'Not me. 'You can stay here. You and Jannie – see if I care.' She ground her cigarette out.

'What would I do in a big city?' Sissie asked. 'I don't know anyone there.'

'You're nuts,' Esther replied. 'I want to go to Cape Town. I want to live in one of those big houses high up on the cliffs. Jannie can fly his kites just as well from there.'

Sissie didn't say anything. She knew her friend well enough to understand that Esther was in one of her foul moods.

The girls had grown up together, practically on each other's doorstep – just as Jannie and Albert had. Childhood friendships like these had crossed many of the boundaries imposed during the apartheid years. Both the girls were exquisite in their own way – Sissie with her sloe-eyes and well-defined bone structure had a quiet dignity that contrasted with Esther's hyperactivity. Although Sissie's slow, elegant quality was enviable, it often drove Esther out of her mind that she constantly had to wait for the other girl to catch up with her. Sissie, so calm, so in control of her emotions, seemed to move at a snail's pace, always lagging behind to observe things around her, while Esther was in a hurry to get where she was going. Impatient with Sissie, Esther would yell at her to hurry.

Esther got up and moved from one rock to the next.

'Why are you so quiet?' she called to Sissie.

'I'm not quiet,' Sissie called back.

'Oh, yes, you are.'

Sissie didn't say anything. She was thinking about her dreams – especially the recurring ones. She wondered, as she

73

sat there, how to interpret the dream she had of Jannie, who had turned into an angel with wings and had fallen from the sky like a stone. She didn't want to say anything to Esther in case something bad happened to Jannie.

Most disturbing of all was the way her dream of Jannie had been interrupted a few nights before by another dream that was so vivid it had remained as clear as a vision for the entire day. The change in her dream had happened so suddenly and so unexpectedly that she had broken into a sweat. One moment she was in the confusion of Jannie and angels and then, abruptly, she and Esther were walking in the veld, engrossed in conversation. She could not remember what they were talking about, but sensed that it had no bearing on the dream of Jannie as an angel.

As they walked, the quiet undisturbed surroundings prickled with energy, as if an electrical charge had been released in their midst. She felt her heart pounding and wanted to open her eyes, tried desperately to awaken from the dream, but couldn't. A figure dressed in a long black hooded robe appeared – she couldn't see the person's face, but knew instinctively that it was a man. The robe he was wearing was tied at the waist with a long piece of thick rope with frayed ends which hung all the way down to the hem of his robe. He was very tall and she realised that he was levitating at least thirty centimetres above the ground. His face was covered by a wooden mask which seemed to be carved out of a chunk of charcoal. The mask had two slits for the eyes and since she could see a bit of white skin exposed through the slits, she knew that the man behind the mask was white.

He did nothing to impede their progress, merely watched them as they passed him. She noticed that he was holding a spectacularly carved wooden staff. Although the man was not in the least offensive or threatening, Sissie knew that she was supposed to be afraid of him – that his presence was a threat of some sort.

Her heart was thumping so loudly that she woke with a

start, her sheets drenched in sweat. The image in the dream remained with her. She could not shed it.

Esther returned to sit with her and Sissie thought briefly of confiding in her. But she changed her mind.

'So, what's going on with you?' Esther wanted to know.

'I told you that there's nothing going on,' Sissie said.

Esther sighed and suddenly fell strangely silent as though the tightly wound spring inside her had worn down. She sat still, absently drawing geometric patterns in the sand.

'I don't remember mine, but are all fathers bad?' Esther asked, looking up from her geometric designs.

Sissie shrugged.

Her father had abandoned them years before. By the time they were old enough to know this, he'd been gone such a long time that no one spoke of him any more. Apart from their mother's ramblings, neither Sissie nor Noelle ever mentioned him. From time to time, thoughts of him crept into her head. Images of him swelled to God-like proportions, and she imagined him a kind and affectionate father. It was a notion that was quickly dispelled by her mother's hatred and her sister's harsh criticism of him. But this did not stop her from wishing that she had known him.

His influence died the moment he walked out of their lives. Killed by their mother's hatred. She had vindictively planted the poison and had set about nurturing it.

When she died, the poison had seeped into every inch of Noelle's body. Not only did she hate her father, but most other men as well. Sissie, who was so much younger, had not been as badly affected by her mother's hatred as her sister.

'Do you remember your father?' Esther asked.

Sissie shook her head and changed the subject. 'Do you think you and Jannie will ever get married?'

Esther shrugged. 'Maybe, maybe not. Maybe we'll have to run away ...'

'I don't think Jannie wants to run away,' Sissie said.

'Then how do you suppose we're going to get married?

My mother hates the Jouberts and his father hates us. I know that given half a chance, my mother would be happy to drive a dagger into Hendrik Joubert's heart.'

'Come on. They don't hate each other that much,' Sissie said.

'Oh, yes they do! If they find us together, they'll kill us!'

'Don't talk such nonsense,' Sissie said sharply, remembering her dream of Jannie plummeting to earth. She dreaded what might happen to Jannie because of her dream.

In the past people had died as a consequence of her dreams.

She always remembered that they thought David was getting better and then one night she had the dream that he had died – and he did. It could only have been because of her. It ate her up. She and David used to be so close that even though David was dead, she still felt that closeness. Some nights she would lie awake speaking to him in her mind, reaching out to him as though they were still connected by a cord more powerful than the umbilical cord that had attached them to their mother. She could sense him around her all the time. Sometimes she'd send her thoughts out to him and at times she even imagined she could hear his sigh, like a low whisper, but, of course, it was merely the rustle of an animal or the stirring of the mimosa tree outside the window.

There were times when the burden of her dreams became too heavy to carry alone and she wanted to share them. But she feared that Esther would not understand. Even though she and Esther had been friends since childhood, the reality was different. Esther was white, and at times she seemed conscious of the divide and ignored Sissie, especially when she was with other whites. Sissie felt terribly hurt when that happened but, when they were alone together again, it was easy to forgive her.

Esther Oosthuizen was different from the others. Rena, Esther's sister, had once told Sissie that she and her sister were independent thinkers. She said that they didn't owe any one any explanations.

'No one gives us a damn thing! So why should we care about what they have to say?' she had said.

But Sissie reasoned differently. She thought that the Oosthuizens were indeed indebted to the townspeople, partly because the church, as well as the Jouberts, supported them. But this was not Rena's reasoning. She said that if residents expected them to bow and scrape, they had another think coming. They could keep their charity – except for Hendrik Joubert, because he owed it to them.

Esther lit another cigarette and then puckered her lips to blow perfect smoke rings into the still air. Sissie watched as the wraith-like rings drifted up, lost their shape and faded. In the distance a sheep bleated and a comet of dust trailed behind a car speeding into town along one of the farm roads.

The following Friday morning a farmer and one of his workers, tracking a jackal, stumbled across a human skull lying in the veld beneath a thorn tree. The rest of the skeleton was later uncovered in a shallow grave nearby. The body had obviously been buried much deeper, but with time erosion had swept away much of the topsoil and had brought the body closer to the surface. The farmer had his worker guard the grave and his grisly discovery from wild animals, while he drove into town to find the police sergeant.

By the time the sergeant and his constable arrived in the police van, word had already spread about the body and some of the more curious residents drove out to investigate. The sergeant officiously asked them to stand back as he and the constable taped off the area with yellow police tape. It was the first time the tape had ever been put to use in Vlenterhoek and the police made a great fuss about the procedure.

They tied one end of the tape to a thorn tree and then cast around for something on which to tie the other end.

Eventually they confiscated a walking stick from one of the residents and, anchoring it into the ground, tied the tape around it. The scene was now cordoned off, just as they'd seen it done on television.

The remains, including the fractured skull, were carefully collected and placed in a plastic rubbish bag. The problem now was what to do with them. The sergeant, who had no investigative experience whatsoever, and had no idea what to do next, decided to transfer the responsibility for the body on to someone else. He telephoned the police in a neighbouring town a hundred and fifty kilometres away to ask for assistance.

Since they were not equipped to handle this kind of situation either, the police sergeant in the neighbouring town advised him to send the remains to Cape Town for forensic examination. The skeletal remains were duly crated and put on to a train for Cape Town the next day.

8

With the finals of the national rugby contest due to be played on Saturday, speculation about the body in the veld was soon eclipsed. There were more important issues to consider – like which side was going to win the match. Small bets were laid and further speculation centred around which one of the coaches would be fired. It was becoming common practice to fire the coach or the assistant coach of the losing side. The announcement of the names of players in the respective teams generated yet more discussion and it was clear that a lot of money was being wagered on the game in the Imperial Bar.

On the Saturday afternoon the streets were deserted, but there was a concentration of parked vehicles in front of the Imperial Hotel, home of the town's only big screen.

The bar, packed with a rowdy crowd of raunchy male patrons, was noisy, the air dense with cigarette smoke. This was how it used to be in the days when Frikkie Joubert played for the Free State. *The* team was still Frikkie's team – it had not occurred to local supporters to switch loyalties. Frikkie's spirit lingered on in old videoed games, long after he had left the rugby fields of South Africa to take on a regular job.

Many of the white residents of Vlenterhoek clung

stubbornly to the past. They relived, again and again, that supreme moment when Frikkie, wearing a green and gold Springbok jersey, played in South Africa's first International home game since their readmission into world sport. They still spoke in awe about what they were doing at the precise moment when he converted the winning try – who had said what and to whom, and in what stages of sobriety they'd been at the time. The same old anecdotes of that day were dragged out and rehashed time and again. At moments like these the locals were eternally grateful to Hendrik, who had had the foresight to install a satellite dish.

People in Vlenterhoek had not shared the passion for the first democratic elections. They were horrified at the possibility of a black government. A year after the elections they didn't care two hoots about a black president being fêted at the World Cup. All they cared about was the team and their hero, Frikkie – even though he hadn't played in that game. That was the year he had been shot.

While fans gathered in the Imperial Bar that afternoon, the four friends were on the ridge. Jannie and Albert were launching the kite, and Esther and Sissie were sitting in the shade under a rocky overhang. Bored and restless, Esther went off to join the two boys. Sissie remained where she was, lazily following the spirited adventures of a beetle. A brightly coloured lizard darted past her outstretched feet.

She watched as Esther and Albert assisted Jannie with the large, intricately designed double kite. Their first attempt at launching it was unsuccessful, and Jannie reeled it in carefully to avoid snagging it on the rocky outcrops. A few minutes later the kite was once again soaring. From a distance it looked like two hawks in flight. Sissie leaned back against the rock. A few fluffy cumulus clouds had sailed into the sky and had momentarily cloaked the sun. Bored with watching the kite, her attention shifted to the clouds and their ethereal shapes. And amongst them she found the image of her twin brother's profile which grew in definition, until it was quite clear: the sharp nose, the curve of his upper lip, just as she remembered him.

Hendrik Joubert, who was part owner of the Imperial Hotel, was standing behind the bar. Prominently displayed behind him were the framed photographs of his son's trophies. In the midst of all these trophy pictures, was an extract from the Rustig Mining Gazette with a picture of a relatively well-preserved Mrs Roussouw wearing a wide, toothless grin.

In bold print, capturing the gist of the story were the headlines:

ONE-HUNDRED-YEAR-OLD VLENTERHOEK WOMAN CREDITS LONGEVITY AND GOOD HEALTH TO HEMELSLAAGTE WATERS.

Crowded into the back of the bar, on either side of the entrance, caps in hand and trying to look as inconspicuous as possible, was a group of non-whites. Under normal circumstances they would never have dared to enter the bar, but today was an exception. They were allowed in for the sole purpose of watching the rugby game. They were not there to drink or to express an opinion. They could slip in unobtrusively and remain invisible throughout, except, of course, if there was a try scored by the favoured side. The white men in the bar, many of them employers of these invisible people, would pretend that they weren't really there.

It was like being transported back to the old apartheid days.

In this final match the Free State was playing KwaZulu-Natal. So far, the game had see-sawed between the two sides and in the final moments both teams were tied at twenty-four points.

Everyone in the bar was about to give up. KwaZulu-Natal was playing well and it seemed that they would once again walk off with the trophy. Then, in the dying moments of the game, just as disappointment was spreading like a rash, Anton de Wet converted a try for Free State. The astonished viewers watched as the ball soared over the goal posts.

It was all over. Vlenterhoek supporters watched on TV as the Free State supporters went crazy with joy. Then they too went berserk, shouting and spilling their beer, whooping and slapping one another on the back.

There was no distinction in the sounds that came from the 'black corner' or from the front of the room where the whites were drinking. The cheering was one indistinguishable cry of pride and love for the sport of rugby.

In Cape Town Rebecca Fortuin was half-listening to the same rugby commentary as she sorted through her clothes. Clearing out her wardrobe was part of the process of clearing out her life. She wanted a change – a clean sweep. She was tired, worn out by six years of political wrangling – not counting, or course, her years of skirmishing in schools and in the streets where battles were fought with rocks and Molotov cocktails.

With her background in grassroots revolutionary politics, it would have been easy to slip into a comfortable position within the ruling party. But Rebecca wanted to make a real difference. The only problem was that her party had become toothless, racked by internal leadership bickering. Her frustration had increased and at times she felt totally wrung out emotionally. As if that was not enough, she had realised that to heal herself emotionally, she had to confront her father. She wasn't considering forgiveness; all she wanted was to make peace, if not for their sakes, then for the sake of her brother Albert.

The rugby commentary continued. She wasn't really interested. Like so many others, she was fed up with the slow pace of transformation in sport. She wondered what it would take to change entrenched attitudes. It was easy to legislate change, but it was not so easy was to change attitudes and that was where the real challenge in the country lay.

There had been high hopes that the Truth and Reconciliation hearings would be the magic formula to create a truly integrated country. They were supposed to be a blueprint for forgiveness. But how could those who had lost loved ones forgive such monstrous acts? She knew that she would never have been able to forgive – not for the things that were done to some of the victims. Forgiveness did not come easily to Rebecca. She was unable to forgive her own father for what he had done to her.

Instruments of death, Rebecca mused, *given absolution: sacramental tears, purple robes – and the Lord said 'Forgive them Father, for they know not . . .'*

She shook her head, trying to clear her mind, but it was hard to shake off thoughts of widow-makers and child-killers who had abused their authority, who had modelled themselves on Hitler's henchmen and had, in some cases, surpassed even their brutality.

They were following orders: it was the times, it was politics, they were merely puppets; the men who manipulated their strings were dead and could not be held accountable; it was the chain of command.

Well, damn! Where does the chain of command end? Were we not all accountable for our actions, Rebecca asked herself.

The Truth and Reconciliation hearings, watched by millions of television viewers, had drawn gasps of admiration from around the world. Here was a country that had emerged from darkness to light, a model for successful transformation in the rest of Africa, and perhaps in the world.

Transformation, Rebecca hissed. So little had changed for the people who really mattered to her: the unemployed, the homeless, the hungry and the victims of a disease that would continue to spread until orphans outnumbered adults. Pharmaceutical companies were now the puppeteers.

She thought of the farm workers: thought of their years of struggle – downtrodden and without hope. The concept of transformation was far removed from their minds as they struggled to eke out a living. People like her father, in his blue-issue uniform, slogging in the fields for a pittance.

What was the trigger for the mechanism that would bring about real and meaningful change? There were often more questions than answers, as parliamentary debates had shown. Where would one find answers in a country that had become bored with the subject of reconciliation? Was there such a thing as genuine forgiveness, or did vengeance linger like a bitter aftertaste? Could she and her father be reconciled? Could she forgive him?

'Damn!' Rebecca thought. 'I suppose I'll have to go to him. If only for Albert's sake.'

The answers to her questions, she realised, lay with her father. She flung an armful of clothes on to the bed.

There had been times, although not often, when she had toyed with the idea of getting out of politics. *Escape* – just another word like *retribution* and *forgiveness*. One more word she'd have to add to the growing list of words that had occupied her mind lately.

She was the first to admit that she needed to get away, as far away from the parliamentary jackals as possible. She had put off for years what she knew was inevitable. She had to rid herself of all the baggage she'd been carrying around from her youth. Her father was at the core of all her problems. She hated the thought of going back to Vlenterhoek to confront him. It was not her way. It had to evolve from something else: a trip that she could justify, something to blot out the pain. Work was her panacea, her escape. Going to Vlenterhoek to investigate the unexplained increase in land sales in the area was just the reason she might need, she thought as she heard a loud roar from the TV and shut her wardrobe door.

The game over, the white patrons at the Imperial Bar pointedly turned their backs on the black contingent who

84

slunk off to continue their celebrations elsewhere, perhaps at a shebeen across the sloot where they could be less inhibited. The whites settled down to some serious drinking.

Albert was at home at the house he and his father lived in on the Joubert farm. He hadn't watched the rugby because he and Jannie had gone off to the place in the veld where the body had been found. After sleuthing around for a while, and finding nothing of interest, they had returned to the ridge and their kites.

The Fortuin house was a small one-bedroomed mud and brick structure. There was no television, only a small portable radio on the kitchen table. Albert slept on a narrow cot in the other room, which served as both dining and sitting room. A small lean-to at the backdoor was used as a bathroom, their water carried in from a tap in the yard.

Albert was finishing his chores around the house late that afternoon when his father, who was not a rugby fan, arrived home. All his father thought of was work, day in and day out – labouring for Hendrik Joubert.

A small area, large enough for a table and a small coal stove was cordoned off from the rest of the room. The Primus stove sat on a wooden crate near the window. On a smaller box next to the Primus stove was a red plastic bucket for their drinking water and a small shelf on top of a cupboard held their plates and cutlery. The bottom cupboard was where their few grocery items were stored. There wasn't much. Hendrik Joubert was not a generous employer. Occasionally Anna Joubert put together a food parcel for them and all Jannie's old clothes usually ended up on Albert's back.

On a small sideboard in the other room, at the foot of the cot where Albert slept, was an early family portrait of his father and his late mother, a fair-skinned coloured woman with three dark, fleshy moles on her right cheek. In one of his books, which he kept in his locker at school, was a picture of his sister that he'd cut out of the newspaper.

'There's no water!' His father growled. He was always resentful that God, who had chosen to give him a second child, gave him a boy too weak to stand up for himself and had to have Esther and Jannie fight his battles for him. This boy was not at all like Rebecca. Not that he was complaining. He never complained.

'I want to wash now,' he said.

Albert avoided his father's eyes.

'The bucket is empty,' his father said pointedly.

'I'll get the water now, Pa,' Albert said hastily.

'What have you been doing all afternoon?'

Albert pretended not to hear the question as he hurried out of the house carrying the red bucket. He filled the bucket three-quarters full. It was heavy and on his way back into the kitchen some of the water spilt on to the floor.

His father took the bucket from him and lifted it on to the bench. Then he filled the basin on the kitchen table and washed the dust from his face and hands.

'Did Pa hear who won the game?' Albert asked, anxious for news.

'Did you not hear it on the radio?' his father asked.

'No, Pa.'

His father sighed, gazed at his son, and shook his head. Then, just for a moment, his expression softened. 'I think it was Free State. I heard all the hooters going off in town.'

'Yes!' Albert said, making the kind of pumping motion he had seen Tiger Woods use. He and Jannie often watched TV in Jannie's room, but only when Jannie's father was not home. *'Dus lekker!* Great!'

His father smiled indulgently. He didn't often smile at his son.

Albert smiled back, a small tremulous smile.

9

Vlenterhoek's unique location provided unusual draughts and eddies of air currents, creating an ideal environment for kite flying. 'Kiting' was a popular pastime in the area and kite lovers from neighbouring communities regularly competed in local competitions for the largest and most unusual kite. The largest festival, which drew competitors from surrounding towns for almost a hundred kilometres, was held in August each year. And although it was still many months away, Danie thought it might be a good idea to send an early invitation to Rebecca.

'Better give her lots of time to fit it into her heavy schedule,' he told Rena.

By the time the invitation arrived in Rebecca's Cape Town office, she had already decided to drive to Vlenterhoek on the upcoming long weekend. Friday was a public holiday and with nothing scheduled for the Monday she had planned to leave on the Saturday morning and return on the Monday morning, in plenty of time for her meetings on Tuesday.

She told her assistant of her plans to drive to Vlenterhoek. 'Just keep it between us,' she said. 'I'd like to slip in and out of town quietly.'

The thought of returning to Vlenterhoek tied her insides

into a quivering knot and she threw herself into work to avoid revisiting all the old emotions.

It was impossible, though, to separate Vlenterhoek from her father. She had hoped that time might have eased the worst of what she had felt for him.

She tried desperately to set aside her personal feelings, to focus on what really mattered – the uncovering of collusion between highly placed government officials and a development company that was apparently buying up property in the Vlenterhoek district.

That was her work.

It was what she did best.

Someone had once told her that had she not become a Member of Parliament, she might have been a good investigative reporter. She knew where to look, which stones to turn up. She could smell the dirt even before anyone knew that it was there. She sensed that there was something going on in Vlenterhoek, something fishy, and she had got wind of it.

With her impending trip to Vlenterhoek, thoughts about the past surfaced, wrapped themselves around her, spun webs in her head and intruded on every level of her consciousness. Unable to sleep, she lay awake at night thinking about her past, about her father, and how the years in Vlenterhoek had shaped her life.

Despite her best intentions to leave early on the Saturday, Rebecca was delayed and eventually left around ten o'clock. She'd left Vlenterhoek at the age of sixteen and had not returned, except for her mother's funeral when her brother Albert was about three years old. After the funeral she and her father had had one more huge fight. He'd hit her and she'd walked out on him and her brother for ever, or so she had thought at the time.

On the sofa in her lounge was a cushion given to her by one of her constituents. It was embroidered in cross-stitch with the words 'Home. Harmony. Love. Trust.' None of these concepts had applied in the home in which she had been raised. There had never been any harmony – her father's violent temper had stilled any protest from her mother. Trust was something she had to learn about later in life – because of her father. There were times when she had wished him dead, had prayed at night that the Lord would take him. But apparently He didn't want him either.

She still blamed her father for her mother's death, for the neglect and hardship they had all endured at his hands. Painful memories like these occupied Rebecca on her drive to Vlenterhoek. So preoccupied was she that she missed the turn-off and drove almost thirty kilometres past it before she realised that she was on the wrong road.

Stored deep in her memory was the fragrance of lavender. Her mother had a lavender plant growing in a small pot. Claiming that it had calming properties, her mother placed lavender around the house, packed it amongst her clothes and sewed it into the waistband of her husband's overalls in the hope that it would have a calming effect on him. But it didn't do a thing for him. The smell of lavender remained one of the few sweet memories Rebecca had preserved through the years and whenever she sprinkled aromatic oils around her house she thought of her mother.

Rebecca arrived around four o'clock on the Saturday afternoon. She drove to her father's house. He hadn't come home from work yet, but Albert was there. He recognised her immediately and was clearly shocked to see her. But when his surprise wore off and he had lost his initial shyness, he told her all about his friends and his life. He also told her that, apart from one Saturday each month, when he worked half a day, their father worked six days a week.

'I'm so glad you came,' Albert said. 'Just wait until my friends hear about this!'

'Albert, no. I don't want you to tell anyone that I'm here or even that I was here. It has to be our secret. I want to find

89

out what's happening in town. I'll come back soon for a longer visit, I promise.'

Albert looked disappointed.

'I have to leave on Monday. I have meetings on Tuesday morning,' she explained.

'Are you here to find out about the Americans?' he asked.

'Sort of. What can you tell me about them?'

'Well, I heard they were coming to town to make a film and then to buy up the town.'

Rebecca laughed.

'It's true,' he told her. 'Everyone is saying that.'

'I think someone made up that story,' she said.

'Do you want tea?' he asked.

'Not now. I want to visit Mama's grave. Can you take me?'

'*Ja*,' Albert said.

'I've brought some flowers. It's very hot in the car and I'm afraid they'll wilt soon. I've got a jar in the car. We can fill it with water.'

'Okay,' Albert said, accompanying his sister to the car.

'We'll leave the car in the shade,' she said and he waited as she parked her car at the back of the house.

She filled the jar with water and with Albert carrying the huge bunch of flowers she had brought from Cape Town they walked to the small cemetery where the farm labourers and their families were interred.

'Who looks after the grave?' she asked, noticing that her mother's grave was marked by a small wooden cross which had a fresh coat of white paint.

'Me,' Albert said. 'And Pa.' He put down the glass jar Rebecca had brought and then arranged the flowers in it.

'So Pa comes to the grave, does he?' Rebecca asked.

Albert shrugged. 'Must do. But I've never seen him here.'

'Who painted the cross?' she asked.

'I don't know,' Albert said.

Then without looking at him, she asked, 'Does Pa hit

you?

'When I don't do as he says.'

Rebecca and Albert cleaned some of the loose gravel and animal excrement off their mother's grave. 'Why don't we roll this rock over there and put it against the cross so it'll stay upright,' she suggested.

Albert looked at the rock and then at his sister. 'It's too heavy,' he said.

'Nonsense,' Rebecca chided. She pushed her sleeves up and, bracing her back, shifted the rock out of its bed, rolled it to the grave and lodged it against the cross. Albert watched in amazement. 'It wasn't that heavy, Albert. Besides, I keep fit,' she said when she saw his expression.

What Albert did not know was that his sister had trained as a freedom fighter in the days when they were still referred to as such. Although bigger and heavier now, much of her bulk was muscle, maintained by regular working out at the gym.

Rebecca climbed on top of a boulder and gazed out over the veld. A number of loud, raucous crows had gathered for a convention in one of the trees. She thought of her life here on the farm, of her mother and the difficult life she'd had. Rebecca had wished so often that her mother had been alive to share in her success. It was largely thanks to her that she had left Vlenterhoek to attend school in Kimberley.

Albert climbed on to the rock and sat next to her. She put an arm around him. Albert was sorry that he hadn't brought his guitar. He told his sister about his music and about the kite festival and how he planned to fix the guitar with the prize money. He also told her about the body that had been found in the veld.

'What body?' she asked.

'A skeleton. No one knows who it is. The sergeant sent it to Cape Town, but they don't know either. There was a big hole in the skull. So big,' he said, creating an open circle with middle finger and thumb. 'They said the hole had been made by an animal. Maybe a jackal.'

'A jackal doesn't have such a big mouth,' Rebecca said. But she wasn't really listening. Her mind was elsewhere – on what might still happen between her and her father.

Her father saw the car parked at the back of the house. One of the other workers had also seen the car and came to enquire about the 'visitor', but he didn't ask too many questions when he saw the fire in the other man's eyes.

When they returned their father was sitting outside on one of the old upright kitchen chairs, his back straight, feet together, hands folded in his lap like a school boy sent to the principal's office. When Rebecca saw him like that, she realised that she was no longer afraid of him – that she was out of his reach and beyond his touch. He could no longer harm her. All she saw now was a broken old man who was slightly bemused by her unexpected appearance.

'Hello, Pa,' she said.

He nodded.

'We went to Ma's grave,' she said.

'*Ja*, all right. It's still there . . . where it was.'

An uncomfortable silence hung between them.

'I'll go help Albert with the tea,' she said when the awkwardness between them became unbearable.

'*Ja*, all right,' her father said as Rebecca went indoors.

Albert poured tea into two chipped enamel mugs. Rebecca took one of the mugs from him and stood at the kitchen window, her father's rigid back square in her sights. Albert added two spoons of sugar to his father's tea and took it out to him. He returned to the kitchen. Rebecca remained where she was and so did her father. With her anger so close to the surface, she thought it wise to keep distance between them and watched from the window as her father thirstily gulped his tea and then placed the mug on the ground next to his chair. Every movement was measured and controlled, as if he sensed her eyes on him.

Albert was aware of the tension between his father and his sister and feared what might happen. He carried the second chair outside and placed it next to his father's chair, then watched anxiously from the window as Rebecca went outside and sat next to their father.

The old man was still perched precariously on the chair. The only acknowledgement of Rebecca's presence was the way his gaze flicked in her direction and then returned to some point in the distance where a flock of sheep was grazing. It was late afternoon, the air so still that one could hear the creak of a distant windmill, smell smoke from charcoal fires and hear the drone of a car on the main road. Rebecca was acutely aware of the heavy oppressive silence between her and her father, making it difficult for her to breathe.

She opened her mouth to speak, but no sound issued. She felt as if every movement, every thought, was unfolding in slow motion. Carefully picking through neutral ground as if addressing one of her constituents, she said, 'It hasn't changed much, has it?' Her eyes, too, were fixed on the distant land-scape.

'*Ja nee*,' her father muttered, leaning slightly forward now and sitting on his hands, his eyes still focused on the horizon.

'How's the wool this year?' she continued, still roaming neutral territory.

'*Ja*, it's all right,' he said, rocking back and forth slowly. His eyes remained glued on some distant point.

'Do you want some more tea, Pa?' Albert asked from the kitchen door.

'*Ja*, all right,' his father said.

Then there was silence again. A donkey brayed from the far end of the compound. Someone flung a stone at it. Startled, it yelped, reared, and took off into the veld.

Rebecca racked her brain for something to say. She wanted to remain in uncommitted territory. She opened her mouth to ask about his work, but instead she said: 'Why did you do it, Pa? Why did you ruin my life?' The calmness of her tone

93

surprised her and contradicted the nervous twitching at the base of her diaphragm. It was the kind of tone she might have used to enquire about his state of health.

Startled by her question, her father moved as if to get up off the chair. But her hand shot out. 'You are not running away this time. You are going to listen,' she said, leaping up and for the first time meeting his gaze. In that split second when their eyes met, all the carefully controlled emotions exploded like the crumbling of a dam wall, releasing torrents of murderous rage. She raised her arm as if to strike him and saw him flinch as he got up.

She lowered her arm. 'I'm not afraid of you,' she told him. 'Not any more. If you hit me, I'll hit back and I'm a lot stronger than you.'

'Then hit me!' he cried. 'Hit me! Why don't you? Kill me, it'll take me out of my misery.' He unclenched his fists and leaned forward on the chair to support his trembling legs. 'Why have you come back? You ran off. Now just leave us alone.'

'It was because of you that I left. Because of you!'

'I don't want to see you! Get out of my house!' he shouted.

Rebecca glared at him. 'I am not leaving here until you apologise for what you did. You ruined my life and you ruined my mother's life.'

'I didn't do anything to your mother,' he cried. 'You were always a wicked child, trying to turn your mother against me.'

'I didn't have to turn my mother against you. She knew what you were doing.'

Rebecca's rage was so intense that she could easily have lifted the chair and smashed it over her father's head. She wanted to. She wanted to obliterate him – from her life and from her nightmares. She wanted to silence the lies in his face.

'I did nothing to your mother,' he said. 'Now get out of here!'

'You didn't have to do anything to my mother. You did it all to me. I could kill you where you stand. The world would actually be a much better place without you.'

'Crazy! Bloody crazy! You and your mother were both crazy.'

'If I was crazy it was because of you. You drove my mother to her grave!' By this time she was screaming at him, her face right up against his. A few curious bystanders had gathered some distance away.

'Your mother died because she was sick.'

'You made her sick. You call yourself a husband and a father. You are pathetic. You are nothing more than Hendrik Joubert's dog. You didn't have the courage to stand up to that man, so you took it out on us. On two women!'

'Go,' her father cried, holding on to his chair. He leaned heavily on it as he struggled to get his breath back. 'Get out and don't ever come back here again.' He was trembling with rage, but there were tears in his eyes. She saw the tears before he turned away from her.

Alarmed by what was happening between his father and sister, Albert stood in the doorway, watching.

'I'm not going anywhere until I hear an apology from you,' Rebecca said following her father who was retreating into the house.

'I have nothing to apologise for. Your mother sent you away and what did you do? You left school and went to fight in the streets like a Godless hooligan. I had to work my hands off to support you and this is the thanks I get. Yes, I was Hendrik Joubert's dog. I still am. But if I don't work, who will support the family? You?' He laughed bitterly. 'You never came home after your mother's funeral. You are much too important. Too good for us now.'

'I didn't come back because of you,' she screamed at him.

He walked away, pushed past Albert and went to his room, slamming the door behind him. By this time Rebecca had lost all self-control. She ran after him and flung her body against the door, but he had locked it from the inside. She hammered on the door with her fists until her knuckles bled. Finally exhausted, she sank to her knees, weeping. Albert helped her to her feet and led her to one of the chairs outside.

'Come, Rebecca,' he said, 'let's go for a walk.' He had found that whenever he got a beating from his father it usually helped to take a walk in the veld. He thought it might help calm Rebecca down too. They walked for a while, following the tracks of the donkey that had fled into the hills. They sat on a rock for a while, neither of them saying anything. Eventually she eased out of her anger, much of it settling like sediment in the bottom of a cup. She wiped her eyes and then got up. On the way back to the house they chatted amiably.

'Are you staying with us tonight?' Albert asked.

'No,' she said.

'Why not?' he asked.

'How can I?

He didn't answer.

'I'm staying at Mrs Naude's B&B,' she said. 'I've already made the arrangements. I'll only be staying two nights. I'll leave early on Monday morning again.'

She saw the disappointment on her brother's face.

'Don't worry. I'll be back soon.'

Her father was leaving when they arrived back at the house. He paused in the doorway, looked at her and lowered his head. Rebecca watched him go, his shoulders hunched, like a man defeated.

She didn't see him again.

The following morning when Rebecca went to the house, Albert told her that their father hadn't returned the night before and that he was worried about him.

'Does he often leave you alone like this?'

Albert shook his head.

'Well, perhaps he had a lot to think about yesterday,' she

said. 'What he did to me and to Ma is something I cannot forgive him for.'

Albert wanted to know what their father had done that was so terrible.

'One day when you're old enough to understand, I might tell you the whole story. For now, he's your father and you have to live with him. But you must stand up to him. Don't let him mistreat you, you hear?'

Albert shrugged. He was accustomed to his father slapping him around, although he'd noticed lately that the beatings were not as frequent as they used to be. He thought that perhaps his father was getting too old and that he was getting too big. He'd grown taller than his father and it might have been a bit difficult for his father to continue hitting him. 'It's okay. He doesn't hit me so much any more,' he said.

'Are you sure?'

'Ja,' Albert said. 'When will I see you again?'

'Soon. I promise.'

Hendrik was returning from town when he saw Rebecca in the yard with Albert. He recognised her from the pictures he'd seen of her in the newspaper and on television. The hair extensions and that walk were unmistakable. He turned into the yard and watched them for a moment before going indoors. He wondered what had brought her back.

Rebecca returned to her room at the B&B. She wasn't hungry and declined supper. Mrs Naude noticed that something was wrong, but respected Rebecca's privacy. She thought she might send a tray to her room a bit later.

Rebecca sat on the edge of the bed dejectedly staring at her hands. She had more or less accomplished her primary objective, and yet she felt empty. The pain was still there. What could she do now? What more was there to do and say to the old man?

When the room finally became unbearably suffocating, she left the house, got into her car and drove out to the ridge. She parked at the bottom and walked all the way to the top. The sun had set and the rocks and bushes were bathed in the surreal light of dusk. Clouds had gathered on the horizon, tinted in shades of pink and indigo. She lingered until the sun had disappeared completely and distant lights from the town twinkled like stars on the horizon. She opened her mouth and, reaching deep inside her, she drew the pain out in one ear-splitting, nerve-shattering scream. Birds roosting in a nearby tree flew out in a panic of flapping wings. She gathered her voice again and screamed once more. She heard the echo ringing back, but not as loudly as the first.

She got into her car and drove back to the B&B. She didn't sleep a wink that night.

She spent most of the Monday talking to Nora Naude about what was going on in the town. Late on Monday afternoon she drove out into the countryside, but did not call to see her father. Instead, she drove around the outskirts of the town looking at some of the property that had been sold. There were no signs to indicate which land had been sold, but she had a map which her assistant had drawn up for her that gave details of the sales.

Although she went to bed early that night she was unable to sleep and read for a long time before she turned out her light. When she finally did fall asleep it was an uneasy sleep and she woke early on the Tuesday morning. She had not intended staying the extra day, but her Tuesday meetings had been cancelled and it seemed a good opportunity to spend more time in Vlenterhoek.

After breakfast Rebecca packed up and left without seeing Albert or her father, but only because she knew she'd be back soon. On her way out of town she stopped at the Hemelslaagte Springs and poked around for a while. She spent about an hour driving around the area, stopping and getting out of her car to check things. By the time she left her shoes were muddied from tramping around the springs.

There was no apparent change and yet she couldn't help wondering why so much of the land around the area had been sold recently. Although she was suspicious about the sales, as far as she could see nothing out of the ordinary was happening in Vlenterhoek.

10

While Rebecca was still poking around the Hemelslaagte Springs, Frikkie Joubert was on his way to Vlenterhoek. The two returnees had missed one another by a matter of fifteen minutes, passing one another on the road, driving in opposite directions – Rebecca on her way to Cape Town and Frikkie on his way to Vlenterhoek.

The digital clock on the dashboard in Frikkie's car indicated that it was nine o'clock.

After nearly thirteen years of absence, Frikkie had finally returned – not to visit his parents, as one might have expected, but to meet two engineers who had driven up from Cape Town to inspect the site at the Hemelslaagte Springs. Frikkie now worked for IRH – International Resort Holdings, a subsidiary of American Resorts Inc which owned holiday resorts in countries all over the world, including health spas in Bali, Tahiti and the Bahamas, and casinos in Atlanta, as well as hotels in Florida and on Australia's Gold Coast.

He wished it had been his idea to open a health resort in Vlenterhoek. But this was one idea he could not take credit for. It was Wesley, the African-American managing director of IRH, the same man who had spent the night at the

100

Imperial Hotel and had been so impressed with the air and the water that he had convinced some of the IRH executives that this would be the ideal place for a health spa. The MD was right about Vlenterhoek. Frikkie had forgotten about the healing properties of the spring water and the healthy air that the locals valued so much. He realised now that nowhere else in South Africa was there a more appropriate place for a health spa than in this small town. The only trouble was that there was nothing else in Vlenterhoek to make the package more interesting. But Wesley said that that was all some people wanted – they didn't want to be taken on sightseeing tours or bused around cities. They wanted to relax and to be pampered and that was exactly what could be offered at a spa in Vlenterhoek.

Because Frikkie had told them that he came from Vlenterhoek, the company had chosen him to put the deal together. He was ecstatic. All he needed now was to pull it off. It was a deal made in heaven, he thought. At last he was being given the opportunity to put together a project big enough to set him up for life. No more knocking at doors, hoping that his name and reputation would carry him through. This was his one big chance and he had to grab it with both hands, he mused with a smile, toying with fragments of speculative thoughts, trying to suppress his sense of rising triumph. He had to take it slowly. There were still some issues to be settled – like the acquisition of two key pieces of land.

As he neared the town, Frikkie felt a tug of apprehension. His right eye twitched uncontrollably and he pressed a finger on it to relieve the tension. He hoped that no one in the town would recognise him. He wasn't quite ready to deal with any of the residents, least of all his family. He'd lost a great deal of hair and was thicker around the waist than he'd been when he was still playing rugby, but he was still recognisable.

It was Frikkie's hope that this deal would be the beginning

101

of a new life for him. He was desperate. This was a last-ditch effort and if he couldn't pull it off, he feared that it would be the end of him. The twitching in his eye continued. He applied more pressure, blinked rapidly and tried to dismiss niggling doubts. It was important for him to remain positive.

International Resort Holdings had promised that if he could acquire the land, they'd throw all their weight behind the planned development. The idea was sound and IRH was the right engine to drive the project. He still felt a twinge of regret that the idea had not come from him. It should have – but there you are. It had taken a stranger to recognise the town's potential. Rugby had been his life. It had taken precedence above all else. But with rugby no longer an option, he'd poured his dreams into making it in the business world and now, specifically, this particular project. IRH had already acquired most of the land surrounding the town and because of their contact in key government offices, permits were already in process. Preliminary studies were almost complete and the directors were delighted with the early engineering reports.

Frikkie remained edgy, concerned about being recognised. He needed anonymity to acquire those last two parcels of land. One of them was a one hundred and twelve hectare parcel, absolutely essential in their plans to build a golf course. But they had not been able to locate the owner and even if they did, it could take months or even years to get the land registered.

The legal department at IRH were still searching. Frikkie believed that the owner of the one hundred and twelve hectares was in all likelihood deceased. The department was still going through death records dating back to the sixties. In the meantime they had placed advertisements in all the major papers, but without success. The company lawyers had even hired private detectives to locate the heirs of the property. There were no tax records to track. It appeared that taxes on that particular parcel of land had been waived in exchange for easement rights to the Hemelslaagte Springs.

Geological reports indicated that most of the underground lake was contained in a granite basin, part of which was located under the one hundred and twelve hectare parcel. With that piece of property they could tap into the underground lake. The second piece of land needed was an eighty-acre parcel that belonged to Suzette's father, Gert le Roux. This land was well located for access roads to the site. The problem here was that Gert le Roux and Frikkie's father were sworn enemies. The feud had started decades ago and had been reinforced by the relationship between Suzette and Frikkie. Even though Suzette was shattered by Frikkie's abrupt departure, no one was more pleased to be rid of Frikkie than Gert le Roux.

As he neared the town, Frikkie felt his chest tighten. He loosened his collar and pressed a button on the console in his armrest. The tinted window slid open and he breathed deeply. He'd been gone for thirteen years and had forgotten how fresh the air was.

Like other young people in Vlenterhoek, Frikkie had left for the city in search of a better life, but things had not always gone well for him.

The first few years after he left Vlenterhoek to play rugby for Transvaal, Frikkie had enjoyed a highly successful career. He had become their star player. Later, he moved to Bloemfontein and played for the Free State side. His career had never looked better than in those few years with the Free State.

Then, one day, in a split second, his life snapped out of orbit – out of the comfortable, suburban existence he had become accustomed to.

Driving home one day, and barely two blocks from where he lived, he was cut off by a dark-blue BMW. Before he could gather his wits, one of the occupants of the car had leapt out and held a gun to his head. They dragged him out of his car. Enraged, and with no thought for his safety, he tackled one of them. A shot rang out.

Three operations, a titanium implant and months of physiotherapy could not restore his knee. For Frikkie, a bullet in the head would have been more humane. Rugby was the only thing he knew or cared about. He suspected, even before the doctor told him, that he would never play again.

As he drove through the town Frikkie observed that not much had changed in Vlenterhoek since those early years when he lived there. It was still a small, one horse town. Except that now, at one of the intersections, a traffic light blinked its interminable signal, like a weary actor performing to an empty house.

He drove past the Dutch Reformed Church with its immaculate gardens.

The abundance of flowers, a mystery to the locals, was explained when the IRH company engineer located the source of the spring, an underground lake which ran almost parallel to the main road. According to the engineer, there was an enormous amount of underground water just waiting to be tapped, enough to green the entire town and the surrounding areas indefinitely.

But, more importantly, there was enough water for a golf course.

IRH had started thinking along the lines of a golf health resort. The geological and engineering studies had been completed some time ago, making the concept extremely feasible. The Rustig Mining Gazette lay on the seat next to Frikkie. On the front page was a picture of the elderly Mrs Roussouw, grinning at the camera and crediting her longevity and good health to the waters from the Hemelslaagte Springs.

Coming back to Vlenterhoek had erased any doubts Frikkie might have had initially about the appropriateness of the planned spa. It was a scintillating day. The air was beautifully fresh and the colour of the sky was a magnificent aquamarine.

The best advertisement for the spa, however, would be the townspeople and their phenomenal good health.

Frikkie was already thinking of foreign tourists coming into town bringing with them American dollars, English pounds and Euros.

Frikkie had sat in on all the planning. But he wasn't too keen on theory. He liked getting in there and mixing things up to get projects done. It was the influence of his rugby-playing days. He left the theory and the planning to others. The so-called experts. He would have enough on his plate trying to get the locals on side.

He could just imagine his parents' reaction if he showed up at their door that day. He remembered how devastated they had been when he had flatly turned down his father's suggestion that he come home after the shooting. He couldn't bear the thought of them feeling sorry for him. It was enough that his wife had left him.

His mother would forgive him. That was her nature. But he wasn't sure what to expect from his father. And then there was his younger brother Jannie, about whom he knew so little.

The geologist and engineer were already on site, surveying and plotting their geological data. Frikkie lent a hand wherever he could, but his responsibility was basically land acquisition. When the job was done the two engineers left, keen to make it to the next reasonably sized town before nightfall. Frikkie stayed a while longer and then drove out into the veld. He climbed to a vantage point and through his binoculars he gazed at the Tweeriviere homestead.

A few of the locals heard about strangers poking around at the springs and came to investigate. But by that time Frikkie and his colleagues had left.

The question on the lips of everyone in town was: 'Who were those men and what were they doing at the Hemelslaagte Springs?'

The inhabitants of Vlenterhoek, who had spent so much time speculating about the Americans, now had something new to latch on to. Some thought that the Americans had returned. They went to see Danie who didn't have a clue what they were talking about.

Why didn't he know? What was the town council hiding from them? The residents demanded answers.

Anxious about these developments, a vociferous group of residents finally cornered Danie as he walked down the main street. He saw them closing in like a tight scrum. His eyes frantic, he searched for a way to escape. But it was too late.

'What the hell's going on?' one of the men asked. The question, the language, the accompanying guttural sounds, and the tone in which it was uttered, turned a simple question into the potential for nasty confrontation.

Danie tried to lower the temperature of the confrontation. 'How should I know? I know as little about what's going on as you do,' he said in a calm and reasonable voice. He thought he knew these people, thought they were friends; after all, they worshipped in the same congregation. But the accusing crowd had been transformed from friends to foe.

'You're the town clerk!' someone yelled.

'What do the Americans want in this town?' The question startled him.

'There are no Americans coming!' he shouted. 'It's nothing but a stupid rumour!'

'You're lying!'

Danie glanced around to see who had called him a liar, but all the faces looked alike: the same gaping mouths yawning with obscenities.

Danie turned and, making himself as slender as possible, slid sideways through the press of bodies. They were still shouting obscenities at him as he disappeared from view.

After school that afternoon Esther went out to the ridge to meet Albert and Jannie. They waited for Sissie, but when it started getting late and she still hadn't shown up, they figured she wasn't coming. Lately, she'd been acting strangely and on a few occasions when Esther had tried to draw her out, she'd snapped at her.

Albert wanted to tell them about his sister's visit, especially after Jannie mentioned that his father had seen his sister at the farm. But Jannie and Esther were more interested in each other than in what he had to say. For the first time he felt like a fifth wheel.

Ignored by Esther and Jannie, Albert took his guitar out of its battered case, tuned it as best he could, considering that the neck had broken again and the frets were a bit lopsided. He'd had the guitar for a long time. He was about six or seven years old when he'd found it lying by the roadside where it had fallen off the back of a truck.

Jannie and Esther listened to Albert's quiet strumming, both agreeing that it sounded flat and slightly off-key, but Jannie was more concerned about Esther.

'W-w-w-w-wh-at's w-w-w-w-wr-r-r-ong? he probed gently, taking her hand.

'Nothing.' Then after a pause she said, 'I was just thinking how much I'm going to miss you when you go off to varsity.'

She had not told him yet about his father coming to their house and threatening them with eviction.

'I-I-I-I'm n-n-n-ot g-g-g-o-ing a-a-a-ny w-w-w-he-re,' he said. 'I-I-I-I t-t-t-to-ld y-y-ou.' Whenever he was agitated his stammer became more pronounced. There were times when his stutter was so bad he could hardly get the words out at all. He had tried all the traditional remedies. He had even endured Mrs Potgieter's singing lessons.

Mrs Potgieter led the church choir and had convinced his mother that his stuttering was caused by air trapped in his diaphragm.

After a great deal of cajoling and pleading by his mother, he had agreed to go to Mrs Potgieter's singing lessons, Doh-Ray-Meeing every afternoon. The singing lessons did nothing for his stutter. It merely subjected him to further humiliation when Noelle told Sissie what he was up to. Sissie told Albert who blabbed it all over town. In no time everyone at school knew about it and used it as further ammunition for their teasing.

He tried to understand his affliction, to function within its constraints, but discovered it was much easier to be silent. He enjoyed silence. He enjoyed being at the computer, surfing the Internet where there was no need for him to speak.

Using his knowledge of computer technology, Jannie was planning not only a huge aerodynamically designed kite for the competition, but was also secretly working on sketches for his hang-glider. Although he had never flown one before, he understood that at a basic level it operated on the same principle as a kite. The hang-glider was a surprise for Esther. He was going to fly it on the day of the big kite competition.

Jannie got to his feet and flung a pebble over the edge of the ridge. He watched it skim and then curve out of sight. Turning back to Esther, he said, 'I-I-I-I d-d-d-don-'t c-c-ca-ca-re w-w-w-what h-h-he s-s-s-s-s-says.'

'Never mind, Jannie,' she said, patting the ground next to her. He drew a frustrated hand through his hair and sat down next to her. She put her arm around him and drew him against her. He slid down, put his head in her lap and gazed at the sky. He felt a warm rush of emotion at being so close to her. He loved her so much. Sometimes the thought of losing her or being away from her was too painful to bear.

Albert picked up his guitar. 'I've got to go,' he said. 'My father will be home by now.'

Esther and Jannie were too absorbed in each other to notice Albert leaving. Jannie took Esther into his arms and drew her to him, burying his face in her hair, breathing in the essence of her. He lowered her gently, his heart thumping wildly as he kissed her. It was always the same; their love-making, though passionate, eager and sometimes fumbling, was bounded by the restrictions she had imposed.

The setting sun was like a red orb against the dusky sky, but neither of them noticed the beautiful sunset. They remained on the ridge, undaunted by threats from their parents, confident in their love for each other.

Portia and Ephemera were sitting on their stoep. Ephemera had been very quiet all day and Portia wondered what was on her mind, if there ever *was* anything on her mind. She seemed incapable of reason. One moment she'd be laughing out aloud and the next crying.

The tiniest things seemed to affect her.

Portia reached out and touched her sister's hand. 'What's wrong, Ephemera? You've been very quiet today.'

'I'm thinking,' her sister said, as if pondering an enormous problem that needed all her concentration.

'Yes, I can see that,' Portia said, her tone gentle. 'What were you thinking about?'

There was a long pause and Portia waited patiently as Ephemera collected her thoughts. Then, with a sigh, she said, 'Do you think Leah still remembers us?'

Portia squeezed her sister's hand again. 'Of course,' she said. 'We're her sisters.'

'But she's been gone for a very long time,' Ephemera said hesitantly. 'Hasn't she?'

'She has.'

'I don't remember her any more. What if I don't know her when she comes?'

'When you see her, you'll know her.'

'Will I? Are you sure?' Ephemera asked.

'Yes, I'm sure,' Portia said.

'What about you, will you remember her?' Ephemera asked.

'Yes.'

Ephemera sat in silence, only her eyes showing signs of restlessness as they flitted around and then came back to settle on Portia.

'You'll know her instantly,' Portia assured her.

Ephemera leaned over and put her arms around her sister.

11

Everything Leah and Charlie owned in Vancouver, including the house, was to be auctioned to recover the money Charlie owed his creditors. The day Leah arrived at the house to pick up a few personal items was the same day the Sheriff arrived with a court order to seize the property. His assistant, a younger, more sympathetic individual, allowed her into the house to take a few personal items. 'But no money or valuables,' he growled.

'There's not much of value in the house,' she told him. 'You're welcome to whatever there is.'

'Just take your clothes. And let me see what you've taken,' the man said grimly and turned away.

As movers carted stuff out of the house, the extent of Charlie's eccentricity was revealed. Bags of rotting fruit, cans of food and drink, things that he, in his mean-spiritedness, had hidden from her, were discovered in the most unlikely places. She offered no explanation, even though the movers looked at her questioningly.

One of them climbed up a tree to retrieve a suspicious looking parcel, only to discover that it contained nothing more sinister than a small box of washing powder.

'How did your old man get the stuff up there?' the man

110

who climbed the tree asked her.

Leah indicated the window winder, a long wooden pole with a hook on the end, used to open skylights. 'That's how,' she said.

She left the movers to their task of packing their household effects while she searched for three of her favourite books: George Eliot, Margaret Lawrence and Pearl Buck's characters were ones she identified with. She had found the three paperbacks lying on top of a dustbin, slightly soggy from the rain. The previous owner of these three little treasures had seemed reluctant to toss them into the bin and had placed them strategically so that someone else would find them – at least that was Leah's theory. She'd read and re-read them countless times before Charlie took them from her and hid them amongst his journals. But the books were hers and she was not leaving without them.

She dragged a chair over to the bookcase and cautiously climbed on it. Starting on the top shelf, she flipped through the journals, working her way over to the heavy mining texts. Trying to keep her balance, she involuntarily grabbed at the bookcase to steady herself and knocked one of the books off the shelf. Her inclination was to leave it lying where it had fallen, but some habits are deeply ingrained and so she climbed down off the chair and picked up the book. She was about to replace it on the shelf when she noticed a folded manila envelope tucked against the backboard where the book had been.

She removed the envelope and opened it. It contained a certificate of some sort, which she could not read without her glasses, and there were also five one hundred dollar bills, obviously part of Charlie's cache. She folded the envelope and shoved it in her pocket. Never mind the young man's instructions that she should remove no money or valuables.

She eventually found her books secreted amongst journals about extraction processes to recover residual copper and cobalt from slag heaps on Zambian mines. She didn't care two hoots about slag extraction. She had her books and the five hundred dollars was like a bonus. It was at least something with which she could start her new life. As an afterthought, and after looking around furtively, Leah slipped Charlie's accounting books and legal correspondence into a rubbish bag. Someone, somewhere, she figured, would be able to tell her what was going on with Charlie's finances, because she didn't have a clue and she needed to understand why they had lost everything.

Apart from a few items of clothing, she took a gold necklace, earrings and Charlie's gold signet ring – the one she had bought for him in happier times when they were first married. It was eighteen-carat gold with a small diamond set in a raised triangle. She slipped it on to her finger. There was nothing else she wanted from the house. She wanted to free herself of everything that connected her to her previous life.

She opened the bag for the man's inspection, but he waved her past without bothering to look, muttering something that sounded like 'Good luck'.

As she walked away she felt as if a weight had been lifted from her shoulders. In the plastic rubbish bag, she'd packed some underwear, a pair of runners, a few pairs of warm slacks, and some sweaters. She had no idea what the future held for her or how she was going to survive. All she had was an intense sense of release – a sense of freedom.

She walked through the gate and turned her back on her misery, leaving it where it belonged – in the past. The house, a ramshackle wooden structure, dark and dank, and wearing a slimy coat of green moss, was located in the upscale neighbourhood of Point Grey. The oaks in the front yard had shed their acorns on the roof and tiny shoots had sprung up in the silt-clogged gutters. The wood shingles were rotted through and during the rainy seasons water had dripped into the house, making life even more unbearable. Charlie had refused to spend a penny on maintaining the house.

Once a young man from one of the real estate companies had come around to ask whether Charlie'd be interested in selling the house. Charlie almost chewed him up.

'I'm never leaving this house,' he yelled. 'Don't you ever come here again! This is my house and they'll have to carry me out of here. That's the only way I'm ever leaving!'

'Well, they did carry you out, didn't they, Charlie?' Leah mused as she walked down the road.

The sun appeared from behind the clouds as the bus arrived. She found a sunny seat at the rear, away from prying eyes, and soon felt her bones begin to warm. She smiled contentedly. For the first time in years she felt alive, as though she were part of this earth, part of its regenerating process.

Although glad to be out of the house, she knew she would miss her long walks through the university endowment lands. There was nothing else she was going to miss about living in Point Grey. No one ever talked to her. All her attempts to make friends were rebuffed by neighbours who regarded them as odd.

They were misfits in this smart upper class neighbourhood where the loudest sound was the soft swish of expensive tyres turning into gated driveways. The neighbours had long wanted them out of there, wanted to see the small, ramshackle house razed and replaced with something more appropriate. But Charlie had refused to budge. He said their shack in Point Grey was worth more than a palace in some middle-class neighbourhood.

What help was this now, she wondered. In the end he'd squandered it all. She shuddered, suddenly cold. She would make a determined effort to shed thoughts of him.

He was dead.

But, like a phoenix, she had risen from his ashes.

She smiled at a woman who had just boarded the bus and snuggled against the plastic bag that now contained all her worldly possessions. The envelope with the five hundred

113

dollars formed a reassuring bulk in her pocket. Bathed in bright sunlight, she felt amazingly comfortable. She was so relaxed that she almost forgot to get off at her stop.

Her time at the shelter was nearly up. They had given her another week to find a place of her own and she had to start looking now.

She ambled back to the shelter, aching with the sheer pleasure of being alive on such a wonderful day – alive and free.

The change in Charlie's health had been slow at first and then, towards the end, his mind seemed to go as well. On the other hand, the seed of meanness in him had been there from the beginning, only she had been too blind to see it. It had taken time for his manipulating ways to became obvious to her. A wedge had slowly been driven between them and in the end it had split them like an axe going through a dried log.

She didn't feel in the least guilty about Charlie being dead. The odd twinge was quickly dispelled when she remembered what he had done to Jock.

A few weeks later, as Leah sat in the social worker's office, the realisation that her circumstances were quite desperate finally struck her. The young man, who had studied the books and legal correspondence she had given him, told her that her husband of forty years had left her penniless.

'I'm not a lawyer, Leah, but this looks as if it is all in order. There are a few subpoenas here that your late husband ignored. He didn't pay any of his creditors. This writ of seizure which the Sheriff gave you is quite in order. He owed a lot of money. More than the property was worth. That's why they seized it. He lost everything in bad mining investments in places like Albania, Australia and South America.'

Leah knew nothing about Charlie's business affairs. But she was surprised to discover what a fool he had been. Charlie's notebooks were spread out on the social worker's

114

desk. The man was still new at the job, and had not yet become hardened towards the steady stream of people who came to his office for assistance. He had taken a special interest in Leah and had devoted more time to her case file than to any of his other clients. There was something appealing about the feisty quality that had emerged after her husband's death. He couldn't help feeling protective towards her.

Leah tried to listen carefully as he explained what he had concluded from Charlie's records, but she was tired and her mind began to wander. Suddenly the irony of her situation struck her and she started to laugh as she hadn't laughed in years. All the held-back misery erupted in tears of mirth.

'That old bastard really did it to me,' she said, finally getting her breath back and dabbing at her eyes with a crumpled tissue.

'I'm sorry Leah . . .' the young man said.

'It's not your fault. I should've seen it coming. And now, of course, after all the fetching and carrying I did for him, I don't have a clue about how to survive out there. Never wrote a cheque in my life, never had a bank account of my own. Never had a penny of credit. I allowed Charlie to control everything – including my life – and now see what it's gotten me.'

'What about your daughter?'

'What about her?'

'I thought you might want to move to Toronto to be near her.'

'She won't be thrilled with that idea.'

'Why not?'

'She could hardly wait to get away from us. I think she was ashamed. I've never met her husband, you know. Besides, I don't want to be a burden to anyone. '

The social worker didn't say anything.

'She's been married thirteen years. I have two grandsons. The eldest is twelve, the youngest is eight. I've never set eyes on either of them.'

'Christ!' he muttered.

'She married some rich lawyer. Told them that her parents were dead. Ron only learned the truth a few years after they were married and he didn't make much effort to meet us. She must have told him about her crazy father.'

The man shook his head. 'What about your sisters in South Africa?'

'Portia and Ephemera? Forget that idea, too, young man,' she said straightening her back. 'I'd rather die than ask them for charity.' She paused thoughtfully. 'But if you need to contact someone in case anything happens to me, they'd be the ones, I suppose.'

'Leah, you'll be sixty-five in a few years and will be entitled to your government pension then. In the meantime we can apply for Charlie's Canada Pension. It's not much, but it will help.'

'How much will his Canada Pension pay?' she asked.

'I don't know. It depends on how long he's contributed. They'll work it out. Also, we'll find out if you're eligible for the survivor's allowance through the old age insurance pension.'

'But I thought you said I'm not eligible for the old age pension?'

'This is not a pension. If you don't have an income it's something to tide you over until you turn sixty-five.'

Leah didn't like working with figures. It always made her head spin. All she knew was that she had nothing. Just the five hundred dollars she'd found in the manila envelope.

'Why do you suppose he did this to you?' the young man asked.

'Who knows,' she said with a shrug. 'Some people are just born nasty. He was a collector and I was just one more thing to add to his collection. I was just some novelty item – one of the novelties you buy in those funny little tourist shops – which ends up in the trash or in a box for the Sal-

116

vation Army.' She paused for a moment. 'That man's soul was twisted from the moment his mother gave birth to him and he just became worse with time.'

The young man smiled grimly. "What about the stuff in the house? I know most of it's been sold, but small things . . .'

She shook her head. 'I don't want anything, thank you,' she said.

The social worker silently toyed with his pen. 'Where will you live, Leah?'

'I'll find something. It's time now for me to stand on my own two feet. They've been very kind to extend my stay at the shelter. I know they've bent the rules for me.'

'You're a good person, Leah. And you've had a bad deal from Charlie.'

'Don't you worry, dear,' she said, reaching over the desk to pat his hand. 'I'm going to get my life sorted out.'

'You know where to find me if you need anything,' he said.

'Sure. And thanks for your help.'

He shut the file and placed it in one of the trays on his desk.

It was one of life's ironies that what she got from Charlie after his death, was more than she ever got from him while he was alive.

12

Leah eventually found a place to stay, a basement suite for two hundred and seventy-five dollars a month. She paid the deposit and the first month's rent.

Although it was small, there was ample sunlight through two of the windows. The kitchen was a tiny nook and the bathroom a shower-stall and a rust-encrusted sink, but the deficiencies in the suite's amenities were the least of her concerns. She was tired – filled with a weariness that seemed to rise from the depths of her soul. All she wanted was a bed, somewhere to lay her aching body.

The landlady, a large woman with a penchant for long flowing caftans, never ventured downstairs. A second door opened on to a steep flight of steps that led to a small grassed area. Leah sat there on sunny days, watching the steady parade of homeless people. Slowly, but with intent and determination, they pushed their shopping carts through the alley, making frequent stops at rubbish bins to search for more treasure. Their carts held everything from plastic bags for instant shelter, to grubby blankets dragged from one sleeping place to another.

An old woman wearing a red toque, men's socks, army boots, and an old grey coat and wheeling a cart with a contrary wheel, became a familiar sight. She'd fashioned a hook at the end of a long piece of wire and by climbing up on to the rampart at the side of dumpsters, she was able to reach in. Using her wire, she foraged for treasure. Later, she separated her bounty into piles: bottles in one pile, cans in another. A third pile was for other usable items which she either traded or sold on the streets. Scavenging, Leah discovered, was a very competitive enterprise and many of the regulars aggressively staked out their territory.

On the first balmy day of spring, Leah dragged out the folding canvas chair she'd rescued from a dumpster in an alley. With a great deal of caution she lowered herself into the chair and turned her face to the sun. The landlady had let her dog out into the yard. A toy chihuahua, usually carried in the crook of her arm, came bounding down the steps and stopped to peer at Leah through small bulging eyes. The uncanny resemblance between owner and dog never ceased to amaze her.

He barked furiously at Leah, who smiled sheepishly, while the landlady waited like a proud mother, calling: 'Here, Chichi.' Leah leaned over, wincing at the sharp pain in her hip, and extended her hand to pet the dog. Her gesture was purely in the interest of landlady-tenant relations, because she was not a dog person. She preferred cats. She enjoyed their independent spirit, and the way they commandeered their space, choosing life on their own terms. Whenever she thought of Jock and his violent end at the hands of Charlie, a lump formed in her throat. She could not get over the sheer evil of the man, who had begrudged her even the little bit of love and affection she'd gotten from an animal.

The dog returned to its owner and Leah sank back into her canvas chair, closing her eyes against the sun – the same sun that was beating down on India and Africa and on the veld at Vlenterhoek. Sometimes it seemed quite mystifying: night here, day there; spring in Vancouver and autumn in Vlenterhoek – where it never got too cold. In winter all one needed was a sweater. One could always bank on sunshine there. The one thing she missed about Africa was the sun. She thought of the farm, surrounded by veld: the veranda, the cool interior of the old house; three dairy cows and five sheep beyond the fenced yard, foraging for food.

She closed her eyes and thought of her sisters, especially Portia, the strong, practical sister; the odd one out with her dark hair, square shoulders and slightly hooded eyes. Always there for everyone else.

Leah felt a pang of regret about the way she had abandoned them. She wished now that circumstances had been different. It was too late, of course. Forty years of possibilities gone, never to be recovered.

All she had of her sisters now were those early images frozen in her mind like ice sculptures. An overwhelming longing crept over her. She wanted to reach out to them. Bloated with pain, with sorrow and an excruciating sense of loss for a life wasted on a man who had died with her curse ringing in his ears, she doubled over in the old canvas chair, buried her head in her hands and wept. A Filipino couple, walking past, hesitated briefly when they saw the woman in the canvas chair on an island of grass sobbing her heart out, crying as though a great tragedy had exploded in her life. They paused only momentarily and then hurried on.

Leah eventually calmed down, folded her canvas chair and carried it back into her suite. One of Charlie's old notebooks was lying on the kitchen shelf and she found a stub of pencil in the cutlery drawer. Tearing a few sheets out of the notebook Leah sat down to compose a letter to her sisters.

A few weeks later, Leah ran into DiDi, a twelve-year-old runaway or, more precisely, DiDi ran into her, almost bowling her over as she hurried around the corner into the alley. Despite the chill in the air the young girl was wearing tight black jeans and a black halter-top. Her face was the colour of

120

bleached bones, her jet-black hair coaxed into rigid spikes like the spokes on a bicycle wheel.

Heavy black eyeliner accentuated her eyes, reminding Leah of the characters in a television show she had once seen. Although she could recall the faces of the characters in The Addams Family, she'd forgotten their names. She was forgetting a lot of things lately.

'Sorry, Grams,' the girl said.

Leah stared at the hoops in the girl's navel. Three silver hoops dangling from her belly-button, a stud in her nose and another in her right brow. Almost as decorated as a Christmas tree, Leah thought, her critical gaze returning to the girl's dark eyes.

'Don't Grams me,' Leah muttered irritably.

'Got a light?' the girl asked.

'Do I look like I smoke?'

The girl laughed and sauntered past. Leah turned to watch her go, slim hips swaying provocatively. She's no more than a child, thought Leah, appalled.

Two days later they ran into each other again. This time the girl was wearing a baseball cap and had once again poured herself into the same black jeans and halter-top. She also had on oversized windbreaker with a hood. At first glance she appeared to be older, but a closer look revealed a body that hadn't developed as rapidly as her attitude.

She was sitting on a low wall, waiting for a bus. Cupped in her hand was a trembling baby bird still covered in down. She was stroking it gently with her index finger.

'Hi,' Leah said.

The girl ignored her.

'Where did you find it?' Leah asked.

The girl inclined her head to the tree next to them. 'Fell out of the nest,' she said.

'What are you going to do with it?' Leah asked.

'Take it home.'

'And where is that?'

The girl shrugged.

Leah watched in silence as the girl continued to stroke the bird. 'I guess the bus is late,' she said, conversationally.

'Yeah. I missed the first one. Where you heading, Grams?'

'I told you not to call me Grams.'

'You want me to call you "dear"?'

'Okay, call me Grams,' said Leah, cheerfully.

'So, where you going?' the girl asked again.

'Downtown.' It was the end of the month and welfare recipients were collecting their cheques.

'You going to collect your cheque or you got a bank account?' asked the young girl.

'Why do you want to know?' Leah asked.

'I can see you don't have a bank account,' the girl said.

'What's it to you?' Leah asked.

The girl shrugged. 'Just easier that way then you don't have to schlep downtown every end of the month.'

'Don't want one,' Leah muttered.

'It's easier,' the girl said. 'Save you all this busing back and forth and standing in line. If you have an address, they'll put your cheque in automatic-like.'

'Aren't you a bit young to know about such things?' Leah asked.

The girl shrugged again and looked away.

Leah didn't dare admit that she didn't know how to open an account, that she had never had an account, and that furthermore she had no intention of admitting this to a total stranger in the form of a bank clerk.

'What's your name?' Leah asked.

'DiDi.'

'DiDi who?'

'Just DiDi. Capital D – little i – Capital D – little i . . .'

Leah raised an eyebrow.

'No last names, Grams, you know, like Madonna or Cher. You don't hear no one going around asking *them* for their last names, do you?'

'Wouldn't know much about that.'

They were silent for a while. Leah sensed a great loneliness in the young girl and felt a keen sense of her own loss – not for Charlie, but for Erica.

Leah and DiDi encountered each other on several other occasions. There were hundreds of street children at this time of the year who spent their nights huddling in doorways and panhandling in the West-End. She'd seen them, like birds, migrating from the east coast to Vancouver Island.

The next time Leah met DiDi, she said, 'Why don't you come meet my social worker? I promise you he's a good guy.'

'Oh yeah . . . there are no good-guy social workers. They're just interested in one thing and that is getting *me* back to my foster home,' DiDi said, her voice hardening. 'And I'm not going back there. No way!'

Leah shrugged. 'How old are you?' she asked.

'Eighteen.'

'You can't be any more than eleven, twelve at the most,' Leah remarked.

'So?'

'Where are you staying?' Leah asked.

'Why the third degree, Grams?'

Leah shrugged. 'I don't have much to do with my time. So I mind everyone else's business.'

DiDi was silent.

'Why don't you come home with me today? I'll pick up my cheque and then buy something to cook. Be my guest. I haven't cooked since I ran away from home.'

DiDi's head shot up, a startled look in her grey eyes. 'You ran away?' She asked, crinkling her nose and almost dislodging the nose-stud.

'Yup.'

'What from?'

'A rotten life,' Leah said.

DiDi grinned. 'Okay. I'll be your guest.'

Later that afternoon DiDi was waiting for Leah in the alley. Leah had returned from cashing her pension cheque and was in the back alley scavenging for empties. Money didn't go far and every little bit helped. In an extravagant mood, she'd spent five dollars and some cents on two lamb chops. She'd been craving a piece of lamb for months now. Leah collected a few more bottles and the two of them trundled the shopping cart home. There wasn't much, just a few items she'd collected from the street – some of it worthwhile, some of it to be discarded.

DiDi wobbled along on her platform shoes.

Leah shivered in her heavy coat. 'Aren't you cold?' she asked the girl.

'Nah,' DiDi shrugged. But she *was* cold, her skin mottled blue and red. She was hugging herself to keep warm.

'Where's the jacket you were wearing this morning?' Leah asked.

'Wasn't mine,' said DiDi.

When they reached the basement flat DiDi poked around the small room. There wasn't much to see and finally she picked up the photograph of Erica and the boys, propped up on the shelf in the kitchen and studied it intently.

'This your family?' She asked.

'My daughter and her kids. Mark and Jeffrey. Mark is the young one, the one with blond hair.' There was a sadness in her tone that the ever-alert DiDi honed in on.

'So where are they now?'

'Toronto.'

The young girl was silent and Leah turned away from her and riffled in a cupboard. 'Here, wear this,' she said, tossing her a sweater.

The young girl accepted the sweater graciously and slipped it on.

After a while she peered down the front of her halter-top

124

and carefully extracted a cigarette. She looked up and saw that Leah was watching her with a disapproving frown. 'Smells like cigarettes down here,' DiDi observed, as she sniffed down the front of her top.

'No smoking in here,' Leah said sharply.

'No smoking in here,' DiDi said, mockingly. But she stashed the cigarette.

'By the time you get to my age, your lungs'll look like the inside of a wood stove,' Leah remarked.

'Why should I worry about that? I'll be dead long before I reach your age.' The calm way she said this startled Leah.

'I have two lamb chops. How do you like yours?'

'I don't eat meat,' DiDi said.

Leah gazed at her and then at the two chops drifting in a pool of oil in the bottom of an iron pan. 'What am I supposed to do with this? I paid good money for it, you know.'

DiDi shrugged. 'Eat it yourself.'

'I can't eat two of these.'

'Give one to the mutt upstairs.'

'One of these is almost as big as he is,' said Leah.

'Yeah!' DiDi laughed, fiddling with her earrings. 'Oh, damn,' she exclaimed as she dropped one.

'I don't like swearing around me, either,' Leah said grimly.

'You don't like much, do you, Grams?' DiDi said with a touch of sarcasm.

'My husband used to swear at me all the time,' Leah said. 'I didn't take kindly to it. He was a mean old sod,' she added.

'You don't know nothing about meanness, Grams.'

'Let me tell you, they didn't come any meaner than my husband,' Leah said.

'You didn't know my stepfather,' DiDi replied dryly.

'Lord, what a life,' Leah sighed. She took one chop out of the pan and set it aside. 'What am I going to feed you, child?'

'It smells awful in here,' DiDi complained, pushing one of the windows open. 'You got baked beans?' she asked, sauntering over to inspect Leah's sparsely stocked cupboard.

'Yup. This will do.' She brought out a small can of beans.

The dog upstairs started to bark.

'Listen to that mutt,' DiDi said. 'Must be smelling your lamb chops. I'll have the beans with bread. You got any bread?'

'In the cupboard.'

DiDi fetched the bread.

'I had a cat once,' Leah said.

'Oh, yeah?'

'Well, he wasn't really my cat,' Leah explained. 'He just came and went as he wished, jumping in through the window. He had this funny tail, sort of crooked, and a chewed-off ear too.'

There was a pause and DiDi asked, 'So what happened to the cat?'

'Charlie kicked him to death,' said Leah.

'Life's funny like that sometimes,' DiDi said. 'That's why I don't love anything or anyone no more.'

DiDi's words pierced her heart and for a moment she was too anguished to look up. She turned off the hot plate. 'Morticia,' Leah said. The name had suddenly and inexplicably popped into her head.

'What?' DiDi asked.

'Nothing,' said Leah. 'I remembered a name.'

'Whose name?'

'The mother in that TV show, The Addams Family.'

'Are you kidding me?' DiDi asked. 'You watch that junk?'

Leah laughed, shaking her head. 'I was trying to remember who you reminded me of.'

DiDi grunted, clearly not impressed at being compared to Morticia.

Leah set the table while DiDi looked on.

She had two forks and a knife and a roll of paper-towel. She ripped two sheets off the roll, folded each into a triangle and placed one at each setting.

'Cool-aid or tea?' Leah asked.

'Water for me.'

They sat down to their meal. Leah with a chop on her plate, DiDi with a serving of baked beans. They ate in companionable silence. Leah felt an affinity of spirit with the young girl. DiDi seemed to have collected a lifetime of experience in a very short span of living. One could see it in her eyes, especially when she was caught off guard and the aggressive, confrontational mask dropped.

After supper DiDi helped Leah with the dishes. She sat around for a while longer.

'You want me to keep the sweater?' she asked as she gathered her things. 'I got to go now.'

'Keep the sweater,' Leah said, almost sorry that the young girl was leaving. She had enjoyed her company. She walked her to the door and stood there watching her climb the steps to the yard. She paused at the gate and waved.

'See you soon,' Leah called.

'Yeah,' DiDi said as she shut the gate behind her.

13

Two months after his first visit, Frikkie returned to Vlenter-hoek. There was still the issue of the two parcels of land to be resolved – both pieces were crucial to the development of the project. Ownership of the larger piece had still not been determined. One of the problems was that some of the records for Vlenterhoek had been lost when land data had been computerised. Frikkie's contact in the Deeds Office was still searching for the owner. The other parcel of land, which belonged to Gert le Roux, was also in jeopardy because of the long-standing feud between his father and old man Le Roux. Frikkie didn't think that the old man, stubborn as he was, would ever give in. As he saw it, the only way was to get at the father through his daughter Suzette. He and Suzette had been friends and lovers despite her father's objections and he hoped that they could still be friends.

All of this was on Frikkie's mind as he pulled up in front of the Imperial Hotel. He turned off the ignition and sat for a moment, trying to gather himself to meet his father. It was going on for twelve o'clock and he wondered whether his father was at the hotel or whether he was still at home.

He got out of the car. The first to recognise him as he entered the hotel lobby was the young Afrikaans waitress.

'My goodness gracious!' she cried. 'Frikkie Joubert! What brings you back to Vlenterhoek?' She threw her arms around his neck and gave him a huge hug. Frikkie and the young woman had been at school together and she had no qualms about greeting him warmly. Even though he was now a has-been, his celebrity status stripped, she still pressed her bosom up against his chest.

'Hello, Hester,' Frikkie said, looking a bit sheepish as he stepped out of her embrace.

'*En toe?* What brings you back here?' she asked again, speaking to him in Afrikaans.

'I've come to see my father,' he said.

'Well, will he ever be surprised. None of us thought we'd ever see you again.'

Frikkie didn't want to offer explanations to the waitress. He wanted to get that first meeting with his father over and done with. He wanted to mend fences because he suspected his father would be of immense help in getting the project off the ground. He still knew enough powerful people to pull strings for them, if they needed him to do so.

He looked around expectantly.

'He's in the bar,' the waitress said.

She watched as Frikkie strode towards the bar.

There wasn't a soul in Vlenterhoek who did not know about the shooting or about Frikkie's subsequent problems.

Frikkie opened the door to the bar and stood in the doorway. Hendrik was behind the bar taking stock. He glanced up and immediately recognised his son. He blinked in surprise, a half-bottle of *Cape to Rio* cane spirits in his hand.

'Hello, Pa,' Frikkie said quietly.

It took a few moments for Hendrik to get over the initial shock of seeing his son.

'Frikkie,' he said. 'What are you doing here?'

'It's a long story, Pa.'

Hendrik put the half-bottle of cane down and very deliberately took a cloth to wipe the counter. It was as if he needed time to put his thoughts together.

'How are you, Pa?' Frikkie asked.

'Well, thank you,' his father said, his tone flat and emotionless.

They studied each other guardedly, circling each other in their minds, like two predators, each trying to establish supremacy over the other.

'How about you?' his father asked.

'I'm getting on, thank you.'

'What are you doing here?' Hendrik asked.

'I came to see you.'

'You must want something,' his father said with restrained anger.

Frikkie didn't say anything.

'Do you know what you did to your mother? You broke her heart.'

Frikkie gritted his teeth.

'You put her through hell!' It was easier to shift the focus to his wife. 'Why couldn't you have come home just once to see her? Instead, you cut her out of your life.'

Frikkie lowered his head. His father stepped out from behind the counter.

'I'm sorry, Pa.'

'Sorry!' His father yelled.

'What more do you want me to say?' Frikkie asked, irritated.

'The day I asked you to come home, you treated me like a fool. So you can just take your damn apology and get the hell out of my sight.'

'Pa!' Frikkie said.

His father covered his face with his hands, his shoulders hunched. When he dropped his hands from his face and saw the shock in Frikkie's eyes, he stepped forward almost blindly and put his arms around his son.

There was a long silence.

'So why are you here? Hendrik asked.

'Work,' Frikkie said.

'What kind of work would bring you here?' His father asked.

'I'll tell you about it later on, Pa. How's Ma?'

'She's going to be very surprised. We never expected to see you again.'

'It was also the last thing I expected. But things change and often we have to change with them.' He looked around. 'Nice place you have here, Pa.'

His father nodded. Frikkie glanced at all the rugby memorabilia his father had collected. 'Jannie must be quite grown up now,' he said.

'We were very hurt when we heard that you were in Vlenterhoek a few months back and didn't come to see us. Why didn't you contact me?' Someone had recognised Frikkie when he was there with the IRH engineers. Hendrik had waited for Frikkie to contact him, but instead his son had slipped away like a thief in the night.

'I'm sorry, Pa,' Frikkie said again. It had taken the entire trip to Vlenterhoek for Frikkie to steel himself against the hurt and anger he knew his parents had built up over the years.

'Sorry isn't good enough, son.'

'What more can I say?' Frikkie asked, a little annoyed with his father for tugging on the same thread. 'I wasn't ready to come home then.'

'And you're ready now?' his father asked with a touch of sarcasm.

'Yes.'

The two men fell silent. Frikkie shifted from one foot to the other. The long drive had caused some discomfort in his knee. He sat down on a bar stool. His father noticed him wince.

'Is the knee still giving you trouble?'

'*Ja*, sometimes. Especially when I've been sitting for a long

131

time.'

'So tell me . . .' his father said. Hendrik suspected that Frikkie was involved with IRH. By this time he'd heard from his network of contacts that large tracts of land in the area had been optioned by a Cape Town company.

Frikkie knew that he could not postpone the inevitable. He'd have to give his father an explanation.

His father opened two beers and they went to sit at a table. Frikkie told his father about his various business interests and how he had become involved with IRH.

'They're a very big company, Pa. They're listed on the New York stock exchange. All we need now to complete the acquisition of the site are the two parcels of land. You don't know who owns that hundred and twelve hectare parcel near the Hartman farm, do you?'

Hendrik thought for a moment. 'As far as I can remember, a fellow by the name of Frans Bosman owns that land. He was a bit of a hellraiser,' he said thoughtfully.

'Do you know where he is now?' Frikkie asked.

'He died years ago.'

'Well, who owns the land then?'

His father shrugged. 'Who knows? Could be anyone. He sold a lot of his land to cover his gambling debts. The Deeds Office would have that information . . .'

Frikkie shook his head. 'It seems that a lot of the transfers have been lost.'

'Why don't you get a lawyer to do a search?' his father asked.

'We have – a whole bunch of them. They've come up with nothing so far. It really is quite a mystery.'

'I'm almost sure Frans Bosman owned the land,' Hendrik mused. 'Maybe he sold it off and it was never registered.'

'That's a bit strange, isn't it?' Frikkie said.

The two men lapsed into silence while Hendrik tried to think of names of contacts who might be in a position to help.

Later that day Frikkie went home with his father. When he walked into the kitchen his mother gave a little yelp of surprise and threw herself into his arms. Overcome with emotion, she clung to him, sobbing.

'Ma, please,' Frikkie pleaded, while his father looked on.

'I always knew you'd come home, Frikkie.' She blew her nose loudly. 'I prayed for you every day. Prayed that the Good Lord would bring you home safely. He always answers my prayers. Here you are.'

Jannie, who was up in his bedroom, heard the commotion downstairs and ran to the kitchen. When he saw his mother's face, he knew without further explanation who the man in the kitchen was.

'Jannie?' Frikkie said, stepping out of his mother's embrace. Frikkie went to Jannie who put his hand out shyly.

'What kind of a greeting is that for a brother?' Frikkie asked, wrapping his arms around him. Unaccustomed to such demonstrative behaviour, Jannie was stiff and awkward. Eventually he managed to extricate himself.

'So, what have you got to say for yourself?' Frikkie asked.

Jannie merely smiled.

'How old are you now?' Frikkie asked.

'Almost seventeen,' his mother answered.

'Let him talk for himself!' Hendrik said sharply.

Frikkie's glance flew to his father and then to Jannie. He saw the look in his brother's eyes. 'Still at school?' he asked, trying to ease the tension.

Jannie nodded.

'It's good to be home,' Frikkie said.

His mother noticed how hollow his words sounded and her heart leapt anxiously. She sensed, instinctively, that something was wrong. She had always known that the bullet, although sparing his life, had shattered more than his knee.

Frikkie sensed that there were problems between his brother and his father. He knew his father well. His father was one of the reasons why he had left home. He felt terribly sorry for his brother.

A few days later, after witnessing a confrontation between Jannie and their father, Frikkie took Hendrik aside. 'The more you criticise him, the more he'll stutter,' Frikkie said. 'Just lay off him, Pa. Give him a break.'

Hendrik did not take kindly to advice, least of all from his children. But in the end he backed off.

Slowly the tension between Jannie and his father began to ease. The one big, burning issue remained Esther. But Hendrik stopped criticising her as well. He managed to swallow hard and say nothing.

'He's a young man, Pa,' Frikkie said. 'He has needs. Don't worry. He's not going to marry her.'

Hendrik had promised his wife that he would not mention Suzette's boy Martin to Frikkie. She told him that Suzette had to sort out her problems in her own time, when she was ready to deal with them. There was no point pushing, it would only create further problems between the two families.

'Just let it be, Hendrik,' she told him.

It was a hard thing that he was being asked to do, but he did leave it alone and for a while the house at Tweeriviere began to feel like a normal household should. But when it lasted beyond the first two weeks, an uneasy calm developed, the kind of calm that came just before a storm.

Portia had long ago given up trying to plumb the depths of Ephemera's mind. There really was nothing behind the glittering smile flashed so eagerly at all and sundry. All her childlike mind wanted was attention. Sometimes Portia had to help her dress and tie the ribbons she insisted on wearing in her hair. A fifty-eight-year-old with flighty, airy gestures that reminded Portia so much of their mother: the vagueness, the mind drifting off on a cloud of whimsy. Those who knew Ephemera twirled their fingers at their temples as an explanation for her outlandish behaviour.

In those early years when her mother and Ephemera lost themselves in a world of literature and poetry, Portia had been left to cope with running the household and managing the finances.

Portia toiled while her mother, wearing a huge sun hat tied with ribbons, read her favourite poems aloud. Both Ephemera and her mother knew them by heart: Lord Byron's 'We'll go no more a-roving' and 'She walks in beauty,' or Christopher Marlowe's 'The Passionate Shepherd to His Love' resounded from the stoep. Seated at her feet, head resting on her mother's knees, Ephemera hung on to every word as her mother gestured beyond the images of an English countryside and the lushness of an English garden to the barren wastes of the veld where their small herd of dairy cows grazed.

Portia knew what was whispered about them. She could hear it in the disparaging way they referred to her as a 'spinster'. An old maid, like an overripe fruit, passed over by discerning hands. She never had the opportunity to find out what she wanted in life, or what her potential was. Never had the opportunity to make herself more desirable.

She didn't have the choices Leah had had.

As she sat on the stoep with Ephemera, Portia gazed out at the landscape, eyes slitted against the pain of her own life.

No family, no children or grandchildren – just Ephemera demanding constant attention. Portia didn't often dwell on the past. She was impatient with nostalgia and with wasting her energy hankering for what might have been.

But when she looked at her sister her expression softened. Poor Ephemera wouldn't know what might have been either. She took her sister's hand. It was just the two of them now. No point holding a grudge against Leah.

The letter from Leah had arrived. She'd picked it up at the post office that morning and left the envelope lying unopened on the table.

'Aren't you going to open your letter?' Ephemera asked,

worrying it like a little terrier.

'No,' Portia said sharply and slipped the letter into the kitchen drawer.

'But why not?'

'Please stop asking questions. You're giving me a head-ache,' Portia groaned, holding her head. Ephemera didn't like it when Portia got one of her headaches. She got very grumpy and had to lie down. She wasn't much fun then. Fortunately Ephemera forgot about the letter. But for Portia the letter was like a heart, alive and throbbing in the kitchen drawer, emitting an irresistible power, drawing her to it, like bait at the end of a fishhook.

When Ephemera finally fell asleep on the swing, Portia fetched the letter and went into her room, shutting the door behind her. She sat on the edge of her bed and opened the envelope. It was a long rambling letter in which Leah told her of Charlie's death. Portia tried to read between the lines, sensing that there was something deeper, something beneath the surface of the words, but for the life of her she couldn't figure out what it was.

She wasn't sorry about Charlie's passing.

She had never liked him and had warned Leah about him, but her sister had refused to listen. Always stubborn and wilful, spoilt to death like Ephemera, she reflected. Then after all their parents had done for her, Leah didn't even have the decency to return for their funerals.

She made her bed and now she has to lie in it, Portia thought grimly. That was what one got for being mulish. Always thinking she knew better than others. Always thinking she was better than others. This was the direction of Portia's thoughts as she read the letter once more and then, taking off her glasses, she sat on the edge of the bed for a long time, the letter in her lap.

14

That summer, when most of the street kids had dispersed, DiDi moved in with Leah; the two of them equally destitute, but needing each other. DiDi had been hanging out with a group of friends, some of whom were into drugs and prostitution. She seemed to be on the cusp. The smallest thing was likely to push her over the edge and Leah couldn't bear the thought of losing her to the streets.

Leah had spoken to her social worker about DiDi. One day when DiDi came home from her wanderings, she suggested once more that DiDi should meet the social worker.

There was a moment of silence as DiDi's face went through a peculiar transformation. Finally, eyes blazing with outrage, she turned on Leah. 'Why did you want to do that?' she screamed. 'What's wrong with you? I told you I don't want nothing to do with social workers! Now you've gone and spoilt everything. Why couldn't you leave it alone!'

Before the shocked Leah could answer, DiDi had grabbed her jacket and was out of the door.

Summer passed and there was no word from DiDi. Leah regretted interfering in her life. She should have left well alone, she thought for the umpteenth time. Leah missed her terribly.

Then one day, about three months later, there was a knock at Leah's door. DiDi stood in the doorway, holding a plastic shopping bag and a small knapsack. She'd been crying, her black mascara streaked across the pale canvas of her face.

'I've come to stay with you,' she said. 'I have nowhere to go, Grams.' She had a kitten tucked into her knapsack. She gingerly lifted the cat out. It clung to her, its nails digging into her hands in sheer terror, ripping the skin and drawing blood.

'Poor thing is terrified,' she told Leah.

Leah took the kitten from her and stroked it to calm it down, but it leapt out of her hands and made a dash into the house, cowering near the bed.

'Come in,' said Leah, opening the door and stepping aside for DiDi to enter. 'Where have you been all this time? I was worried about you.'

'I got a job planting trees on Vancouver Island.'

Nothing more was said. Leah was just happy to see her again.

DiDi and the kitten both found a home with Leah. DiDi named the small black and white cat, with its one green eye and one brown eye, Spots. There were some wild moments when the dog upstairs sensed the presence of the cat. And when the landlady asked her whether she was keeping a pet in the basement apartment, Leah lied.

Spots settled in, but DiDi became restless. Sometimes she stayed away for days on end and just as Leah was going out of her mind worrying about her, she'd pitch up, unannounced. If Leah wasn't home, she'd wait on the step outside the kitchen door, even though she knew where the key was hidden.

DiDi reminded Leah of Jock, who had come and gone as he pleased. One never knew when DiDi was going to turn up either. Leah never complained. She was always happy to see her and so, of course, was Spots, who immediately scaled her leg like a mountaineer, digging his claws right through her denims. Leah eventually cured him of this terrible habit and he learned to lie quietly on a cushion. But he had clearly been as traumatised as DiDi by life on the street. Eventually DiDi also began to settle and stayed with Leah for longer periods.

One day, aware of DiDi's intense scrutiny, Leah looked up from a magazine she'd scavenged from one of the dumpsters.

'What's up?' she asked.

'How old are you?' DiDi asked.

'Don't be personal. It's not polite.'

'Oh, sure! But it's polite for you to get personal with me. Always asking me questions.'

'Well, there's a difference . . .'

'Oh, yeah . . . like what?'

'A generation gap.'

'Simple question, Grams. How old are you?'

'Sixty-three,' she said. 'If it's any of your business.'

'You look twice that age,' DiDi said with her usual candour.

'One hundred and twenty-six?' Leah asked, laughing.

DiDi pulled a wry face. 'Well . . . almost.'

Leah playfully tossed the magazine at her.

'It's your face and your hair. Let me show you how to do your hair.'

Leah hesitated.

'I know how to do hair,' said DiDi. 'I worked for a hairdresser.'

'When?' Leah asked.

'A few months ago,' the girl replied nonchalantly. 'Before I went to the island.'

'Where?'

'Downtown.'

'You had a job,' Leah asked, astonished, 'and you never told me?'

'Yeah, cleaning the place, sweeping up the hair and doing all the shitty work ... anyway, what does it matter? I quit, didn't I?'

'Why?' Leah asked.

'They were full of crap.'

Leah didn't pursue the matter.

DiDi opened her tote bag and took out a comb. It was a very expensive-looking comb. No doubt a souvenir from the hairdressing salon, Leah thought wryly.

'Come over here. Come sit by me and I'll style your hair.'

'You said you were only a sweeper ...' Leah started.

'I saw what they were doing. Easy stuff, man. I'm a quick learner.'

She took Leah's thick grey shoulder-length hair, which she usually wore tied back in a ponytail, swept it back off her brow, brushed it well, braided it and tied it in an elegant knot at the top of Leah's head.

'I'm going to teach you to have some style,' DiDi muttered.

'I'm not piercing my navel,' Leah said quickly.

'Not that, silly!' DiDi laughed. 'You're too old for stuff like that. I meant style for a woman of your age – to make you look younger.'

'What for?' Leah asked dryly.

'Well, you never know when it'll come in handy. You've got to look sexy. Okay?'

Leah made a disdainful sound, took a deep breath and slowly let it out. If agreeing with her meant that DiDi would stay off the streets, she'd agree to anything.

The next day DiDi brought home a parcel in a plastic bag. 'This will look great on you. I found a neat place to shop.'

'What is it?'

'Don't have a fit. I got it at the Thrift Shop,' DiDi said, extracting a straw bowler from the bag. 'They've got all sorts of nifty things. You won't believe.'

'I don't believe,' Leah said, her suspicions aroused. 'You

sure you didn't pinch this off the rack somewhere?'

'Honest to God, Leah . . . Cross my heart and hope to die.'

'Take it back, DiDi. We barely have enough money to eat.'

'You can't take things back to the Thrift Shop. Everything is a final sale. Besides, don't worry . . . I'll find a job . . .'

'What? Panhandling?' Leah asked, irritated with DiDi's breathless insistence.

DiDi paused, her expression crestfallen.

'I'm sorry,' Leah said, quickly. 'I don't know what came over me. I really am very sorry. I didn't mean to hurt your feelings.'

'Yeah, right,' DiDi said and then, seeing Leah's expression of consternation, she burst into laughter. 'Where do you think I got the money from to buy you this stupid hat?'

She was incorrigible, Leah thought, and loved her all the more for it.

DiDi got Leah doing pelvic exercises and sit-ups and slapped her shoulders back when they slumped from tiredness or from anxiety. The young girl was a tough taskmaster and slowly Leah felt a change in her health. Her hip felt a lot better and she was beginning to recover some of her shattered self-esteem. It was amazing how much better Leah felt about herself just being around DiDi, who asked so little in return.

One day DiDi picked up the photograph of Erica and the boys, and looked at it intently. 'Do you love your daughter?' she asked.

'Of course I do.'

'Does she love you?'

Leah took a long moment to think about the answer. 'You never expect your children to love you, DiDi. You just love them enough and hope that some of the love will be returned to you. You also hope that someday your children might just love *you* enough to forgive you for being their mother.'

DiDi listened attentively. She didn't say anything, but Leah could practically hear the cogs grinding in her head.

'I dreamt of my father the other night,' DiDi said. 'He died a long time ago. Then my mother got married again.' She paused, her eyes clouding with a sadness that touched Leah. 'He took me to the exhibition grounds once. They had all these great rides. Boy, did we ever have a great time.'

'When did he die?' Leah asked.

'A long time ago. I don't remember exactly when. I wish I could remember the whole dream. I didn't actually see my father's face either. I just knew it was him.'

Leah didn't say anything.

'I woke up too soon,' DiDi said. She sat down and Spots climbed on to her lap, curled up and went to sleep.

'That's the worst thing about dreams. You always wake up too soon.'

'Yeah, I guess,' DiDi said. 'I always dream. Not that I can always remember what the dream was about. When we were on Vancouver Island, we slept in tents and I dreamt about my father too. My mother and I used to go over to the Island every spring and summer. She used to take me along even when they were protesting about the way the trees were being cut down. I loved those days. We were happy then. Tree Huggers, that's what we were. Then she remarried.' DiDi's eyes wandered off and she fell silent.

Leah reached for her hand and squeezed it lightly. But DiDi got up quickly. Spots leapt off her lap with a squeal of protest. Without another word, DiDi left. Leah let her go. There was nothing she could do to stop her. Holding on to DiDi would have been like trying to clutch a fistful of air. She lived her life on her own terms and coped with her pain in her own way. Leah could only let her know that she was there for her if and when she needed her. It suddenly occurred to her that it was more than she had ever done for her own child. But Erica was the one who had pushed her away, who had dreams of her own which did not include her parents. It was different when she was young. The two of them were close then. They were allies in a miserable household. She

142

couldn't blame Erica for going off the way she had, and even for cutting them out of her life, although it hurt so terribly.

For a moment she toyed with the idea of visiting Erica, but sensed that by now the gulf between them was much too wide to be bridged in one leap. Perhaps what might work, she thought, was bridge building – one step at a time, starting with a letter. She reached for Charlie's old notebook and found the pencil. Then she changed her mind. It didn't seem right for her to write a letter to her daughter using a pencil.

'Tomorrow,' she said to Spots, 'I'm going to buy a pen and write that letter to Erica. Right?'

Spots nuzzled her and Leah picked him up and went to sit on the bed with him. A sense of loneliness welled up in her and she had to fight the inclination to cry.

'Damn,' she muttered. 'I'm becoming a real old baby, aren't I?'

15

Leah's letter had given Portia a great deal to think about as she bustled through her workday. One thing she knew for certain was that Leah was family and that families stood together in times of need and trouble. They were there for one another, no matter what their history. It had taken her a long time to come to this conclusion, just as it had taken her a long time to decide what the best approach might be if, indeed, Leah did need help.

Portia was not prone to rash decisions. She took her time about everything. One of the ideas she toyed with was sending Leah a ticket, especially in view of Ephemera's persistence about Leah coming home. There was the little bit of money she'd saved through the years and she thought it might be enough to get Leah there. It took another few weeks but when her mind was made up, she sat down to write Leah a letter with the offer of a plane ticket.

Portia, who had never been on a plane, had no idea how to go about making travel arrangements. As far as she knew, the only person who'd been on an overseas trip was the dominee, and that wasn't really overseas; he'd merely flown to Kenya to visit family who were farming there. The dominee, a tall, lanky man in his mid-forties, with a craggy

144

face and piercing grey eyes was not someone she was particularly fond of, but she was desperate and there was no one else she could turn to.

The dominee, who rarely got the opportunity to apply his knowledge in areas other than his ministry, sprang into action. He moved like lightning, much too fast for Portia's comfort and she had to slow him down, dampen his enthusiasm, so to speak, because she needed time to measure each and every step.

Fearing interference from the locals, she swore the dominee to secrecy, but like all secrets, this one, too, began to leak and soon little threads of the story, thin and wispy like cobwebs, were spun around the town.

By the time Portia had finished talking to the dominee, many in the town knew that Leah was coming. As soon as Danie got wind of the news, his eyes glazed over and he became preoccupied. He now had something to look forward to, something to add a bit of fizz to his otherwise dreary life, or so he thought, as he studied his profile in the hand mirror. When Leah married Charlie and left Vlenterhoek, Danie was devastated.

Danie exercised more vigorously. He wanted to look good. Not just good, but so spectacular that when Leah saw him, she'd realise what she'd missed by not marrying him.

Danie was the furthest thing from Leah's mind as she carefully read Portia's letter. It had taken three months to reach her by surface mail. The tone of the letter was muted and Leah understood that her sister had a great deal to be angry about. She herself had been in quite a state when she wrote to Portia after Charlie's death, her thoughts so jumbled that perhaps Portia hadn't been able to make any sense of it.

Portia was suggesting that Leah visit them in Vlenterhoek. If Leah agreed, she was quite willing to send her the money for the ticket. Leah studied the careful, childlike writing and knew that it had taken an enormous effort for her sister to sit down and write that letter. Portia had only a basic education. She could read and write, of course, but nothing more than that – she'd been too busy taking care of them to spend time on her own education.

It was all too much for Leah. She put her head down and wept.

She decided that she would not mention the letter to DiDi. She didn't want to give the young girl the impression that she'd even consider accepting Portia's offer. She had no intention of abandoning DiDi just so the streets could reclaim her. Her familiar restlessness was visiting DiDi once more and Leah guessed that it wouldn't take much to draw the young girl back to the streets.

Leah pulled the suitcase out from under the bed. The envelope was hidden under a tear in the lining. She withdrew it, opened it, and took out the certificate. The five hundred dollars was long gone.

Carefully supporting her spectacles in their broken frames, she studied the certificate. For the first time she noticed that it was no ordinary certificate. It was a bond, a 'Strip Bond', payable to the bearer in the amount of five hundred US dollars. She hadn't a clue what the bond was for, but it was clearly worth its face value – at least five hundred US, which to her was a lot of money. She knew that the US dollar had greater value than its Canadian counterpart.

Leah read it again, wondering if it was fake – another of Charlie's diabolical jokes – her heart leaping one moment and sinking the next. She feared that approaching the authorities would only result in them taking it from her, just as they had taken her home and all her possessions.

Leah developed a headache. Her hands trembled and suddenly her arthritic hip started acting up. She got up and paced around her small room. She left the bond lying on the bed and went to pour herself a drink. On an impulse, she'd bought a bottle of cheap wine for a special occasion. The appropriate opportunity to drink the wine had never presented itself until

146

now.

She unscrewed the aluminium cap on the bottle, sat down and poured wine into a cracked coffee mug.

She was expecting DiDi home soon and returned the bond to the suitcase, tossing the letter in as well. She poured herself another drink, and began to relax. There was no point worrying about the bond now. There was nothing she could do about it until morning. With this thought, Leah fell asleep.

When DiDi arrived, she saw the open bottle of wine on the table and gave Leah one of her quizzical looks.

'What's this? You turning into a wino now?' she asked.

'No. I just needed something to pick me up.'

'Looks like it knocked you out instead.' DiDi screwed the cap back on to the bottle and returned it to the cupboard.

Leah rolled off the bed, her hip suddenly very painful. There was no reason to tell DiDi about the bond or the letter from Portia. There was no point building the girl's hopes and then having them dashed if the bond was nothing more than a worthless piece of paper.

'So you're back,' Leah said irritably.

'What's wrong with you?' DiDi asked.

Leah was silent. She pressed her hand into her lower back trying to ease the ache – a dull, throbbing, constant pain like toothache.

'It just ticks me off,' Leah said, 'that you come and go as you please.'

DiDi raised a mocking ring-studded brow.

Leah manipulated her hip as she limped around the room, trying to regain some mobility.

'Okay, okay,' she said. 'I'm a bit snarly – so shoot me.' Leah was beginning to sound more and more like DiDi.

Then she noticed for the first time that DiDi had put a plastic shopping bag on the cluttered counter.

'I brought us some stuff to eat.'

Leah peered into the bag. It contained a carton of milk, a loaf of bread and a packet of potato chips. She put her arms around DiDi and hugged her. The young girl did not respond, but nor did she withdraw as she might have done before. Leah sat down at the kitchen table as DiDi related her day's events, but her mind was preoccupied. The idea of going to Vlenterhoek was beginning to take hold.

Frikkie was back and forth between Vlenterhoek and Cape Town. Whenever he was in Vlenterhoek he stayed at his parents' home at Tweeriviere.

On the surface he and his father appeared to be getting on well. Hendrik Joubert had forgiven his son. Frikkie's project had seduced him, and had brought forgiveness into his stony heart. All he could talk about now was 'the project'; 'a lucrative opportunity'; 'money could be made hand over fist'. In the process of lending support to his son, he carved out a niche for himself. 'A slice of the pie', was the way he thought of it.

The question of ownership of the one hundred and twelve hectares of land remained a mystery.

Frikkie eventually decided that the time was right to see Suzette – not that he hadn't tried to do so before; he'd telephoned twice and had driven past the house on several occasions. He had stopped short of visiting her at the Glory Café only because he feared a public confrontation. He sensed that she was still very bitter about the way he had left town and that she had expected so much more of their relationship.

Finally, knowing that further delay would only make matters worse between them, he went to see her. Suzette's anger, contained for so long, rose to the surface and she bristled with hostility as she confronted him on the doorstep.

'So,' she said scornfully, 'you've finally deigned to visit.'

'It's not what you think,' he said, her tone immediately putting him on the defensive.

'And what do I think?' she said testily, as she led the way into the house.

Frikkie smiled sheepishly. 'I have tried. I tried to call . . .'

'Of course. This is such a big town . . .'

'Please, Suzette,' he said, lifting his hands in a gesture of surrender. 'I didn't come here to fight.'

They sat down opposite each other – he on the sofa, she in her father's easy chair. They were close enough for her to reach out over the coffee table and touch him, something she had often dreamt about. Instead, her hands remained tightly clasped in her lap as Frikkie explained to her why he had left Vlenterhoek so suddenly.

As she listened to him, she wondered why he had not thought that she might have felt as trapped as he, and why he expected her not to be upset about the way he'd taken off without a care in the world, while she was left with the responsibility of raising a son.

'I heard you were married,' she said.

'Yes. It didn't last long.'

'Any children?' she asked.

He shook his head.

'I heard about what happened to your leg.'

'So much for the new South Africa,' he responded with resentment.

'I'm sorry,' she said, smiling politely.

He shrugged. 'I want to get on with my life.'

'Why have you come back?' she asked. Her question was so abrupt that for a moment he was speechless, his startled eyes on her face.

'The resort development is an important project. It'll bring a lot of money and progress to this town. Who knows, it might even bring people back.'

'You'll never get my father's land,' she said quietly. 'Especially now that he knows you're involved.'

'I don't understand why he hates me so much. What did I do to him? He already hated me when you and I . . .'

'It's what your father did to him and his brother. Your father stole my uncle's land and that's why he shot himself. Pa will never forgive you or your family.'

'But I had nothing to do with it.'

'I know. It doesn't matter to him. You're a Joubert.'

Frikkie realised that it was hopeless even to think that Suzette might help him change her father's mind. He could see that this meeting was going nowhere and it was time for him to leave. He still had to make a few phone calls, but he couldn't seem to get up off the sofa, and it wasn't only because his leg was stiff and painful. Suzette had changed. She was so calm, so content, and still so beautiful with her brilliant blue eyes and blonde hair. He noticed that she'd put on a bit of weight and that her face had plumped out. He wondered why she wasn't married and whether there was a man in her life. He'd heard that she'd had a child. Frikkie wrenched his attention away from her and got to his feet. He didn't want to be there when her father got home. He was about to say goodbye when Suzette's son, Martin, entered the room.

'So this is your boy,' he said, offering his hand to Martin. Suzette, too emotional to speak, nodded as Martin took Frikkie's hand.

'He looks like a fine boy, Suzette,' Frikkie said when Martin left the room. He wanted to ask about the boy's father, but felt that he didn't have the right. Perhaps the man was married. He'd heard rumours about her and another man. He turned away without further comment.

He didn't stay long after that. Suzette seemed distraught and he didn't want to upset her further.

Early one morning, some weeks later, an older model, slightly battered blue Mercedes Benz with Cape Town plates, drove into town. The solitary occupant was a man in his mid-sixties. His love of good food and beer were responsible for the paunch which rested firmly against the steering wheel. In his khaki pants and work boots, he was indistinguishable from the locals.

The volume on his CD player was turned up, blasting the

still air with Puccini's 'Madam Butterfly'. Occasionally, moved by the music, he released the steering wheel to conduct the orchestra.

Lying on the seat next to him was a Nikon camera with an assortment of additional lenses. He slowed down as he reached the rusted signboards on the outskirts of town, then reversed and stopped in front of one of the signs. After looking around, he reached for his camera and got out of the car. In the distance he spotted a huge red kite flapping in the breeze. He took pictures of the kite, the landscape, some landmarks and the WELCOME TO VLENTERHOEK sign. He looked purposeful and interested in his surroundings. And all the while the aria from 'Madam Butterfly' filled the air.

From their position at the top of the ridge, Jannie and Albert saw the dust thrown up by the speeding car. They also saw it stop. Jannie wished he'd brought his binoculars. Albert, who was resting against a rock, strummed on his guitar which sounded flat and off key. 'I can't fix it,' he said, disgruntled, as he screwed and unscrewed the frets, playing with the tension in the strings.

'I t-t-t-to-ld y-y-ou we-we-we-'d u-s-se t-t-the p-p-pr-ize m-m-money t-t-to f-f-fix it.'

The Mercedes continued on its way into town, the driver turning the volume down as he slowly cruised along the main street, swerving around a dog lying asleep in the middle of the road.

He stopped at the lights. The light turned white and the Mercedes continued for two more blocks, made a U-turn and then parked in front of the Imperial Hotel where the driver got out and took some pictures.

He spent about fifteen more minutes exploring the town. Then, as quietly and inconspicuously as he had arrived, he drove out of town. It would be some time before the residents learned that the 'location scout' had been and had left with several rolls of exposed film on the seat next to him. There

151

would be no opportunity for the anxious Danie Venter to show off the town's attributes or to influence him in any way.

The initial reports about the town had been reliable. It would be the perfect setting for one of the segments of the docudrama 'Ambiance', the story of a legendary Indian dancer from a small village in India, who became internationally renowned for her fusion of Gypsy, Rajastani and Middle-Eastern traditional dance styles. Segments were being shot in Rajastan and in Dubai. The local producers had searched for months for the ideal landscape, with just the right kind of light, to film the South African segment. Josh had not only personally sought out this particular location, but was also one of the producers of the South African-Dubai co-production. After reading the article about Mrs Roussouw and the Hemelslaagte Springs, he'd come to investigate and it was indeed as incredible as described. He knew instinctively, without even seeing his developed pictures, that the colour would be stupendous.

The location scout drove back the way he had come, the aria from 'Madam Butterfly' once again splitting the still air as it followed him through the veld. He was relieved that he had not met any curious townsfolk. He hated their questions. They were always about money.

Later that same week the town of Vlenterhoek finally found out why, over the past few months, there had been so much interest in their small town, and especially in the Hemelslaagte Springs.

One morning they woke up to find that a 'NO TRESPASS-ING' sign had gone up along one of the dirt roads leading to the springs. The residents learned for the first time that many of the absentee owners had sold their land at huge profits.

Gert le Roux heard about the fence and the sign and went to fetch his wire cutters. Stories circulated about the development and Frikkie explained what IRH was trying to do for the town. Opinion was split. Some wanted progress; others thought that progress would come at too great a cost.

Many people thought that Frikkie Joubert had betrayed them. It didn't matter what his reasons were, he'd given up rugby and they still felt resentful about the fact that he hadn't come back to Vlenterhoek. Their disappointment was like an itch that just wouldn't go away.

In his capacity as town clerk, Danie tried to allay their fears at a meeting called by IRH. The way the meeting went, it seemed that he, rather than Frikkie, was there to represent IRH interests. The development was a good opportunity and he wanted to push it, especially since there were no other prospects on the horizon.

There were a lot of stony faces at the meeting as he tried to present the positive side of such a huge development. He emphasised issues like jobs, prosperity and the importance of putting Vlenterhoek on the map.

The dominee was there and so was Gert le Roux. The meeting, almost evenly split between those who wanted the development and those who didn't, became loud and rowdy. The aisle was the boundary separating the two sides. There were a lot of raised voices, some insults were hurled across the aisle and later several chairs were flung across the same divide. The police sergeant and his constable had to be called in to restore order. But the furore continued, spilling out on to the town office lawns. Never before had there been such a commotion in town. Everyone was caught up in the melee. It was as if the town had lost its collective mind.

16

Leah agonised for several days before she approached one of the volunteers at the Seniors Resource Centre. Ron was a man in his late sixties. She'd spoken to him on a few occasions and he appeared to be honest and knowledgeable.

Although she was not a frequent visitor to the recreation centre, she occasionally used the facilities when she needed information. This was one such occasion. She tried to think of an easy way to slip her question into a conversation with Ron, but there didn't appear to be a subtle way of approaching the subject and so she came right out and asked: 'Do you know what a bond looks like?'

'Why?' he asked tentatively.

'Well, do you know what one looks like?' she pressed.

'It looks like a certificate – what kind of a bond are you talking about?'

'I don't know,' Leah said. 'It says it's for five hundred US dollars.'

'Do you have such a bond?' he asked.

'What if I do?' she demanded.

'Let me see it. I can't tell you unless I see it,' he said.

She shook her head.

'What are you afraid of?' he asked.

154

'They took everything from me,' she said quietly.

He understood. He'd been through a lot of living himself and knew what went on in the lives of some of those who came to the recreation centre. In fact he'd seen Leah around and had introduced himself to her, but unlike the others, she hadn't volunteered any information about herself and this had intrigued him. 'I won't know what you have until I see it,' he said gently.

She opened her purse and removed the bond, holding on to it for a moment before relinquishing it to him. She'd heard about the scams perpetrated on seniors and had been warned to be careful. But there was something in Ron's eyes that put her at ease.

'Don't be afraid,' he said, taking the bond from her and studying it. 'It's like a bearer bond, so you don't have to worry. It's yours. It's as good as cash. It says Strip Bond, right here. See?' he pointed this out to her. 'Never heard of one like this before, but it looks genuine. Why don't you take it to a bank? They'll verify it.'

She dropped her head, clearly reluctant.

'They're the only ones who can help you, Leah.'

He handed the bond back to her. She folded it and slid it into her purse. Unsure of what to do next, she waited for him to say something.

'Do you have a bank account?' he asked.

'No.'

'Okay. Look, I'll take you to the bank. I have some time before lunch. Can you wait a few minutes?' He glanced at his watch. 'I have a few things to do first.'

'I'll wait out there,' she said with a sense of relief, as she got up out of her chair and walked to the door, her purse firmly clasped under her arm.

The investment manager at the bank took the bond from her and gave her a receipt. She explained that the bond was a perfectly legitimate document, but that it had to be sent to

155

the main branch for verification. 'They stopped issuing these about fifteen years ago,' she said.

She suggested that Leah open a bank account. 'It'll be so much easier,' the investment manager assured her. 'We'll be able to put the money directly into your account.'

'I don't want an account,' Leah said firmly. 'I want the cash.'

The woman glanced at Ron, looking for support. 'It's not safe to walk around with so much money, Mrs Barker,' she said. 'It would be much better to have an account. You can withdraw whatever you want, whenever you want.'

Leah leaned towards Ron and whispered, 'I don't know how . . .'

'They'll help you,' he said.

She hesitated again and then nodded. 'Okay.'

Her details were taken and for the first time in her life, she owned a bank account and a banking card.

'We have to convert the US bond to Canadian dollars. Interest will be compounded,' the woman said as she accompanied Leah to the bank machine to demonstrate its use. 'Your permanent card will be sent to you in the mail,' she said. 'When you turn sixty-five you will be eligible for your old age pension. It really is a good idea to have an account. Your pension can then be paid directly into it. You'll be able to draw on your account from any of our machines, using this card,' the woman continued.

Leah remembered nothing. Everything was a blur. She tried to concentrate on what the woman was saying, but her mind kept drifting to the question of how much money this piece of paper would realise. She didn't dare ask.

'You can't use the machine now, of course,' the woman said. 'There's nothing in your account. But in a couple of days you'll be up and running.' She gave Leah a bright smile. 'Don't lose your card, Mrs Barker, and don't give anyone your password. If you want to invest the money, one of us will be quite happy to help you.'

156

Leah was dazed. There was so much to remember.

'That wasn't so bad, was it?' Ron asked as they left the bank. 'If you feel like it, we can have a coffee at the Starbucks across the road.'

But Leah didn't want coffee. She had a headache and wanted to get home to rest. All in all, the day had been terribly stressful. 'Another time,' she said.

He understood. She looked pale and wan. He drove her back to the Seniors Resource Centre, dropping her at the bus stop. 'Come in any time and we'll have that coffee,' he said.

'Thanks, I will,' she said as she got out of the car.

On the way home, she thought about the day's events and hoped there would be enough money to pay for DiDi's ticket.

But she was still not ready to share the news with her. She wanted to wait a few days to make sure that the money had actually been deposited into her account.

Leah went to the bank on the Friday, handed her card to the teller and asked for the balance in her account. She almost collapsed with relief when she discovered that she had a little more than three thousand dollars credited. She was sure it would be enough to pay for DiDi's ticket.

On her way home Leah stopped at a travel agency and enquired about the cost of an air ticket to South Africa. It seemed she had enough money for *two* airline tickets. It was a tremendous relief because she was reluctant to accept money from her sisters, knowing that they, too, were struggling. She felt a whole lot better about making the trip now that she would be able to pay her own way.

That night Leah prepared a bean salad with a variety of canned beans she'd picked up from the local grocery store. She'd also splurged on a head of lettuce, a cucumber and some tomatoes. She bought herself a steak. Unlike DiDi, Leah craved meat.

When DiDi returned later that evening the table was set with two new plates and two glasses. Leah had bought orange juice for DiDi and wine for herself. She knew that DiDi drank alcohol, but didn't want to encourage her.

'What's this?' DiDi asked as she entered the door and saw the table. 'Are we having company?'

Leah was bursting with impatience.

'Hang on to your hat, girl! You and I are going to South Africa.'

'Yeah, Yeah . . . Yeah,' DiDi grinned. 'Are we hitch-hiking or what?

'We're going to fly.'

'You're kidding . . . right?'

'No. I'm serious.'

She told DiDi the whole story.

'Neat O,' DiDi said. 'Totally awesome.' Then she leapt up, grabbed Leah and the two of them did a little jig together.

They were making so much noise that the dog upstairs started yapping. The landlady rapped on the floor. DiDi picked up the broom and cheekily banged on the ceiling. Their celebration continued, interrupted occasionally by the landlady pounding on the floor. Neither of them cared. They were both ecstatic.

But it wasn't as easy as Leah thought. There were other complications, like passports and the fact that DiDi was not yet eighteen and would require parental consent to travel. Leah spoke to her social worker and he promised that he would assist with DiDi's travel documents.

'What about Spots?' DiDi asked.

'I'll find him a good home,' Leah promised.

While Leah was occupied with making plans, DiDi was going through her own emotional crisis. One afternoon, when the arrangements were well under way, she told Leah that she had changed her mind. Instead of going to South Africa, she said, she wanted to head east to Ontario with a group of her buddies. They were planning to hitch-hike across the country.

Leah pleaded with her, but DiDi insisted that this was

158

what she wanted and that nothing Leah could do or say would change her mind. With this dramatic reversal still ringing in Leah's ears, DiDi walked out and stayed away for a week. It was a week of tremendous anxiety for Leah, who wasn't sure whether DiDi was serious about the trip east, or whether she was just being her usual contrary self. Although Leah worried about DiDi, she knew that the young girl was more capable than she of surviving on the streets. But the scourge of drugs remained a threat.

Leah began to think about cancelling her plans and when DiDi finally deigned to visit she told her this, but DiDi argued that there was no point in Leah staying in Vancouver because she'd be alone. It would be best for her to accept her sister's offer. As usual, her advice was sound and, as always, showed surprising maturity. But Leah wasn't going to let go that easily.

'Come with me, dear,' she said. 'I need your support. You know how people walk all over me. I don't think I could bear Portia bullying me. There's always been this issue of my parents.'

'What about your parents?' DiDi asked.

Leah sighed. 'I never went home for their funerals.'

'That's okay, isn't it? I mean they're dead anyway. It's not as if they're going to know whether you were there or not.'

Leah smiled. 'Thanks. I needed that. But I don't think Portia sees it the same way. It's been very hard for her to accept the fact that I didn't go back. She sets very high standards for herself and for others. It would have been the decent thing for me to do. But Charlie wouldn't let me. Anyway, I hate funerals. Funerals and weddings. Such a fuss and then it's all over and you're buried – in both cases.'

'I like weddings,' DiDi said. 'Must say I'm not so fond of funerals. I went to my stepfather's funeral. It was the pits. I was glad he died.'

'Why?' Leah asked.

'Never mind,' DiDi said sharply.

'So?' Leah asked. 'Will you think about coming with me? I have enough money for your ticket.'

'Yeah, yeah. I'll think about it,' DiDi said dismissively.

'Well, don't take all year. I've got to know soon. It would be nice to leave in the fall.'

'Stop nagging me,' DiDi said sharply. But Leah saw the sliver of a smile in her eyes, softening the harshness of her words.

Portia was about to transfer the money when she received a telegram from Leah to say that she had enough money to pay for her ticket and that it wasn't necessary for her to wire money. Portia was relieved because by the time the bank had made all its calculations, converting rands to Canadian dollars, it sounded like it was going to cost her a fortune. She had almost changed her mind, almost had second thoughts, but the dominee was at the bank with her and she didn't want to give the impression that she was a total idiot – especially after he had gone to so much trouble.

Very early one morning, about two weeks after his initial visit to Vlenterhoek, the location scout Josh returned with Ian, the producer. He and Ian were there to make arrangements and to get the necessary permits to film in the town.

Josh was driving and humming Puccini's 'Nessun Dorma' while Ian studied the photographs. It didn't bother Ian that Josh was an opera buff, but it drove others mad.

Ian continued to scrutinise the photos, identifying the various landmarks on their way into town. He was holding the picture of Jannie's kite when he happened to look up and saw the same kite hovering in the sky above the ridge.

'What a magnificent sight,' Ian cried. 'We've got to get a few shots of that kite. It's fantastic.'

'Let's get the meeting with Venter over and done with first,' Josh said.

It was early morning and the town was just beginning to stir as Ian and Josh slowly drove along the main street. An employee at the Glory Café was removing the shutters.

Mrs Venter was behind the counter and two of the assistants had just arrived to start work when Ian and Josh pulled up outside the café.

The first few school buses arrived as the two men entered. Petronella peered at them over the top of her glasses, lips puckered, eyes darting around like a curious mole peering out of its burrow.

'Good morning,' she said, her lips stretching into a smile.

'Good morning,' Ian replied and ordered two cups of coffee.

'And how are you today?' she asked, pouring the coffee into two Styrofoam cups.

'Fine, thank you,' Josh muttered.

'Are you visiting or just passing through?' she asked, although she suspected that they were people from the film company.

Neither of the men said anything.

She paused, coffee pot poised, waiting for a reply. Ian gave her a thready smile, paid for the coffee and thanked her. He and Josh walked out on to the veranda and stood there drinking their coffee.

They continued into the street and stared down the length of the almost deserted ribbon of tarmac.

Petronella watched them through the big plate glass window in the front of the café. When she caught sight of the camera on the front seat of Josh's Mercedes her suspicions were confirmed and she quickly disappeared into her small office to phone her husband.

Danie, who had already showered and dressed, hotfooted it over. He was an early riser, often at his desk in the town office before eight. Not that there was a lot for him to do, but he liked to get there early, sometimes to read the paper and take his time easing into the day. It was also good for his image: a town clerk who took his job seriously.

Danie met the two men in the street in front of the Glory Café and escorted them to his office. Rena had not yet arrived. She usually got in at nine o'clock. Danie and the two men were still there when Rena arrived an hour later. News had already spread around town and she knew when she looked at Danie's closed door that the two men from the film company were in there with him, 'negotiating'.

This was the word that Danie bandied about afterwards, as if the deal had been closed because of his skilful manoeuvrings.

The cast and crew were to arrive within two weeks when everything had been finalised. It was estimated that it would take about two days to rehearse and that they expected to be in town for between eight and ten days.

Danie explained sheepishly that there might be some problems, but that everything would be taken care of. 'Heh, heh,' he chuckled, to cover up his embarrassment at being part of a town so small in its size and thinking. 'This is our first experience, after all. But it will not be our last, heh, heh, heh.'

Ian smiled. He could see how hard Danie was trying and felt sorry for him.

'Don't worry,' he said. 'We won't back out of this deal. We like what we've seen.'

Danie breathed a sigh of relief, removed his handkerchief from his pocket and dabbed his brow.

'The only problem, as I see it,' said Ian, 'is the telephone system . . . but . . .'

Before he could finish his sentence, Danie jumped in. 'It is not a problem. We'll have someone on the exchange twenty-four hours a day, seven days a week.'

He had told them earlier that the exchange closed at midnight. The town council had decided years ago that it was a waste of time and money to keep it open all night. To their

162

way of thinking, no one had any business making phone calls after midnight.

'We all have cellphones,' Josh said.

'Reception's not that great,' Ian said. 'There's only one transmitter. I saw it as we drove through the mountains. We might not always have a signal.'

Danie put his hands up to stop any debate. 'We will work it out. Not to worry,' he said with a broad smile, mopping his brow again. The business about the phone could be sorted out. He didn't want any further complications. For a moment there was silence. Danie puckered his lips and thoughtfully massaged his head.

The next question came from Ian. 'What about accommodation?' he asked.

Danie nodded vigorously, beaming at the two men. 'There is lots of room. We have the hotel. We have Nora Naude's B&B. There are also many households who will take in guests. They have said so. So it's nothing to worry about.'

The rest of the meeting went smoothly. Josh and Ian omitted to mention that the dancers were Indian and that most of the cast and crew were people of colour, including the cameraman Vusi. Neither of them considered this relevant. What they *did* say was that their client was very wealthy and would spare no expense in producing the film, that 'Ambiance' was three-part documentary of dance set against various backgrounds and settings. A one-hour segment was to be set in South Africa.

It might have contributed to Danie's understanding of the project if they had told him that the dancers would wear colourful costumes, shot against the muted colours of the landscape. Music was to be a fusion of Indian and African sounds, much of which was to be taped in a sound studio in Cape Town. Two of the musicians would accompany the crew. One of these was a well-known drummer, Thabu, and the other a sitar player, Ravi.

Eventually the men emerged from Danie's office. Rena

smiled and nodded her head at them. Both men acknowledged her. Danie was all smiles as he shook their hands and
walked them to the door. 'Do you know the MP Rebecca
Fortuin? She is from this small town,' he said, indulging in
some name-dropping.

'Is that so?' Ian said, but did not comment further.

The two men exchanged a few more pleasantries with
Danie and by the time they left, Danie was positively
beaming.

That Sunday the church was packed. News about the film
company's expected arrival had spread to the outlying farms.
While they waited for the service to start, people gathered
outside in small groups. All sorts of speculation flew around
the churchyard: who had extra space in their homes? How
much could they charge? And who was to do the catering?
Speculation continued long after the church service ended,
over midday meals and over coffee or beer long into the
evening.

17

One night when Sissie, drenched in sweat, awoke from a particularly harrowing dream, she crept into bed with Noelle – something she hadn't done since she was a child. Squeezed up against her sister in the narrow cot, she felt safe and protected, but the moment she fell asleep, her dreams returned. She thrashed around until Noelle was pinned to the wall.

'Wake up, Sissie!' Noelle cried, shaking her sister by the shoulders, but Sissie was a heavy sleeper and it took some effort. Sissie rolled over on to her back, gasping for air, and with a strangled cry she opened her eyes.

'It's only a dream,' Noelle said, climbing over Sissie to light the lamp.

Trembling, Sissie drew her legs up to her chest and lay curled up like a centipede.

Noelle stroked her brow.

'I can't go back to sleep again,' said the distraught Sissie.

'I thought you'd stopped having bad dreams.'

Sissie shuddered. Noelle gathered her in her arms and held her. It was the first time since her mother had died that she had felt any kind of emotion. For the first time too she felt something akin to love and a connection so strong that it left her aching.

Sissie had sensed from the time that her dreams about Ivan started that there was a connection between her dreams and the body that had been found in the veld.

This same feeling eventually took Sissie into the veld. She thought that if she could unravel the mystery of her dreams, and how they tied in with the discovery of the body, her nightmares would end.

A piece of yellow police tape was still knotted to the tree where the body had been found. The grave had been filled in and smoothed over and, apart from that piece of yellow tape clinging so tenaciously to the tree, there was no evidence whatsoever that anything untoward had happened there.

Sissie had gone about thirty paces in the direction of Herman's Rock, her eyes scanning the ground, when she spotted something in the sand, half-hidden by an elephant plant. She dug it out with her ballpoint pen. It was a badly damaged identity book of the kind that all South Africans carried. The pages had been ripped out and all that remained was the last page on which a few numbers were still visible. The rest of it had been destroyed.

Sissie took the book to the police station and explained where she had found it. She led the sergeant and the constable to the place, where they conducted an additional search, but nothing else was found. The ID book was immediately dispatched to the forensic laboratory in Cape Town. The sergeant sensed a new tension in the case. He felt a twinge of excitement as they awaited the report.

About six weeks later the report from Cape Town arrived. The sergeant read the report several times and then, looking very official, he went to see the Erasmus girls. Noelle was home when the sergeant arrived and she knew immediately why he had come.

He dispensed with the preliminaries in a very sensitive manner and then explained that he required a sample of her hair for forensic testing. This would be compared with some of the body material that the pathologist had found on the skeleton. The pathologist thought that the body belonged to their brother Ivan, because a set of identity numbers had been lifted off the book Sissie had found. But they needed one final test for confirmation.

A few weeks later the results were confirmed and Ivan's body was returned to Vlenterhoek.

Anna Joubert insisted on helping the girls with the cost of burying their brother.

'Stay out of this,' her husband warned when he heard of her plans.

'No. He deserves a decent funeral.'

Hendrik was silenced by the calm determination in her voice.

'I've known for a long time,' she said. 'It's the least we can do.'

Ivan was buried in the cemetery in town. Anna promised the girls that she would pay for a small, simple headstone.

Sissie returned to the grave two weeks later, laying sprays of bougainvillaea on the mound. Even though she still didn't quite understand the significance of the dream, she knew now with absolute certainty that she had been meant to go into the veld, meant to find the ID book. It was even more significant that Sissie's dreams ended with its discovery.

On the long flight to South Africa, Leah had ample time to think about her life. In the seat next to her, DiDi was firmly plugged into the in-flight movie. Leah dozed intermittently, struggling to get comfortable, but it was hard to find comfort in such confinement. Eventually she raised the blind to gaze through the window, but all she could see below were clouds.

'Shut the blind,' DiDi hissed.

With a sigh, Leah sat back and pulled the blind down, plunging them into darkness once more.

'Can't you see we're watching a movie,' DiDi muttered.

Leah shut her eyes, pretending to be asleep, but images rolled off her closed lids. She sighed. She had put all her hopes in Charlie, and for what? The pain of her wasted life consumed her. She turned her head to hide her tears. She felt so miserable, so alone. A hand closed over hers, squeezing it affectionately. She returned the pressure. She still did not want to turn her head for DiDi to see her tears.

'You okay?' DiDi asked.

'Yeah, sure,' Leah said. 'Can't you see I'm sleeping?'

DiDi, who missed nothing, saw Leah's hand go up to her eyes and the surreptitious way in which she dabbed her eyes.

'Think I can have some wine?' DiDi asked mischievously, trying to distract Leah, when the drinks trolley approached.

'No way. You're under age,' Leah said, turning to smile at the girl.

'What a drag,' DiDi replied, replacing her headphones.

When the cabin attendant asked them what they wanted, DiDi hesitated for just a moment and glanced at Leah.

Then she smiled sweetly, crinkling her nose and causing the nose stud to droop lopsidedly. 'Coke, please,' she said and laughed as Leah exhaled.

'You're much too uptight, Leah,' DiDi said as the trolley rolled on to the next row of seats.

'The trouble is I never know what to expect from you,' Leah said.

'Have I ever let you down?' DiDi asked.

Leah thought about this for a long moment. 'I guess not,' she said.

'Exactly,' DiDi said triumphantly, as if nailing a huge issue of immense significance.

The rest of the flight was uneventful. They both slept intermittently.

They had an eight-hour layover at Frankfurt. There was no point leaving the transit lounge. They had no money for transport or shopping. DiDi was restless and went for a walk. It was hard for her to be still for too long. The nine hours of confinement in the cabin had already set her on edge.

Leah found a seat in a quiet corner. So many thoughts wrapped themselves around her. She wondered what DiDi would think of Vlenterhoek. Now that they were on their way, she worried how the unorthodox young girl would fit into the small, narrow-minded community.

Leah and DiDi flew into Cape Town where they spent two days taking in the sights. DiDi seemed to like Cape Town. She said that in some ways it reminded her of Vancouver. But before DiDi could become too comfortable in Cape Town, they took the train to Vlenterhoek.

When they stepped off the train at Vlenterhoek, DiDi was wearing her tight jeans and a cut-off top exposing her navel with all its artefacts. Leah was wearing a light summer frock with a gathered skirt belted at the waist, sandals, a straw bowler and a look of easy confidence.

Portia withdrew stiffly from Leah's warm embrace and greeted DiDi coolly. She instructed the porter to take their luggage to the car.

'Neat O,' DiDi said when she saw the vintage Ford. She walked around it, inspected it and smiled her approval at Portia.

Portia was alarmed and dismayed that Leah had arrived with extra baggage. A child, a strange creature that she could not make head or tail of. She couldn't understand a word the girl said and was irritated by her precocious behaviour.

Ephemera, thrilled at seeing Leah, linked her arm through her sister's, holding on to her as if she was never going to let her go again.

Stories about Leah's arrival spread through the town like a bushfire. Everyone wanted to see the girl Leah had brought with her.

Portia remained distant and cool towards DiDi. Leah

explained that it was part of Portia's nature. She'd never been an outgoing person.

'I don't think she likes me,' DiDi remarked.

'Nonsense,' Leah admonished. 'I know her. You just have to get under that tough shell. She's really quite sweet once you get to know her.'

DiDi guffawed. 'You gotta be kidding!'

Leah wanted Portia to like DiDi. She desperately wanted the two of them to get along.

'I like Ephemera,' DiDi said. 'I think she's got something special.'

Leah had not expected to find Ephemera so removed from reality. There had been no warning that her young sister had snapped the way she had. When Leah saw her at the station and realised that there was nothing but empty recognition behind her smile, she was taken aback. It was only when they got home and when she and Portia were sitting on the stoep while DiDi entertained Ephemera, that Portia explained the situation to her.

'I didn't know what to do about her,' Portia said. 'She's been like that ever since Mother died.'

'I'm sorry, Portia,' said Leah. 'I didn't know.'

Portia shrugged. Resentment leaked from her in the dullness of her eyes, in the way she sat so perfectly erect, so still, studying her hands loosely clasped in her lap. Leah looked at those hands: work-worn and roughened, nails permanently stained from working in the soil, and she felt her guilt surface. She wondered if her sister would ever forgive her for having stunted her life. But then, by the same token, what did she have out of her own life? Nothing but misery.

'I'm so sorry that I didn't come home for the funerals, Portia. Charlie wouldn't let me. I wanted to bring Erica to meet you, but he wouldn't let us come home.'

Portia made no comment.

'My life with him wasn't easy,' Leah continued, then her words petered out. She didn't want to sound like a victim.

Besides, Portia too had had a difficult life. She couldn't help but admire her sister and the remarkable way she had coped with everything, including Ephemera. She had to be given her due. Leah reached out and took Portia's hand. Portia sat like a stone Buddha, her hand frozen in Leah's. There was no forgiveness in that hand. Not yet.

It took about two weeks for Leah to recover from the long flight. DiDi, younger and more resilient, recovered much more quickly. After a few days she was out exploring. Leah eventually raised the subject of DiDi's dress.

'Just a few centimetres lower and you'll be naked,' Leah remarked, fearing that if DiDi wore her pants any lower her pubis would be exposed. DiDi was stubborn. No one was going to tell her what to wear. She refused to give up her short tank tops or to remove any of the rings attached to her body.

'I'm not taking my navel ring out for nobody,' she said firmly and that, as far as she was concerned, was the end of the matter.

18

Overt admiration for Leah from one section of the Vlenterhoek community did not preclude strong feelings of resentment from the other. Among the former were those who
envied her air of worldliness and sophistication. This surprised
Leah, since she had never regarded herself as either. On the
contrary, largely thanks to Charlie, she felt extremely
inadequate.

Danie, blind to reality, saw only the woman he had loved
so many years ago. They had both aged, of course, she more
gracefully than he, he thought wryly as he drew a hand over
his brow. Although he would have liked nothing better than
to throw himself at her feet, he didn't dare approach her. All
he could do was admire her from a distance. He still carried
around a picture of her in his head as she'd been in her youth:
the pretty face and the pert nose, long blonde hair worn in a
ponytail or hanging loose to her shoulders and a figure that
had turned many a young boy's head. Now she wore her
grey hair in a braid that swung down to her shoulder blades
and she carried herself with a dignity that one couldn't help
but admire.

'You look fantabulous,' DiDi remarked. This was one of
her new expressions.

There was no doubt that Leah had something special, a *je ne sais quoi*, some might have remarked had she been in a more sophisticated environment. Nevertheless, even here in Vlenterhoek, these qualities were noticed as she walked down the main street with DiDi trailing a few steps behind, making all sorts of rude comments about the residents under her breath.

Some admitted, albeit grudgingly, that there really was something quite regal about Leah's demeanour – in her posture and in the way she held her head. Leah wondered what they might have said had they seen her a few years before.

It was largely due to DiDi's efforts that she had turned her life around.

Whenever Mrs Potgieter saw her, she screwed her lips up in a distasteful sneer. She had never liked Leah – as far back as their schooldays when the boys had buzzed around her like bees around a patch of petunias. Her late husband Walt, besotted with Leah, might never have noticed her, had Leah not left Vlenterhoek.

Because of their history, Mrs Potgieter was understandably critical of the fuss that was being made about the other woman. While Leah had traipsed 'overseas', the rest of them had stayed in Vlenterhoek. Now that she had decided to return – forty years later – everyone was leaping through hoops for her. Mrs Potgieter silently wished that she had stayed away for good, like some of the others who had left, never to be heard of again.

The more reticent of the residents asked Leah polite questions about her life overseas. *Overseas* – a vague mysterious place far beyond Vlenterhoek's horizons.

DiDi attracted attention wherever they went,

'Is this a weird bunch or what?' she remarked to Leah. 'Don't know if I'm going to like being here. They give me the willies. It sure is weirder than anything I've seen on the streets of Vancouver.'

'Shush,' Leah said sharply. 'I don't want anyone hearing you say such things.'

'Why not? It's the truth, ain't it?'

'Maybe. Maybe not. Just give it a chance, will you, before you become judgemental.'

'Well, what the hell you think they are?' DiDi demanded.

'Please try to curb your tongue, dear. These people aren't used to swearing and cursing. My sister won't be as tolerant as I am.'

'All right,' DiDi said, when she saw the anxiety in Leah's face. 'But if this keeps on much longer, I'm out of here.'

Some of the women, with a spiteful glint in their eyes, put their own spin on how Leah had kicked the dust off her heels and had moved first to Zambia and then to Australia, finally settling in Canada. They speculated that DiDi might be Leah's illegitimate child. One of the women thought that there was an 'illegitimate' feel about DiDi.

Speculating about Leah became more interesting than the soapies on TV. This was real life. Interactive entertainment. They could watch their victim squirm. But they under-estimated Leah's strength of resolve. Nothing they said or did could affect her. She'd been through hell and had survived.

The more level-headed residents did their calculations and realised it was highly unlikely that DiDi was Leah's child, even though the possibility might have been an interesting one, especially since it would have taken the Hopkins sisters down a peg or two.

Those who tried to get close to DiDi eventually gave up. It was difficult to communicate with her. Jannie, Albert, Esther and Sissie had initially been wary too, but it was Albert who made the first move. His music transcended language barriers. Like DiDi, he couldn't read a note of music. He was self-taught and because of this one thing they had in common, their friendship was instantly assured. Esther and DiDi also had something in common – they both thought that Cape

Town was a much more desirable place to be. But DiDi was really intrigued by Sissie, with her strange look-into-your-soul eyes.

The only person who had not quite thawed was Portia, and DiDi stayed out of her space. 'Hey, man, it's her life,' she told Leah. 'She got to do what she got to do. I won't beg her to be nice. Me, I stick with Ephemera. She's great. Doesn't listen much and doesn't speak much, but she sure don't hurt my feelings like Portia.'

Leah and Nora became friends. Later, when things started happening in Vlenterhoek, Leah explained to the bemused Nora that everything in life was subject to cosmic influences. It was a Leah philosophy – an almost karmic philosophy with a bit of astrology tossed in – something she had adopted from the hippie movement of the sixties and seventies. Leah, living in the heavy-metal era of computers and cyberspace, was a late-blooming hippie.

On the third Sunday of the month, a special day of worship, a large crowd was expected at the church. Portia and Ephemera got themselves ready and invited Leah and DiDi to accompany them, but neither wanted to attend the service. They were both tired of the snide comments that followed them wherever they went and thought that a confrontation in church might be more than either of them could bear. There was no telling how DiDi would respond and Leah thought it better to be safe than sorry. As it was, DiDi had already shocked Portia with the declaration that she wouldn't be caught dead in church.

Many among the large crowd of worshippers had come out of curiosity, expecting that the newcomers would be present. The other drawcard was the fact that with the film company's imminent arrival, a fiery response was expected from the dominee. One of the other notable absentees was Hendrik Joubert. Jannie was there with his mother – he and Esther stealing glances at each other from behind their hymnbooks.

Ephemera, always restless and easily distracted, turned in her seat to gaze at the congregation. The dominee did not like distractions during his sermon and Portia tried to keep her sister still. Ephemera leaned forward and wiped the dust off her shoes with her handkerchief. Portia had to take her sister's hands in hers. The dominee was at the dais, about to deliver his Sunday sermon.

A hot and heavy silence had settled over the congregation. Portia retrieved a small fan from her handbag and proceeded to fan herself as they waited. The dominee adjusted his spectacles. They waited again as he opened the Bible and searched for the appropriate passage.

Suddenly a child cried. His eyes fanned over the congregation and fixed on the source of the disturbance – an infant cradled in its mother's arms. The dominee glared at the culprit over the top of his glasses as the mother got up and tiptoed out of the church.

This was merely the warm-up for what was to follow. He was clearly incensed that strangers were coming to the town to corrupt the residents and especially the young people. There was a shuffling of feet and a clearing of throats as his flock awaited the expected lambasting.

'Do we want strangers coming to our town?' he cried.

The congregation, thinking this was a rhetorical question, did not respond. After a momentary pause, he answered his own question: 'No! We don't want or need strangers in our midst.' His words resounded through the cavernous interior of the church.

'Fornicators, drunks and drug pushers. We read about it all the time and see it on our television screens. Is this what we want for our children? Is this what we want in Vlenterhoek?' His gaze swept over the upturned faces. Some of them lowered their eyes.

'Do we?' he shouted again, as if they were hard of hearing.

In response there was a general shaking of heads and a

great deal of muttering.

Esther's mother looked equally fiery. Esther lowered her head. Portia continued to fan herself. The interior of the church was hot and beads of perspiration appeared on many brows. Women discreetly patted their faces with their handkerchiefs.

'They'll come into our midst as disciples of the devil – disguised as film-makers, seducing our girls and our women, tempting our men with money and pleasures, crowding the bars, breaking up our homes,' the minister cried passionately. 'Is that what we want?' He scanned the faces around him once more.

There was a moment of hesitation and then the congregation was galvanised. There were shouts of: 'No! No!'

More shuffling and shifting of feet occurred. Members of the congregation glanced around them and a general restlessness crept into the hall as the dominee cast his eyes over them once more, before abruptly shutting his Bible, removing his glasses, folding them and returning them to his pocket.

After further lusty hymn singing, the service ended and worshippers began to drift out of the church.

The dominee thought that the matter was settled, that he had convinced them about the perils of harbouring strangers. Had they not seen for themselves what the two strangers in their midst had done to the peace and quiet of this small town? Clearly, he was referring to Leah and DiDi and everyone knew it. DiDi with her navel and nose adornments, a disgraceful spectacle, had become his bane. He would have loved to put her on a train with a one-way ticket out of town. He berated himself for the part he played in getting them there. It galled him that he had assisted Portia, had encouraged her to bring her sister home. Well, it was up to him now to rectify his mistake. There could be only one way to deal with the situation: his way.

But, as usual, the dominee had underestimated the people of the town, and the tenacity of the two visitors. And he had hugely underestimated the power of greed.

Portia and Ephemera returned from church and described the scene to Leah and DiDi.

'As soon as they see the bucks, they'll change their tune,' DiDi told Leah. 'There's lots of money to be made. You can rent your house out for thousands. That's what a friend of mine's mother did on the Sunshine Coast.'

'But that's dif . . .' Leah started.

'She made pots of money. And they painted it too. Must say she wasn't too happy with the purple colour, but they promised to paint it back to its original colour . . .'

Leah could see that DiDi was getting carried away. She tried to cut in again, but DiDi had the floor and was not going to relinquish it easily.

The next day DiDi continued her story on the steps of the Glory Café. 'You can make loads of money,' she told some of the kids gathered around her. Some of the adults stopped to listen as she expounded on the merits of working as a film extra. 'Any fool can do it,' she assured those who were nervous about being filmed.

'I did it a couple of times. Like I said, I didn't like it so much because you had to do all that waiting around. Couldn't handle that.'

By the time she finished telling them about her very brief acting career, a few of the young people who fancied themselves as actors, had already transported themselves to Hollywood.

There was an atmosphere of muted excitement throughout the town. No one wanted to be too obvious out of respect for the dominee, but emotions eventually overran any consideration they might have had for him.

In the midst of all this anticipation, Rebecca arrived in town late one afternoon. Her first stop was at the farm. Her father was home. She'd deliberately gone there first to test herself.

She felt no anger. It was as if the earlier confrontation with her father had purged her. All that was left now was an empty space. She knew that she wasn't ready to fill that space with forgiveness. But at least the anger had subsided and with it some of the emotional turmoil that had thrown her life into such chaos. It was an important step to effect emotional healing. This was what her friend, a psychologist, had told her. A sense of calmness and of peace had settled over her and she was better able to cope with her life and her work. When she pulled up at the house, she had fully expected her father to be as belligerent as ever. He was sitting outside on the kitchen chair, staring into space, when she arrived.

'Hello, Pa,' she greeted him.

He nodded. There was a long pause and then he grunted, 'Hello.'

Albert heard her voice and came out to greet her. 'Sis, I'm so glad you've come,' he said. 'The kite competition . . .'

'I know,' Rebecca said. 'I came in time for it. But go and look what I've got for you in the car.'

'What is it?' Albert asked.

'Go and see for yourself.'

Albert returned hugging a brand new guitar to his chest. His face was glowing.

'Pa, look what Sis brought me,' he said, his eyes sparkling with excitement. With a huge smile, he held the guitar out to his father for inspection. His father gave it a cursory look and nodded.

'Isn't it fantabulous?' he asked.

'*Ja nee*,' his father sighed. 'It looks good.'

Rebecca watched her father through the corner of her eye and noticed that he had extended his hand to touch the instrument. He ran his hand over the glistening surface and nodded again. Then he smiled as Albert started to pick out a tune.

Rebecca slipped away to the kitchen. She watched through the window as Albert entertained his father with an Afrikaans folk song. His father seemed to enjoy the music and tapped his foot, his lips parted in a smile that exposed the gap in the front of his mouth. The sides of his face crinkled in folds. It was the first time that Rebecca had seen her father smile and she watched the transformation with amazement. The smile lasted only for a while and then his usual scowl returned.

'Hey, Sis, it sounds fantastic,' Albert cried, coming into the house. 'It's the best present I've ever had. It really is. Wait until the others see it.'

Rebecca stayed for a while. Her father didn't have much to say and Rebecca was tired from the long drive.

'I'll come by tomorrow,' she said.

'Aren't you staying here?' Albert asked.

Rebecca shook her head. 'I've already made arrangements to stay at Mrs Naude's Bed and Breakfast.' Albert was clearly disappointed, but didn't say anything. Their father remained silent, seemingly resigned to everything that was happening around him.

'I'll come and see you every day,' she said to Albert. 'And if you want to, you can come and see me at Mrs Naude's. Okay?'

'Okay,' Albert said. Although he was disappointed, he seemed to understand.

'Night, Pa,' she said.

Her father responded with a grunt while Albert walked her to the car, carrying his precious guitar.

19

The next morning Rebecca stopped by at the Glory Café. Portia's vintage car was parked outside. DiDi was sitting on the step waiting for Portia who was in the Portuguese Buy & Save. The young girl watched with some curiosity as Rebecca approached.

'Hi,' DiDi said when she spotted Rebecca. 'Where you from?'

Rebecca stopped in her tracks. The young girl's attitude and manner of speaking was clearly foreign. 'Cape Town. Where are *you* from?' Rebecca asked, smiling at the girl's impudence.

'Vancouver,' the young girl offered by way of explanation. 'We're visiting. We spent a few days in Cape Town. Nice City,' she said.

'What's your name?' Rebecca asked.

'DiDi. What's yours?'

'Rebecca Fortuin.'

'Hey, you're Albert's sister, aren't you?'

'Yes. How did you know?'

'I know everything,' DiDi responded. 'It's just a piddly town. Nothing much happening here that I don't know about.'

Rebecca laughed and went in to the café where Mrs Venter immediately recognised her. Suzette le Roux was there too, waiting at tables. She also recognised Rebecca even though she had changed quite dramatically in the intervening years – she was a lot heavier than Suzette remembered her as a young girl. She still had the same round face, though, with laughing eyes and a gaze so direct it could pin you down. It was what DiDi would have called a nail-you-to-the-wall look.

'How are things, Suzette?' Rebecca asked when Suzette brought her a menu.

'Fine,' Suzette said, sitting down in the chair across the table from her. 'I've just got a moment. God, Beckie, I haven't seen you in years. How are you? I heard you were in town a while ago. What are you doing back? Are you staying a few days?'

Rebecca nodded.

'I honestly didn't think I'd ever see you again,' Suzette said. 'I'd heard you were in the government. One of the fat cats *nè*?'

Rebecca laughed. 'No. One of the lean hungry ones.' And then she patted her ample midriff. 'I'm with the People's Party.' She gazed at Suzette for some sign of name recognition, but there was none.

The two women fell silent, trying to bridge the divide of time and place. It was easy for Rebecca to reconnect with Suzette, with whom she had always been comfortable.

'How's your son?' she asked. 'He must be quite big now.'

'Twelve.' Suzette smiled proudly. 'He's at boarding school but he's home now for the holidays. You must come around so you can meet him.'

'I'd love to,' Rebecca said. 'And what about Frikkie? Does he know?'

Suzette lowered her eyes. 'He's back in town with the people who want to build the resort.'

'*Ja*. I know about them.'

'There's a lot of trouble about it. But Frikkie is determined.'

182

Rebecca saw the pain in Suzette's eyes. 'Don't tell me . . . Suzette!'

'I couldn't.' She shook her head. 'We didn't . . . he doesn't know about Martin.'

'I don't believe this.'

'I couldn't bring myself to tell him. You know that he left soon after I fell pregnant. It was that time you came for your mother's funeral. I didn't want to tell him so he would stay just for that reason. It wouldn't have been right. Besides, you know how my father feels about him. My father hates their guts – all of them – all the Jouberts. Doesn't matter which one of them is involved. I swear, I was afraid. My father said if he ever showed his face again, he'd kill him.'

'That stuff goes back such a long time. Who would have thought he'd still hold a grudge?'

'My father will take that grudge to his grave. He knows nothing about forgiveness.'

Rebecca lowered her eyes and toyed with her ring. Finally she looked up. 'Does your father know that Frikkie . . .'

Suzette nodded before Rebecca could finish her sentence. 'He made me swear never to tell anyone,' she said.

'What a mess,' Rebecca said dryly. 'And now Frikkie's here and he doesn't know he has a son.'

Suzette nodded. 'I couldn't tell him . . . I promised my father.'

'That was silly, Suzette. You're depriving Martin of a father. I know what it's like growing up without a father – or with one that you hate.'

'It's better that Martin doesn't know,' Suzette said, pushing back her chair as a customer entered. 'We'll talk again,' she said.

Rebecca watched as Suzette returned to work. She hadn't expected Suzette to end up as a waitress. She had had so many dreams for the future. The two of them were good friends when they were children, even in the days when there were boundaries separating them.

Portia, dressed to the hilt in white gloves and hat, came into the café and walked over to greet Rebecca. DiDi had evidently told her that she was there. The two women shook hands and Rebecca invited Portia to sit down, but the other woman declined, saying that DiDi was getting impatient.

'I hope you'll stop these people,' she said, surprising herself with her audacious approach. She'd never before shown any interest in the coloured families in town, but Leah's arrival with the child had brought about subtle differences in her thinking. 'If anyone can do it, you can.'

Rebecca watched as Portia walked out of the café to her vintage car and, with a gloved hand, conscientiously signalled her intention to pull away from the kerb.

While staying with Nora, Rebecca learned about the ins and outs of the development issue and especially about the problems Frikkie had encountered in acquiring the two key pieces of land. In fact, Nora brought her up to date with all the town's news.

'Leah, one of the Hopkins sisters, came from Canada for a visit,' she said. 'She brought a streetwise child with her.'

Rebecca didn't know Leah. She had left Vlenterhoek before Rebecca was born. 'I met the young girl at the Glory Café,' Rebecca said. 'She looks like quite a character.'

'You should hear what comes out of that child's mouth,' Nora said.

'I can imagine,' Rebecca laughed.

The conversation returned to the issue of the one hundred and twelve hectares.

'The deed is lost. No one seems to know who the owner is. Frikkie's already done a search in Cape Town. That's what Danie Venter says – he's the town clerk. But you've already met him,' Nora said.

'Yes, I met him in Cape Town.'

'He says it's going to take months, if not years, to sort out that scrap of paper. He blames it on the new government.'

'It would be nice to blame all the woes of this country on the government, but that would be stupid, wouldn't it? It would merely be blaming the government because they're black . . . besides, I don't want to be lumped in the same camp as Frikkie.'

Nora didn't say anything.

'How do you feel about this development?' Rebecca asked.

'I have mixed feelings,' Nora said. 'I know it's important for the town to grow . . . but it's going to change things. I like the town as it is, but that's me.'

'Lots of people like the town exactly the way it is,' Rebecca said. 'But we need the jobs such a development might bring. People here are so poor. I guess we have to find a developer who'll be fair to the community. There's no point selling out to companies who'll bring in their own people. In the end such a development will only profit outsiders.'

'And you think that's what Frikkie's doing?' Nora asked.

'Yes. He and his father are only thinking of themselves.'

'What are we going to do about it?' Nora asked.

'I don't know yet, Nora,' Rebecca sighed wearily.

'You'd better think of something soon,' Nora said, 'or else it'll be too late to stop them. IRH have already been throwing money around. They've bought up most of the land around the Springs. Many people are nervous, probably because of Frikkie Joubert . . . but that's another story . . . Then there's Hendrik Joubert who now has his claws properly into the situation.' She paused and then said, 'I know that deep down most of the people feel the same way I do – they want to keep things the way they are.'

'I have to think this through. I can't risk being associated with IRH. On the other hand, I have nothing in common with the old conservatives either . . . you know the ones I mean.'

'Yes. We have our fair share of them here.'

'There's got to be an alternative,' Rebecca continued thoughtfully.

'And what might that be?' Nora asked.

'I'm not sure. I have to think it through. Remember, I've only just got here . . .'

'You've got to work quickly, Rebecca, or it's going to be too late for us.'

'A court order might give us a bit of time,' Rebecca said. 'I might have to call in a few favours.'

Nora wasn't quite sure what she meant and so she said nothing.

'Do we have an automatic exchange here, or do we still have to go through a local operator?' Rebecca asked.

'A local operator,' said Nora.

'Damn,' said Rebecca. 'If I know these operators, they listen into every word of your conversation.' She dug through the contents of her handbag and found her cellphone. Excusing herself she went out on to the stoep to try to find a signal.

On the day of the kite competition people started gathering early in the morning, staking out choice spots on the top of the ridge. Events like these were usually an excuse for a huge picnic. Families from outlying areas arrived, ballooning the population. Visitors arrived in campers, bakkies and buses. They unloaded cooler boxes stuffed with beer and boerewors. This, by local standards, was a big event, where prizes were given for various categories of kites. Jannie and Albert had entered for the most unusual kite. Theirs was a large red kite shaped like a jet. It was Jannie's aerodynamic design and it was supposed to outpace all the other kites.

After the initial bustle of settling in some of the men stripped off their shirts and settled down with their beers, while others started their barbecues. Soon the smell of barbecued meat filled the air. The younger children energetically pursued their games. Older boys, barely into adolescence, collected in herds to ogle scantily dressed girls who had congregated to make snide comments about their lanky, pimple-faced counterparts.

Frikkie cornered Rebecca just as Albert and Jannie were preparing to launch their kite.

'Don't put obstacles in my way,' Frikkie said gruffly, perhaps a bit too gruffly because he immediately got Rebecca's back up. 'This project is good for the town and you, of all people, should know that.'

'I'm not a fool,' she replied, coldly. 'I know what you're up to.'

'And what am I up to?' he asked scornfully.

'You have a lot more to gain from this project than the townspeople do.'

Frikkie, well known for his quick temper, especially on the rugby field, kept it in check now. 'What do you mean?' he asked.

'Oh, for God's sake!' she snapped impatiently. 'Don't play dumb. I hear the same self-serving arguments day after day. In my job, I've heard it all!'

'I think it's just sour grapes because you and your party didn't think of it first.'

'Do you really think that no one suspects you and your father of collusion? It's on everyone's lips.'

'Whatever the case, you can't stop me now.'

'Watch me,' she hissed.

Frikkie glared, contemplating the situation for a moment, and then backed away from further confrontation. He hadn't factored Rebecca into the equation. 'Rebecca, do you know what a project this size can do for the entire district?' he asked.

'Don't give me that,' she said. 'You're thinking only of the profit margin – how much you and your father can pocket out of the project.'

'You seem to have all the answers,' he said. 'But you're the one who doesn't have their interests at heart. You're about to ruin the only opportunity they have to improve their lives. These, people . . .' he began, spreading his arms to embrace the town . . .

'Which people?' she interrupted curtly. 'Whites or blacks?'

'All of them,' he said.

'Why don't I believe that? The trouble with this town is that it's too white. But I promise you one thing, Frikkie. You're not going to get away with this. We'll make damn sure when local elections come around next year, that some of our own people are on the council. It's time that the butcher retired from the job of mayor.'

Frikkie shook his head in disbelief. 'Just so the town can be bankrupted. Look what's happening in towns that have black councils. How many of them are solvent? How many of them have money to pay for services? Who do you think pays taxes here? Where will the money come from to run this town? In a few years it'll be as bankrupt as the rest of the small towns. One of the reasons why IRH have been drawn to this area is because the council is in good shape. We may not have surplus money, but at least we're not in the red.'

'What you're forgetting is that for the first time blacks are receiving services – services that the whites take for granted. You talk about taxes. How can you tax the unemployed? Does it make sense?'

'Exactly my point,' Frikkie said. 'That's why I'm working so hard to get this project going. It will create employment.'

'Frikkie, don't give me that crap. We both know why you're doing it.'

'I can't do it without investors. And they are in it for the money, not out of the goodness of their hearts. For a good, viable project we need investors with deep pockets.'

'And you?' asked Rebecca.

'Of course I want to make money out of it. I'd really be stupid, not to want something out of it for myself, wouldn't I?

'I want to see it done in an equitable way – so some of the money goes into the local economy. I want to see locals

188

employed.'

'That's what I want too,' Frikkie said.

'I've seen this happen elsewhere,' she said with a weary sigh. 'The only ones who benefit are the big corporations and all their workers usually come from outside. That's not going to happen here. Not while I have anything to say about it.'

'Know what I think?' he asked.

She didn't say anything.

'I think these people should have someone to look after their interests,' Frikkie said, the set of his shoulders indicating he had himself in mind.

'How long were you gone?' she asked with a touch of sarcasm. 'You couldn't care less about the people of Vlenterhoek. What do you know about them?'

'And I suppose you know because you stayed here?' he asked sarcastically.

'I know because I'm one of them,' she said firmly.

'You're soft in the head,' he said dismissively. 'Why don't you go back to Cape Town where you can have a good time at the taxpayer's expense. That's all you politicians are good for, anyway.'

'I'm staying to make sure the people here are not shafted by you and your company,' she said tersely.

'Do whatever you want, but stay out of my way,' he said, his face flushed.

'Frikkie, you are not going to ruin this town.'

'And you think that's what I'm trying to do?'

'Whatever it is, it's not going to happen,' she told him.

He might have had some choice words for her had it not been for the fact that at that precise moment Albert's kite was released into the air amidst exclamations and shouts of appreciation. Jannie was nowhere to be seen, though. Other kites soared into the air, pitching and rolling in minor skirmishes, creating a colourful tapestry in the sky.

'You've never been able to see the obvious, Frikkie,' Rebecca

189

said, her calm, controlled voice belying the anger she felt as she blocked his way. 'You're so engrossed in your own tragedy that you haven't been able to see the tragedy of the other lives around you.'

'What are you talking about?' he asked.

'Suzette and Martin.'

'What about them?'

'When are you going to realise that Martin is your son . . .' She didn't finish her sentence because at that precise moment, Jannie launched his hang-glider from the other side of the ridge. There was a shout and people surged forward to watch as Jannie glided across the airfield. The windsock, which had earlier indicated a brisk westerly breeze, now hung flaccidly.

Jannie felt the wind drop. For a brief instant he hovered and then one of the metal bars on the frame snapped. The glider dipped and bucked.

'Push with your legs, Jannie!' DiDi cried. He didn't hear her.

Esther screamed.

Jannie heard her scream and for a split second remained poised in the air like a bird, and then he plummeted to earth.

Esther screamed again.

Frikkie ran to the edge of the ridge. He scrambled down the embankment, slithering part of the way down the ridge. Albert followed. The two of them were the first to reach Jannie who was lying very still.

Frikkie loaded his brother into his SUV and drove to the small hospital in the next town, about an hour's drive away. Esther sat in the back seat, Jannie's head in her lap. There was a huge, gaping laceration on his brow, which was bleeding profusely. Using a towel she applied pressure to the wound to staunch the bleeding. There were other injuries too, one of them a broken shoulder.

Jannie was unconscious when he was admitted into

hospital. Doctors took X-rays and tried to reassure the family. Jannie's parents arrived in their own vehicle. Esther sat in the waiting room while the doctor examined Jannie in the emergency room. He was still unconscious. Fearing something more serious than concussion, they admitted him to the intensive care unit. Esther waited. No one had spoken to her. When Anna Joubert saw her, she ignored her husband's angry gaze, took Esther's hand and the two of them went up to ICU together.

For a day or so Jannie's accident overshadowed everything.

The next day Frikkie returned to Vlenterhoek. There was nothing much he could do at Jannie's bedside. His task was still to persuade Gert le Roux to sell. Failing this, IRH had decided that they would go ahead with the development, regardless of whether or not they had the Le Roux property. They would develop what they had and bully their way through the remaining issues while they tried to find the owner of the one hundred and twelve hectares.

In all the time that Jannie was unconscious, Esther never left his side. She and Anna sat with him, on either side of his bed, anxiously watching for signs of recovery. Hendrik was still hostile, but Anna had convinced him that it would be in their interests to have Esther there. With her at his side, Jannie was sure to recover.

Three days after the accident Jannie regained consciousness. The first sign was a slight twitching of his fingers in Esther's hand. Esther felt the movement and called Anna, who summoned one of the nurses.

Esther was still holding his hand, her anxious expression fixed on his face as he opened his eyes. The accident had brought them so much closer. All Esther wanted now was to be at Jannie's side and she didn't care where this was: whether it was Cape Town or in Vlenterhoek. Nothing mattered any more. All she had now was Jannie and she was never going to let him go.

191

'Esther,' he said. 'I'm so glad you're here.'

It took a few moments before Esther and Anna registered that Jannie had spoken his first words without stuttering.

20

Sissie was devastated. Jannie's accident happened exactly the way she had seen it in her dream. The fallen angel. Her dreams now gained new significance. With all that had happened she was beginning to see the dreams for what they were – presentiment rather than cause. She wondered later whether telling Jannie about her dream might have prevented the accident.

Her nightmares ended, but the question remained of how her brother had died and why his body had ended up in a shallow grave in the veld. The same question also troubled the police sergeant. But, to all intents and purposes, the case was closed. Death by misadventure, was the conclusion in the coroner's report.

The film company arrived in a convoy of buses and trucks. It was seen wending its way into town along the detour. Part of the tarred road was being resurfaced and had already been closed for several weeks. Everyone seemed to know immediately that the distant cloud of dust signalled the arrival of the long-awaited film company.

News seemed to travel by bush telegraph and almost immediately the main street was congested with traffic – cars and trucks parked everywhere – some of them even triple-parked. Most of the arriving vehicles had Cape Town and Durban licence plates. The Imperial Hotel was thrown into bedlam with crew and helpers trotting in and out, lugging film equipment. The corridors and lobby were stacked with boxes, trunks, lights and dollies. By midday waves of heat rose from the surface of the tarred road, but no one seemed to notice. Donkey carts and a variety of vehicles had all stopped to gawk, causing a major traffic jam.

The townsfolk had anticipated the arrival of the film company. But when the crew and cast alighted, they were stunned. Virtually all the new arrivals were non-white – Indian musicians in long flowing *kurta* shirts, female dancers in brightly coloured saris, African and coloured musicians and crew in brightly coloured shirts and denims.

The last vehicle in the convoy was a white GT Golf, driven by the Indian actress-dancer. With her was her choreographer who doubled as her wardrobe lady. Both of them were wearing saris.

As the young dancer alighted from the car, one of the town's older residents, an eighty-eight-year-old army veteran, directed a stream of chew-tobacco spittle into the ground. The offensive missile landed with a plop, forming a small crater in the sand right next to the dancer's foot.

'These guys are full of beans, aren't they?' DiDi remarked loudly, turning to Sissie for confirmation, but Sissie merely shrugged. The reaction did not surprise her. She'd grown up amongst these people.

By this time a large crowd had gathered: young children, mothers in frumpy dresses, grandmothers with tightly curled hair, old men and women well into their eighties. With frantic faces, they were all searching for Danie and for an explanation. School kids out of uniform, in tight jeans and short skirts, hung out, enjoying these surprising developments.

For a moment the consternation was stilled as the two sari-clad women walked to the entrance of the hotel.

194

Intrigued, Esther and Sissie pressed forward. The young Indian woman, clearly the star, glanced around with a shy smile, only to be met by stony-faced bystanders.

There was clearly not enough accommodation at the hotel for everyone. It was decided that the crew and cast of lesser status would stay in trailers parked on the rugby grounds.

The townsfolk protested. In their eyes rugby was sacrosanct and the grounds consecrated. Many of them were still enraged at having a whole contingent of non-whites descend so unexpectedly on them. Some of the offers for accommodation in private homes were quickly rescinded.

The Imperial Hotel was soon filled and so was Mrs Naude's Bed & Breakfast.

Mrs Potgieter who had earlier indicated she wanted to earn some extra money, had told Danie that she would be happy to open her house to guests.

However, when Danie and Ian approached her to accommodate the cameraman Vusi, who was one of the few people still needing a place to stay, she baulked, her eager smile turning into a scowl when they told her who the room was for.

Danie pleaded with her, explaining that all the available rooms had already been taken.

'No,' she said firmly.

'But you said . . .' Danie argued.

She shook her head determinedly.

Danie did not appreciate being embarrassed in front of the other man. 'You said . . .' he repeated.

'I know what I said . . .'

'I trusted you. I thought . . .'

'This is my house and I don't want them here.'

'Why not?' Ian asked. 'And what do you mean by "them"?' But he had a sinking feeling he knew what she meant. Confronted with enough evidence of racist attitudes when they arrived in town, he was not altogether surprised by her reaction. There was no point arguing with her.

'They're noisy people . . .' she said through her gritted teeth.

'But he's alone. How could he possibly be noisy?' Ian asked, unable to restrain his indignation. 'All we need is one room.'

'They smoke too much. I don't want smokers in my house.'

'Vusi doesn't smoke,' said Ian quickly. 'I can vouch for that.'

'It's the smell . . .'

'What smell?' Ian asked, his temper rising.

The woman's eyes were shuttered and he knew that he was not going to get anywhere. She gave him no time to respond. She gathered herself and stalked off, nose in the air.

The only one left to hear Ian's protest was Danie and he was red-faced and silent. He had already done everything he could to resolve the situation. There was nothing more he could do. If Mrs Potgieter didn't want Vusi in her house, he couldn't force her.

'It's OK,' Vusi said afterwards when Ian explained apologetically. 'These people know nothing about the outside world.'

'It's not OK,' Ian muttered.

'Don't worry, man, I've made arrangements to share a trailer with one of the guys. It's only for a week or so and you're not going to change that woman's attitude in that time.'

The switchboard was jammed with calls, most of them local calls or calls from the outlying areas. Fortunately all the visitors had cell phones. The local transmitter was for the benefit of the Rustig Mines, and because of the hills around the town, there were many dead spots. Roaming gained new meaning in Vlenterhoek as people drove around in their cars trying to locate a signal.

Communication with the outside world presented the biggest problem of all.

Danie realised that their antiquated phone system was something he'd have to tackle once and for all, especially if they hoped to entice business groups to the area.

He thought it might be something he could complain about to the government – to the Ministry of Tourism, he thought at first, but then remembered that it would be Ministry of Post and Telecommunication. Things were always changing. Just when you got used to working with one department, the government would change it to another. In the old days things were relatively simple and straightforward if one had the right channels. Now things were changing so quickly. Every time you turned around there was another change and when they couldn't find things to do they occupied themselves with changing the names of streets, towns and provinces. And at what cost! In the meantime poverty was rampant. Changing the names was not going to sort out the country's problems. Were they so afraid of the past, Danie wondered, that they had to obliterate it completely? There were no sacred cows any more. He thought how much easier it might have been having Rebecca on side. It was always the small Afrikaner towns that got the short end of the stick. And, after all, who paid the taxes?

Jannie recovered and returned to his life and his kite-flying hobby. He was out on the ridge one morning with another of his designs, trying to get it airborne. The huge kite, in the magnificent colours of the new South African flag, suddenly lifted and rose, dipping and diving – an exquisite sight against the muted colours of the veld. Esther watched where she was skipping along the surface of the flat rocks. She hardly ever let Jannie out of her sight these days. There were still physical signs of Jannie's mishap. The large bruise on the side of his head had faded to a brown patch. The stitches on his brow had been removed, and only the scar remained.

Ian and the film director, who had driven out to inspect some of the locations, saw the kite and then noticed a hawk hanging in the air just above the kite. On the road ahead of them two suicidal field mice darted across the road, right into their path. Ian swerved but could not avoid hitting one of them.

The hawk swooped.

Esther saw Ian's four-by-four and drew Jannie's attention to the vehicle that had driven up the back of the ridge and parked about a hundred metres from them. When Jannie saw the strangers, he withdrew like a crab into its shell. Esther smiled shyly and swept her hair back, tucking it behind her ear.

'That's a pretty sharp kite you have there, lad,' Ian said.

'Jannie makes the best kites in the whole world,' Esther replied proudly.

'How would you like to build and fly one for us?' the director asked. 'The only problem is we'd like to have it by tomorrow. Think you can do it?'

Jannie cast a frantic glance at Esther.

'Of course,' Esther said confidently.

Jannie remained tongue-tied. Although he no longer stuttered, the habit of silence was hard to break.

'We'd like to shoot some of the scenes out here tomorrow. We'd like one exactly like that,' Ian said, indicating the kite which was now lying on the ground at Jannie's feet. Jannie hesitated, looking at the faces as they waited for him to respond.

'Tomorrow?' The effort of saying that one word exhausted him almost as much as it used to do when he still stuttered. It was no longer the physical effort, but the psychological bridge that he had to cross each time he opened his mouth.

He took off his glasses and absently started to clean them while a beaming Esther stood next to him. The director had clambered to the top of a huge boulder and was surveying the landscape. It was magnificent. He couldn't get over the quality of the light.

They left with a promise from Jannie that he'd have the

kite ready for them the next day.

Portia, who had for years supplied baked goods for every function in town, was contracted to do the baking for the Imperial Hotel. Leah volunteered to help and Noelle, who had occasionally helped her in the past, agreed to do so again. The kitchen at Hopkins Landing was a hive of industry from long before sunrise to long after sunset. The fire in the coal stove burnt almost non-stop. Leah was usually up long before daybreak, helping Portia. Leah was no longer that self-centred, bright-eyed, young girl Portia remembered and, having heard some of her story, she couldn't help feeling sorry for her.

But Leah didn't want her sister's pity. 'Charlie's death freed me,' Leah explained. 'It was hell being married to him. But it's all over now and I seldom think of my life with him any more.'

She and Portia often talked about the past, especially when they were alone together. She felt regretful about the way Portia had sacrificed her life for the family and now, in the twilight of her life, she had another responsibility – Ephemera. That morning, chatting amiably – they had started baking before Noelle arrived. It was still dark and the two sisters shared some precious time together in the kitchen.

As Portia made the deliveries, she mulled over the conversation, and marvelled at the way Leah had changed.

'I still have to go through all the papers Pa left in the trunk,' Portia had told her when they spoke about their father.

'I'll help you,' Leah volunteered.

'I'm glad you're here,' Portia said simply. It was more than she would normally have admitted. 'You can see for yourself, Ephemera isn't much help.'

Albert was hired to help when he mentioned to DiDi that he needed to make a few bucks. He accompanied DiDi and Portia on the delivery route. He and Jannie had lost the kite competition, thanks to Jannie's accident. He'd had his heart set on sharing the prize money with Jannie and even though he had a new guitar the money would have been useful. Instead they had nothing to show for all their effort – except Jannie's bruises and scars.

Portia felt a glow of satisfaction as she carefully negotiated the ruts in the road. She loved being busy and being paid for her efforts. It gave her a feeling of accomplishment.

'You've been very helpful, Albert,' Portia said. 'They want the rolls for breakfast,' she added conversationally.

'So, what am I?' DiDi asked. 'Chopped liver?'

Portia looked puzzled for a moment. Although she had discovered that DiDi, under all her bluster, was a likeable child, Portia still thought her peculiar and wasn't always sure how to respond to her.

Finally, she understood DiDi's comment and with a wry smile, said, 'You too, DiDi. I'm glad you're here to help me.'

'I can do a lot of things,' DiDi bragged. 'I did a lot of things in Canada.' But she did not elaborate.

'Like what?' Albert prompted.

'Like being a hairdresser.'

'Oh, sure. You a hairdresser?' Albert said sceptically. He had already adopted some of DiDi's speech patterns.

'Sure, I was. Ask Leah.'

Albert, who admired DiDi's pierced body, asked, 'Can you make a hole in my ear?'

'What for?' Portia demanded.

'I want to wear an earring,' Albert told Portia.

'Are you mad!' she cried. 'You're a boy. What do you want with an earring?'

'It's very fashionable in Canada,' DiDi said. 'Everyone wears earrings,'

'Ja, I saw it in a magazine, Miss Hopkins,' Albert explained.

'Your father will kill you first,' Portia said.

Albert sighed. 'He won't even notice.'

'What about your sister? She'll notice,' Portia said.

'She'll understand. She's cool.'

200

Portia rolled her eyes.

DiDi didn't say anything. She sensed that there were undercurrents in Albert's relationship with his father. She knew about these things. Her stepfather had abused her sexually for years, which was why she had sought refuge in the streets.

There was silence for a while. Then DiDi said, 'You're a good baker, Miss Hopkins.'

'It's a lot of work and if it wasn't for the money, I wouldn't be doing it,' Portia told her. 'They don't have a baker at the hotel any more. He left too.' Her remark was directed at Albert in the front seat and DiDi in the back, but she never once took her eyes off the road.

Albert raised an indifferent shoulder.

'No one wants to stay in this town any more. As soon as they have a bit of money, off they go,' Portia continued.

Albert was quiet. His thoughts were far away – off in the distance where he thought Jannie would be testing the kite he'd made for the film company. But he didn't mind DiDi's company. Not at all. As they drove towards town he scanned the ridge, but there was no sign of Jannie or the new kite.

'You mustn't be a naughty boy too, Albert,' Portia continued. 'You must stay here with your father. Poor Moses. All he has now is you. Your sister won't stay long. There's nothing here for her. She has to be in Cape Town. But why is she not staying with you? I see she's staying at Nora's place. The film company could use an extra room, especially with Katryna Potgieter not wanting that black in her house.'

Albert glanced at DiDi in the back seat, but didn't say anything.

After a while he said, 'I suppose you were baking all night.'

'My sister helped me,' Portia said.

'Don't forget I helped too,' DiDi said.

Portia smiled into the rear-view mirror. DiDi was beginning to worm her way into Portia's heart in the same way she'd found a place in Leah's heart. 'You ate most of the cake dough. I'm surprised you don't have a stomach ache today.'

'I can eat anything,' DiDi said, patting her flat stomach. 'Concrete constitution,' she added with satisfaction.

They lapsed into silence again.

Portia drove slowly and very sedately, her gloved hands firmly anchored to the steering wheel as she meticulously avoided the potholes.

'You'll earn good pocket money, Albert, if you come out every morning.'

Albert looked at her. 'For how long?' he asked.

'Eight days.'

'Okay,' he agreed.

Danie told anyone willing to listen about the tough negotiating he had done. The truth, however, was that he was so eager to open up the town, that he would have waived the fee for the permits. Ian had indicated that they were only going to be there for eight or nine days and that three days would probably be used for rehearsals.

Mrs Venter, expecting to make breakfast for hordes of people at the Glory Café, had ordered twenty-four dozen eggs. Suzette advised against the large order, but Mrs Venter said she knew what she was doing.

After the first two days she suspected that the anticipated rush was never going to materialise. The film crew were up early, long before she opened, many of them hard at work by the time her day began. On the third day she opened earlier, but by that time it was too late, as many of them had already established a pattern of grabbing breakfast at their lodgings.

There was no place for her to store the eggs and she realised with a sinking feeling that she'd have to throw them out. The bread could at least be frozen, the milk as well. But the vegetables were bound to rot before she was able to use them.

'How could I have been so silly,' she said to her husband, who tried to comfort her. But it was hard to comfort Petronella when her mind was occupied with making money.

Many of the townspeople had thought that money would

drop into their laps like manna from heaven. In the beginning they'd had no idea that the price they'd have to pay would be putting up with the non-white contingent.

They were all over town, crowding the streets, causing congestion and invading their rugby field. Not to mention the litter. Never in their wildest dreams did they expect that, for a short period of prosperity, they'd be expected to change their attitudes and put aside their prejudices.

There were some, like the Afrikaans waitress at the hotel, who didn't mind the invasion. She was making a lot of money in tips. Asked to work overtime, staff returned for the evening shift and worked until midnight or until the bar closed. The visitors were generous tippers.

By this time DiDi had become very friendly with Sissie and Esther, and had become a part of their small group. Prior to the arrival of the film company Leah, DiDi, Esther and Sissie, had started taking afternoon walks into the veld. Esther and DiDi were alike in many ways, but it was Sissie that Leah was drawn to – Sissie with her calm, quiet manner and her dark eyes that seemed to change from black to pewter, depending on the light.

Sissie was still preoccupied with trying to understand the cause of her brother's death. She and Noelle spoke about Ivan quite freely now. It was as if his memory had finally been released, the silence shattered.

But Noelle still didn't want any part of Sissie's theories about his death.

'He's dead now,' Noelle said firmly. 'Just leave it alone. Let him rest . . . Please! I don't want to hear what you have to say. I'm not interested in your dreams. I don't want to hear about them any more.' She shut the door on any further speculation from Sissie.

The one good thing that emerged from it all – both the good and the bad – was the cessation of her nightmares. Her dreams now were quite ordinary and she no longer feared going to sleep. Thanks to Leah and especially DiDi, whose company she enjoyed so much, any lingering negative images disappeared. DiDi, with her acid humour, was unlike anyone Sissie had ever known. No one in her experience was as candid as DiDi, who said exactly what was on her mind. DiDi was free of the kind of constraints that muzzled most other people. She was a free spirit who darted around the town; her raucous laughter could be heard a block away. Those who did not approve of her or her behaviour (and there were many), looked on dourly, their expressions screwed up with disapproval. But the more they criticised DiDi, the more she taunted them.

Leah stayed clear of the commotion caused by the arrival of the film people. But not DiDi. On the second day she got herself a job on set working as a runner – fetching and carrying, going wherever she was needed. It was easier for the crew to use her rather than any of the locals, because she spoke English. In any event, she bossed the locals around shamelessly. She tried to find jobs for Sissie and Esther too, but there wasn't much to do those first couple of days when the dancers and musicians were rehearsing. On the third day, however, the director asked Esther and Sissie to dress in Indian peasant costumes. Esther declined. She had suddenly lost her confidence and became shy and awkward. The director thought that both girls would add an extra dimension to the segment and DiDi urged Esther to take the part.

'You'll look great,' she said. 'Really, you will.'

But Esther shook her head.

'They'll pay you.'

Nora Naude was the one who eventually persuaded her. 'You'll be wonderful, Esther,' she said. 'Just remember everything I've told you about walking tall – head up and shoulders back.'

The girls were made up appropriately. Esther, whose face was darkened and who donned a dark wig, looked like any sari-clad Indian woman from Kwa-Zulu Natal.

'Why would you want to look like a *Koelie meid*?' one of

the local women asked her.

This was the derogatory term still used by some whites to refer to Indian women. But the girls were having so much fun that no insulting remark, in any language, could offend them.

It was a walk-through part and DiDi, who claimed to be enormously experienced, talked them through it.

Both Esther and Sissie looked sensational. The director was wild about them. The next day six of the Indian dancers in their colourful costumes prepared for their first shoot. The musicians, the drummer and the sitar player were working through their music, a fusion of African and Indian sounds, while the dancers were warming up.

All of this was happening on the rugby field and a group of curious spectators had gathered to watch. Some were entertained, others grumbled about the dancers damaging the turf. Most didn't quite know what to make of the amazing spectacle of brilliant colours, whirling brown bodies, and alien music.

Later that day the level of irritation amongst the towns-people was pushed up a few notches when several blocks in town were cordoned off. A harassed-looking police sergeant was trying to control the traffic. Tempers flared because some of the residents regarded this closing off of the town as a personal affront. This was their town and nobody had the right to stop them from using their post office.

Parked trucks blocked the entire street and the sidewalk while the film crew carried their paraphernalia into the post office, the only building of interest to be included in two of their shots. Some residents were offended that the brass plaque at the entrance to the post office, which explained the building's historical significance, was covered for these shots.

Not only were the irate residents not allowed to use the post office which was closed for a few hours but, to crown it all, they had to walk around the trucks which monopolised the road and the sidewalk.

Two locals were eventually employed to control and divert traffic. An agile sixty-year-old, given a bit of authority and with a whistle in his mouth, directed traffic like a frenetic signalman on the deck of a distressed vessel.

'I came to use the post office,' a resident complained. 'Now I'm told it's closed for the day. Someone's going to hear about this.' She turned, looking for Danie, who did a quick U-turn and disappeared the way he had come. She went after him, walking briskly to catch up with him, but he had already vanished into a building.

There were a lot of complaints that day.

People yelled at the temporary traffic officer as if he had turned traitor. He simpered like an idiot, trying to reason with them, explaining that it would only be for a few hours. But people became incensed and insults flowed freely.

'What is everyone making such a big deal about?' DiDi asked Sissie and Albert. 'This happens every day in Vancouver. We have all the world's crazies right there in the downtown area. You should see them. One day I saw this guy talking, like he was talking on a cellphone, like he was talking up some big business deal . . .' she paused. Sissie and Albert stared back uncomprehendingly. DiDi's lips parted in a grimace. 'You don't understand a word I'm saying, do you?'

Albert shook his head. 'You speak too fast. We'll teach you to speak Afrikaans.'

'Right,' she said grimly. 'Picture me, speaking Afrikaans.' Sissie giggled.

Albert became DiDi's shadow. His devotion increased when she pierced his ear and gave him a small stud to wear. Sissie recommended a piece of fern stem to thread through his ear until the hole healed. It was a good idea. His father didn't notice.

Eventually he was able to wear his stud, but took it off at school and whenever his father was around.

'What's the point of having an earring if you can't wear it?' Esther wanted to know.

'You know what everyone will say,' Albert reminded her.

One evening Nora invited Leah for dinner. She had prepared one of her specialities, a leg of Karoo lamb, roasted to perfection, with a medley of vegetables.

Josh, who had arrived two days after the rest of the crew, had missed the controversy about accommodating Vusi. At dinner that night they once again rehashed the incident. Nora tried to downplay it. 'These people just don't know any better,' she concluded.

'Don't you think it's time for them to change?' Leah asked.

'You should know what the townspeople are like, Leah,' Nora said. 'What about Portia? She's one of the culprits. Her mind's as closed as the rest of them.'

'I don't approve of my sister's attitude, Nora. In fact we've exchanged a few words about that. But in the six weeks I've been here, she's mellowed considerably.'

Nora raised a sceptical brow, but the conversation moved on to other things.

Throughout dinner, Josh's attention was on Leah. For the first time in the years since his wife's death he opened up and spoke about his son, who worked for an oil company in Calgary in Canada. Leah said she'd never been to Calgary. She'd never been anywhere with Charlie – except when they moved. In all their years of marriage they'd never spent a holiday together.

Josh drove her home after dinner and they sat talking in the car for a while. She looked so vulnerable in the soft light of the moon that Josh had to resist the temptation to take her in his arms. Instead he leaned forward and planted a kiss on Leah's cheek. Flustered, she got out of the car and hurried away. He waited until she had climbed the steps to the stoep before he drove off. Leah's flushed cheeks and the brightness in her eyes were not noticed in the dark.

Across town the bar at the Imperial Hotel was crowded with both cast and crew. There were only a few locals present, perhaps because it was a weeknight. Vusi and his assistant cameraman Dirk were in the bar, quietly enjoying a beer and watching rugby on the big-screen TV. Raucous laughter rose above the sound of the TV and the air was thick with smoke. The two men were relieved that they would be finished shooting in four days' time.

Most of the crew were uptight. What had become known as the 'Vusi Incident' had affected them all.

Mrs Potgieter had almost single-handedly ruined the town's opportunity to get on the tourist map. Had it not been for diplomacy on either side, the episode could have escalated into a major incident, and might even have made the newspapers.

Vusi remarked that Vlenterhoek was like another planet.

The residents would have been surprised at this. They considered themselves perfectly normal. The visitors were the ones who were alien.

Vusi and Dirk were still chuckling about the fuss the locals made about the Hemelslaagte Springs. One would have sworn, Dirk said, that the film crew had come to steal the water. He and Vusi had listened in amusement when Ian stressed that they should stay out of the Hemelslaagte area.

While Vusi and Dirk sat quietly in the bar with their drinks, two local troublemakers drove into town, clearly intent on making mischief, since it was unusual for them to come into town during the week. Neither of them had the money to buy drinks in the bar so they had their bottle of cheap brandy, wrapped in a brown paper bag, in the bakkie. By the time they entered the bar, one of them was decidedly unsteady. With a few drinks under his belt, he was all bravado.

Anyone paying attention would have seen that the drunk was up to no good. But no one noticed him staggering over to the bar where Vusi and Dirk were sitting.

Reeking of cheap liquor, the man leaned his elbow on the

counter top and brought his face up close to Vusi. 'What you doing in here, man?' he demanded. Losing his balance, his propped elbow slipped and his face almost hit the counter top. He made a huge effort to collect himself and was about to start on Vusi again.

'Hey, man, lay off,' Dirk snarled.

Vusi ignored him, which enraged his antagonist.

'Go sit down,' Dirk said dismissively. 'You're drunk.'

Barely able to stand, the man squared his shoulders and leered drunkenly. 'Who you calling drunk?' he slurred, almost knocking Vusi's glass over. 'Who you think you're talking to?' He paused dramatically to glance around the room, but there was so much noise that no one paid any attention to him.

Dirk turned back to his drink.

Vusi remained very still, his powerful shoulders hunched over his drink. He didn't look up.

'How come you're hanging out with the darkies?' the drunk asked Dirk, giving Vusi a sly look. Then he ventured a big swing with his fist. Dirk saw it coming and instinctively turned, catching the man's arm with one hand and at the same time punching him in the solar plexus. The drunk dropped like a felled tree and lay sprawled on the floor.

His mate started to move towards Dirk and Vusi, but when he saw Vusi get out of his chair and he saw the bulk in his shoulders he hesitated.

'I'm glad it was you who punched him,' Vusi said as he finished his beer and stepped over the man's prone body. 'I would have killed the clown.'

The drunk's mate dragged him to the bakkie parked outside. His nose was bleeding and he was sobbing pitifully, muttering dire threats against the strangers. Thoroughly humiliated, the two troublemakers got into their vehicle and drove away.

209

21

Leah and Portia were on their knees in the spare room, the contents of their father's trunk spread on the floor.

'I'm so sorry,' Leah said.

'About what?' Portia asked.

'About Ephemera – and you having all that responsibility.'

'It's okay,' Portia shrugged.

'How do you cope?'

'She's my sister. I love her,' Portia replied.

Leah turned away, guilt suffocating her.

'It's all right,' Portia said. 'Really. You don't have to feel bad. You had your own life and you had problems with Charlie. Now and then when things get too much for me I have someone come out and keep an eye on her while I go into town – maybe stop for a cup of tea at the Glory Café. Or I go for a drive. We've managed.'

For a moment the awkwardness between them returned and they unpacked the rest of the contents of the trunk in silence.

'I can't open this box,' Portia said, lifting a smaller box out of the trunk. 'I don't know what I did with the key. But take a look at this.' She indicated a sheaf of papers lying in the trunk. 'Maybe you can make sense of it. The key must be somewhere. I'll go see if I can find it.'

It was amazing, Leah thought, they way people expected her to know so much – expectations based purely on the fact that she had lived abroad. What did she know about these things, especially about documents? She'd never set eyes on a legal document until Charlie died. Despite her youth, Leah reflected wryly, DiDi probably knew more than she did.

But she gave her sister no hint of these self-doubts as she paged through the file of documents.

They were vaguely familiar, like the ones she'd seen amongst Charlie's papers.

'These are old files and accounting records in Pa's hand-writing,' she said when Portia returned.

'I found the key,' Portia said. 'I suddenly remembered that I put it in my dressing table drawer.'

'Here,' Leah said, holding the locked box out to Portia.

Portia inserted the key and jiggled it in the lock. The lid snapped open. They took it to the table and sat down to examine the contents.

The two women went through every scrap of paper. At first glance, apart from a note written by someone named Frans Bosman, it didn't appear to contain anything of significance. It was only when they took a closer look that they realised the note ceded two hundred and seventy-six acres of land to their father, Alistair Hopkins, in payment of a gambling debt. The signatures of two witnesses appeared on the bottom of the page, below the signatures of their father and Frans Bosman. Neither of the women was able to identify the signatures of the witnesses.

The land was described as bounded on one side by the Hartman farm and on the other by the De Villiers erf. The third boundary was the town boundary near the Hemelslaagte Springs.

Portia was stunned.

She had suspected for a long time that their father had had a gambling habit. The pack of playing cards she'd found in the trunk had offered proof of this, but she'd always been reluctant to believe he was capable of such weakness and, in her opinion, such treachery.

Leah sensed Portia's dilemma. She knew her sister had a blind spot about their parents and had never wanted to acknowledge what they were really like – their mother trapped in a world of candyfloss and their father finding escape and excitement in the intense world of gambling.

'Do you think this piece of paper is legal? Portia asked.

'It says so right there,' Leah said. 'See . . . it says "this is a legal and binding document" but I'm no expert. We'll have to ask someone who knows about these things.'

'Like who?' Portia asked.

'I don't know. I was hoping you could suggest someone.'

'What about the dominee?'

'I don't think he'd be too thrilled about having to make a decision on a gambling debt,' Leah remarked. 'Remember what he said in that famous sermon of his.'

Portia said, 'His bark is often worse than his bite.'

'I wouldn't take a chance on it.'

'I just can't accept that Pa did this.'

'I thought you knew,' Leah said. 'Surely Ma must have known . . .'

'If she did, she never said anything,' Portia replied.

'Must say Ma never paid much attention to what was going on around her . . .'

Portia didn't say anything. Leah was right, but she'd never had the time or the energy to speculate about her father's activities.

In the end they made an appointment to speak to Danie Venter. 'After all, he is the town clerk,' Leah concluded. 'He should know about such things.'

Danie confirmed that the note would hold up in a court of law. It was signed and witnessed and he even recognised the names of the two witnesses, although both of them were now dead.

'What now?' Portia asked.

'If I were you,' Danie said, 'I'd see a lawyer.' He suspected quite rightly that this was the one hundred and twelve hectare parcel of land that IRH so desperately wanted. He was tempted to tell Leah how valuable the land was, but resisted. He needed to think this through carefully. It was best, he thought, if he kept his nose out of it, in case things went wrong. He didn't want anyone blaming him, especially not Leah.

Leah told Rebecca about the document and she asked them not to tell anyone, not until she could figure out what to do next.

'Come to Cape Town with me,' she suggested to Leah. 'You can speak to a lawyer there.'

Leah hesitated. She didn't want to go to Cape Town.

'You must go,' said DiDi.

'But what about you?' Leah asked.

'I'll stay,' DiDi told her.

Two days later Leah accompanied Rebecca to Cape Town. Rebecca had made both Leah and Portia promise that they wouldn't do anything about the land until they had spoken to the lawyer and until Rebecca was able to come up with a plan. She hadn't made much progress in Vlenterhoek, what with the phones not working properly and her access to e-mail restricted by down times. But with the information she now had, she thought it would be easier to sort out the legalities in Cape Town.

The kite scene was done on the fourth day of shooting. Jannie was ecstatic about the five hundred rand they paid him for building the kite in record time. Since he felt responsible for losing the competition, he felt obliged to compensate Albert and gave him two hundred rands. The rest, he said, would go towards the cost of the new software he was saving for.

Albert pranced around the girls, gleefully waving the two

hundred rand at them.

'What are you so happy about?' Sissie asked. 'You didn't even earn it. Jannie had to work for it. Not you.'

'But I helped him,' Albert cried, aggrieved. 'Didn't I help you, Jannie?'

'Sort of,' Jannie said.

'You see! You see!' Albert shouted, his integrity intact.

Shot at sunset, the kite scene was filmed at such an angle that the kite seemed to fly into the setting sun. It was magnificent. Ian and the director were both thrilled with the images they'd managed to capture. It was almost as good as the segment shot in the desert in Rajastan.

The following day some of the dance scenes were shot and many of the townsfolk gathered to witness the event. Because they had never seen anything like it before, they felt awkward and there was a lot of tittering and derogatory laughter. Some of the locals had been hired for smaller jobs, including an Afrikaans schoolboy who was operating the clapboard.

'Silence!' he called officiously. '*Amjance*. Take ten.' There was some snickering and the ruddy-faced boy lost patience and yelled 'Shut up!'

To maintain order the spectators were moved back forty metres from the cameras. A huge bonfire had been built to capture the dancers in silhouette. The drummers beat out their haunting rhythm. Those who had never seen such dancing before had to admit, albeit grudgingly, that the scene was very moving.

The scenes with the horses were shot on the fifth day.

Jannie and Albert were in charge of the horses. It was their job to ensure that the horses were brought to the set on time.

Josh felt inexplicably restless while Leah was away. He spent quite a bit of time on his own, his thoughts miles away. On a few occasions he drove to the ridge where he sat in his car gazing out over the veld and the small town, and feeling strangely sad and contemplative as he listened to his music. In the few days that he'd been in Vlenterhoek, he'd grown accustomed to having Leah around. Her absence, regardless of how brief it was, seemed to leave a void in his life. He couldn't figure out what was happening to him. All he knew was that each time he thought of Leah, his heart skipped a beat. He hadn't felt this way since he was a young man.

The following day, in the middle of one of the crucial scenes, a shepherd and his flock moved right across the shot.

'Cut!' the director yelled angrily.

The shepherd was an old man and was so bemused by the commotion all around him that he came to a dead stop in the middle of the shot. Several of the crew were hastily dispatched to move him and the flock out of the way. The interruption had ruined the rhythm and there were several takes. By the twentieth take, the young clapboard operator had shouted 'silence, shut up' so often that he was quite hoarse.

On the seventh day the last bits were done, like close-ups and a few interior shots. In the midst of all this activity, an old African woman stepped on to the set. The director looked up when he heard Vusi's exclamation.

To his amazement, the woman proceeded to sit down right in front of the camera while they were setting up for a tracking shot.

'What the hell's going on here?' the director shouted.

Vusi shrugged and spread his arms.

'Well, why don't you ask her?' Ian yelled.

Vusi spoke to the old woman in Xhosa. He spoke quietly and respectfully, addressing her as 'Mama', while the rest of the crew waited impatiently.

The woman became quite emotional as she gave Vusi her explanation. She removed her headscarf and, to the consternation of those watching, started wailing loudly.

'What the hell?' the director demanded.

'*Tula, Mama,*' Vusi said in his most reasonable voice, trying to silence the old woman, so that he could convey her explanation to an irate Ian.

The old woman continued her histrionics, quite undaunted.

'She says,' Vusi began, 'that her husband is a thief, that you paid her husband for the use of the horses. They weren't his horses. They were her horses and she hasn't been paid yet.'

'But we paid her husband!' Ian snapped.

Vusi shook his head. 'It's not going to cut any ice with her, Ian. She wants to be paid and she won't leave until you've done so.'

'Oh, crap!' Ian muttered. But he could see that the woman had settled in and had no intention of moving. She was still wailing, although less vigorously than before.

Ian opened his wallet and took out a fifty rand note. He handed it to the old woman, who studied it, looked at the wad in Ian's bulging wallet and shook her head, firmly rejecting his offer. She said something to Vusi.

Vusi grinned. 'She says it's not enough,' he said.

Ian gave her fifty more, closed his wallet, returned it to his pocket and walked away. When she saw that there was nothing more forthcoming, the woman carefully folded the two notes and stowed them in the bodice of her dress. Then she picked herself up, carefully brushing the dust off her skirt, and limped away.

The eighth day was a wrap.

The dancers packed up, and DiDi, Sissie and Esther said goodbye to the star and her choreographer, rather sadly because they had got to know and like the two women.

Life was going to be boring. For a few days Vlenterhoek had simmered with all sorts of intrigue, undercurrents of possibilities and lots of excitement.

Naturally, a number of people were happy to see them leave. One of these was the dominee.

Petronella Venter was one of those who was sorry to see them go. She had made as much money in that one week as she would normally have made in six months of local business. It didn't matter that she had donated eighteen dozen eggs to the church and had thrown out all the salad vegetables that had wilted in the heat and the bananas that had rotted on the shelf.

The last few shots of the landscape were taken and the trucks were packed and ready to pull out. The rugby field was vacated. A local crew had been hired to clean up and the 'honey truck' came by to empty the portable toilets for the last time.

Ian looked around as he and his crew prepared to leave. He was satisfied. Without even having seen the 'rushes', he knew that the South African segment was going to be phenomenal.

Some of the residents stood around, scuffing the toes of their work boots in the dust. Although they would never have admitted as much, especially after all their complaints, some of them actually felt a twinge of regret about the visitors leaving.

The film company had provided a lively diversion. Some of the residents had almost become used to the commotion, the trucks in the streets and, above all, the extra money that had been brought into the town coffers and into their pockets.

Danie Venter came to say goodbye. He regretted the two incidents that had cast a pall on what was had otherwise been a very successful enterprise. Mrs Potgieter's refusal to accommodate Vusi had been unacceptable, and so was the drunk's behaviour in the bar. Still, it hadn't caused too much damage, not as far as he could tell. He hoped that the few unpleasant episodes would not deter others from coming – he could already imagine requests pouring in to use

Vlenterhoek as a film location.

Ian promised he'd be back to screen the film as soon as it was ready.

Danie Venter waved as Ian got into the four-by-four and the director got into his red Toyota and Josh in his blue Mercedes.

Leah and Rebecca returned the day after the film company left. The rugby field, like the town, lay still and deserted.

Danie had to settle for cricket on TV. Had it not been for the fact that his paramour's husband was home for a visit, he might have sought solace and comfort in her arms. He felt dissatisfied with his life, a new feeling for him, and hankered for more. All the hankering, however, was futile. His life was slotted into the Vlenterhoek rhythm.

It was as if he had dug a hole for himself, a hole with steep sides that would take another lifetime to climb out of. He realised now, as he sat in front of the TV, that the feeling of dissatisfaction had been creeping over him ever since Leah arrived.

He knew that his life was never going to be the same again. Even the young woman was no longer enough to keep him interested. He had already felt his interest in her flagging and it had nothing to do with the fact that their relationship was such a carefully guarded secret, especially from the husband who worked at the Rustig Mines – a mean brute of a man likely to kill both of them if he ever found out about them.

Danie was looking for more than a sexual relationship. He'd never had any kind of relationship with Petronella. There had never been any warmth or tenderness between them. Petronella, who came from a strongly Calvinistic background, knew nothing about love and affection. He had concluded long ago that she didn't have a warm bone in her body.

Just seeing Leah again had awakened so much awareness in him – made him realise how little he had in life. How little he'd settled for.

With all this time on his hands Danie once again gave IRH some consideration. He was not averse to making money and it had occurred to him the moment Leah and Portia had first approached him with the note, that the two hundred and seventy-six acres was the same one hundred and twelve hectares that Frikkie was interested in. He remembered that in those days land measurement had been in acres, not hectares.

He suspected that the original deed to this land registered to Frans Bosman, had been lost in the Vlenterhoek office. He was disappointed that this had happened, even though it was before his time as town clerk. He had always taken pride in his work and the work done during his term of office. Although he hated the idea of something like this sullying his good reputation, he was not averse to making profit out of it. He was convinced that there was something in it for him, either on a profit-sharing or on a commission basis. He figured that if he could represent the Hopkins sisters as an agent, he could negotiate with IRH and earn a commission. He'd work hard for the commission because he had no doubt that it would be tough negotiating with IRH. But, most important of all, he'd be helping Leah. The idea took hold, grew, spread like a vine in his head, growing until it was all he could think of.

He was already well into formulating his plans when he realised that not only was he going to require a great deal of diplomacy, but trust and goodwill as well. He knew that he'd have to be very skilful if they decided they wanted him to assist them in negotiations. If this didn't work out maybe they'd be more inclined to sell the land to him than to IRH, especially in view of the hostility between the company and some elements in town. Money, of course, was the big issue, but Petronella had money in the bank and a loan was also possible. There were so many things to consider, so many contingencies to cover. He'd have to talk the whole idea over with Petronella. No doubt she'd want to take credit for his idea again. Oh, well, he thought, there were more ways than one to skin a cat.

But Danie did not take Rebecca into account.

The big issue on the minds of the residents was not about land, or the development in Vlenterhoek, but about Leah and Josh and the fact that they'd had dinner together at Nora's place. For days the local women strung out all the possibilities and suppositions about Leah's love life.

Mrs Potgieter had a sore jaw from speculating. 'So, what now?' she asked with a smirk. 'He's gone, left her high and dry. Serves her right.'

'It's exactly what happened all those years ago with Charlie Barker,' someone remarked. 'I knew a long time ago that she was a loose woman,' another commented.

Petronella, struck mute by a bout of laryngitis was unable to gloat about her plan for making money out of the Hopkins sisters, nor could she contribute to the gossip that raged in the café about Leah and Josh. By the time Petronella recovered her voice, Josh had left town and the subject had already been hammered to death.

All were agreed, however, that the visit by the film company had been a very interesting experience in more ways than one.

With the film company gone DiDi became increasingly bored and restless.

'When are we going back, Leah?' she asked.

'Oh, DiDi, my dear child . . .'

'I'm bored, Leah,' DiDi complained. 'Bored right out of my skull.'

'DiDi, please be patient . . .'

'Patient? We've been here for nearly six months already. You planning to stay here for ever or what?' she demanded.

With a sigh of exasperation, Leah said, 'Another month or so . . .'

DiDi gave an involuntary shudder. 'I ain't staying here much longer. This place sucks.'

'Please DiDi . . . I've got to sort out the land business with Portia. She needs my help. I can't let her down.'

'I'm sorry I came,' DiDi muttered petulantly. 'Why did you drag me here with you? I didn't want to come. You forced me. I hate this place. Everybody always yakking in *Afri-kaans*.'

'I thought you were having a good time,' Leah said, disappointed.

'Two weeks tops and I'm out of here, Leah, I'm telling you now.'

'I'll see what I can do . . .'

'That's not good enough.'

'For once, stop being so selfish and self-centred,' Leah scolded. 'We've come a long way just to rush back because you're bored. There are still a few things that I have to settle with my family. You can understand that, can't you?'

'I'm not asking you to go back with me,' DiDi snapped. 'You think I can't fly back on my own? I'm not a baby. I can get back on that plane and fly to Vancouver. Any time. It's no big deal.'

'Okay, okay,' Leah said. 'Let's just sort things out here and I promise we'll head back as soon as we can. Besides, you're under age, you can't be traipsing across the world on your own. You have to be eighteen.'

'I can pass for older . . .'

'No, you can't. Your date of birth is in your passport.'

'Oh, darn!' DiDi glared at Leah, muttering further expletives under her breath before stalking off to sulk in a corner.

Leah imagined that DiDi's reaction on returning to Vancouver would have been to find her friends in the street and perhaps lose herself in a cloud of drug-induced indifference.

DiDi had admitted to smoking pot, but denied taking anything more lethal than that.

221

'I haven't been shooting up,' she'd said, holding her arms up for inspection when Leah questioned her about her drug habits. 'I'm not that crazy. I seen what it does to the kids I hang out with.'

'Are you sure, DiDi?'

'Absolutely.'

That was some time ago and Leah had no choice but to accept DiDi's word.

Now, with a pang of gnawing anxiety, she watched DiDi march off.

One afternoon, soon after the departure of the film company, Danie went to visit Leah. They had met on several occasions and had talked briefly, but she'd always been curt with him. Danie, however, was not easily discouraged. This visit was an opportunity to delve a bit deeper, perhaps to find again that young girl that he had been so hopelessly in love with. He also felt the need to talk, to open up and to have a real discussion for a change. The kind of discussion that would perhaps stretch his mind – might stimulate him, might open windows and, more importantly, might indicate whether the sisters would consider using him as an agent or else sell the property to him. Either way, Danie hoped to make a tidy profit. It was his ticket to freedom – to start his life afresh somewhere else, as far away from Petronella as possible.

From the moment Portia opened the door to his knock, his behaviour was impeccable. He feared that the slightest hint of impropriety would be the death knell of any hopes he might have of charming Leah. Leah, the sophisticate – the overseas woman. Danie had no intention of giving her the impression that he was just a small-town *mampara*.

He said that he had come to ask her for some suggestions on how to turn Vlenterhoek into a tourist destination. After all, it was an accepted fact that she knew about such things, he added jovially.

DiDi was out with Sissie and Esther. Portia made the tea and then came to sit next to Ephemera while Danie sat on the sofa next to Leah.

They talked for a long time. How could she explain to this man that she knew nothing about the world; that his faith in her was misplaced; that she was still basically a small-town girl; that her world had been restricted to four walls; that it was only with Charlie's death that she had ventured out into the real world and had begun to experience life and discover who she really was.

Danie's gaze was riveted on her with such expectation that Leah told him what she thought he might want to hear. It wasn't much and she felt self-conscious about her lack of experience. In the end as she lifted her eyes to him, she said, 'That's all I can tell you, Danie. DiDi probably knows a lot more than I do.'

'*Ag* no. You've been a big help,' Danie said graciously.

Leah smiled apologetically. 'Sorry. I don't know what more I can say. Have you thought of placing an ad in the paper? I agree with you that this is a lovely town . . .' she faltered.

'I have put an ad in the Cape Town newspapers,' Danie said. 'But I need to do more. Wouldn't you please . . . please come to Cape Town with me – I want to talk to the Fortuin woman again. She rushed away so quickly. I didn't get a chance to talk to her.'

'Danie, I've just been to Cape Town. Why on earth would I want to go back there again?'

Neither of the sisters gave any indication that Rebecca was a key figure in their plans and that she was expected back in town soon. The less Danie knew about their business, the better, Portia had warned Leah.

'She's here quite often,' Leah said. 'Why don't you speak to her yourself? Better still, invite her to the screening of the film. I'm sure she'll be interested. She did come for the kite festival, after all.'

Danie's eyes lit up. 'That idea is a very good one.'

223

They drank their tea. Then placing his cup on the table, Danie looked directly at Portia. 'Have you discovered anything more about the land?' he asked.

'Not really, and we haven't had much time to do anything about it,' Portia said sharply. 'You can see how busy we've been.'

'What happened in Cape Town?' he asked.

'The lawyers are working on it,' Portia said.

Leah watched Danie closely. Perhaps Portia was right about him, she thought. Maybe he was an opportunist.

Danie nodded, waiting. But Portia said no more on the subject. There was an awkward silence and Danie coughed and cleared his throat, politely putting his hand to his mouth.

It occurred to Portia that she had never seen Danie so well groomed or so polite. She gazed suspiciously at him and Leah.

'If you're interested in selling, let me know,' Danie continued. 'I can help.'

Leah and Portia exchanged glances.

'Yes,' Portia said. 'We will let you know, but for now we are not interested.'

'I see,' Danie said, a smile covering his disappointment. He was so sure they'd be anxious to sell.

Danie feared that the longer the delay in obtaining the land, the better chance there was of them discovering its real value. He wondered now, as he sat in their front room how he could get his hands on the land – get his offer in before anyone else, especially IRH and Frikkie, found out that they owned it. It wouldn't take long for the news to get around.

Danie sat with puckered lips, massaging his head, trying to focus on how to approach matters without casting suspicion or doubt on his motives.

But before he could put any of his thoughts into perspective, Portia rose, slapping the hem of her skirt down. Tall and forbidding she stood in the centre of the room, flesh turned into stone, hands locked around her wrists as she waited.

Danie glanced up, hesitated and then took his cue.

'We will let you know if we want to sell,' Leah said as Danie got up off the sofa. She smiled and Danie's spirits were buoyed.

For a moment he forgot about the land because he realised that she was still in there – the young girl who had fascinated him so.

If only ... He quickly shrugged the thought out of his mind. No use dwelling on the past now. There were things to be done. Phone calls to make to Cape Town.

Ephemera, who had sat quietly throughout the conversation, had observed the dynamics between her sisters and Danie with great interest. She saw Portia rise to her feet, saw her standing there waiting for Danie to take his leave. Then just before they reached the door, she leaped up, rushed to Danie and, with all the enthusiasm of a young child, threw her arms around his neck and gave him a resounding kiss on the cheek.

They were all taken completely by surprise. Portia, shocked and scandalised by Ephemera's behaviour, led her away. Leah could hardly contain her mirth. But Danie looked a bit sheepish as he left the house.

22

When Danie had left, Portia turned to Leah and, using one of her quaint Afrikaans expressions, said, 'That man still has a candle burning for you. But that doesn't make him any less of an idiot. I don't know how Petronella has put up with him all these years. And now I hear he's running around with some other woman.'

'The gossip in this town never ends, does it? Anyway, who'd take a chance like that, especially with Petronella at the other end?'

Portia smiled grimly.

Leah laughed. 'I'd forgotten what it's like living in a small town where everyone knows everyone else's business.'

'There's nothing wrong with the town,' Portia grunted. 'It's the people.'

'You're right. Poor Danie. I never liked Petronella. Reminds me of an old crocodile.'

'That man's as sly as a fox – don't you encourage him,' Portia warned.

'Why would I? You said he's an idiot,' Leah chuckled.

A small twitch at the corner of her mouth was the only hint of a smile from Portia. Leah realised how much Portia had changed since she and DiDi arrived. She felt a lot more comfortable in her sister's company now. DiDi's verdict was that Portia was okay. Leah couldn't remember ever seeing Portia so pleasant, so obliging and so ready to laugh. She had always wondered what had happened in Portia's life to turn her into a bitter old maid. One never questioned Portia about these things. Her stern bearing tended to discourage intimacy or familiarity and one knew instinctively that there were areas of her life that were out of bounds. The wall between Portia and her siblings had gone up a long time ago – when they were still children.

She was so much more pleasant now. But then, just as Leah was having kind thoughts about her sister, Portia, as if sensing it, immediately set about crushing it.

'He thinks he's quite a ladies man. I told you he's been cheating on his wife. Well, it's quite disgraceful. Poor Petronella has been totally humiliated.'

'Petronella knows how to get mileage out of every situation,' Leah said.

'That's a terrible thing to say,' Portia said sharply. 'What gives you the right to judge others?'

'I didn't mean . . .'

'Don't try to ruin someone else's life because yours turned out a failure.'

'A moment ago we were joking . . .' Leah said, astonished.

The cheerful mood was completely destroyed. In a matter of moments, Portia had undergone a complete transformation.

'But you know what Petronella is like . . .' Leah retorted.

'What do you know about our lives here? Besides, it's absolutely scandalous for a woman of your age to encourage another man. A married man too. Don't you think you're too old to be flirting? Pull yourself together, Leah, for goodness sake!'

'Don't be ridiculous, Portia!' Leah cried, scalded by her sister's insinuation.

'You're behaving exactly like the kind of woman they say

227

you are,' Portia said as Ephemera entered the room. 'Go and lie down,' Portia snapped at her.

Leah felt the blood rush first to her head and then to her tongue, but she closed her mouth, trapping her angry response.

'Why are you shouting?' Ephemera demanded.

'You've always been so selfish,' Portia continued. 'You've only ever thought of yourself!'

Ephemera started to cry. DiDi, who had just come in, heard the raised voices. When she saw Ephemera standing in the middle of the room looking frightened and confused she took her hand and led her outside.

Leah bit back her retort and walked out of the kitchen, slamming the door behind her. A heavy atmosphere once again descended over Hopkins Landing. It felt just like it did before a Karoo storm.

Overwhelmed by the shift in her sister's mood, Leah sought refuge in her mind in the gentle lushness of the University Endowment lands in Vancouver, the soft rain and the long walks she used to take through the tall wet grass and the dripping canopy of trees.

'You're too old . . . you're too old . . .' the refrain hammered at her.

With Portia's words still ringing in her ears, Leah changed her opinion, instantly rescinding her generous defence of her sister.

'No wonder she's been alone all these years,' Leah muttered angrily to herself.

'Who?' DiDi asked coming up behind her.

'No one,' Leah said sharply.

'What were you and Portia arguing about?' DiDi asked.

'Nothing,' Leah said again.

'Okay,' DiDi said. 'I'm going to get a drink of water. You want something?'

Leah shook her head.

DiDi returned to the stoep with a glass of water. She paused in the doorway for a moment, then she said, 'This place sucks!'

In the distance a cloud of dust signalled an approaching vehicle. A short while later a slightly beaten-up and rusted green bakkie pulled up at the gate. Jannie was driving and Esther was sitting next to him in the front. Albert and Sissie were in the back.

'We just came to see DiDi, Tannie,' Sissie said to Leah. All the young people addressed her as *Tannie* and they did so respectfully, with a touch of veneration, for she had ventured far beyond Vlenterhoek and had returned to tell the story.

'Jannie's going for a drive with Esther,' Sissie said as she and Albert clambered out of the back of the vehicle.

'We won't be long,' Esther called with a nonchalant wave.

'Whose truck is that?' Leah asked.

'Jannie's father,' Albert told her. 'His father will kill him if he knows he's taking Esther for a drive.'

'Oh, stop it,' Sissie said, impatiently. 'You're always going on about things. His father won't find out – not unless you open your big mouth again.'

'Me? Never,' Albert said.

It was a beautiful afternoon and Leah joined the young people under a eucalyptus tree. Sissie sat on the ground, a little apart from the others, legs drawn up, head resting on her knees, her thoughts clearly somewhere else.

Leah's exchange with Portia had driven home to her the realisation that her life was no longer in South Africa, but in Vancouver. She couldn't shrug off the years she'd spent there.

The struggle to survive had changed her and she could not turn the clock back. She'd learned her lesson the hard way with Charlie. He'd changed her, but not always in the way he had intended. She'd learned through DiDi that life was short and that one had to make the best of one's time on earth.

'Life is for the living,' was one of DiDi's favourite expressions.

Maybe DiDi was right, Leah thought. Perhaps it would be best for them to return home.

Albert took his guitar out of the battered case. It was the new guitar, the one his sister had given him. Using the hem of his T-shirt, he carefully wiped the dust off the glistening wood and then tuned, twisted, strummed and listened, smiling with satisfaction at each adjustment.

'It has a lovely sound, Albert,' Leah said. She'd heard him play the old guitar.

'*Ja*,' Albert said proudly. 'It's fantabulous.'

'Play something for us, Albert.'

'What do you want to hear?' Albert asked.

Leah thought for a moment. 'I don't know. Play anything you like.'

Albert postured, lowering his head shyly.

'Hey, don't be full of sh . . .!' DiDi began impatiently.

'DiDi!' Leah groaned.

Albert strummed and improvised a Country and Western piece.

'Where did you learn to play like that?' Leah asked.

'From the radio.'

He played for a while and then handed his guitar to DiDi. DiDi did her own tuning and fiddling and then picked out a tune.

Sissie leaned back against the tree. There was a faraway look in her eyes. Watching her, Leah wondered about her silence and the inner calm she projected to the outside world, yet from the moment she'd met the young girl, Leah had sensed an inner turmoil. It was such a contradiction.

Portia and Ephemera came to join them, interrupting her thoughts about Sissie. Portia had made sandwiches and they had an impromptu picnic in the backyard. Ephemera had forgotten the episode of unpleasantness and was radiant with the joy of having people around her.

Portia was quiet, almost sorry about the things she'd said to Leah, but she was not one for apologies.

230

Jannie and Esther returned and joined them. Jannie's father was no longer such a threat to their relationship. Perhaps relieved at having Jannie return to 'normal' after the accident, he had become a lot more tolerant of both his sons.

Jannie had recovered completely, and his stutter was gone. The doctors had no rational explanation for this. The locals thought it a miracle. But Jannie remained unsure about whether his recovery was permanent.

'So what about that hang-glider idea?' DiDi asked Jannie. 'You can't just give up like that, man.'

'*Ja*,' Jannie said, still a bit shy and awkward with girls other than Esther.

Esther was sitting with Sissie and couldn't hear their conversation.

'What happened? Why did you luck out?' DiDi asked.

Jannie took his time answering; he first had to figure out what the question was. 'I'm not sure,' he said. 'I think the design was wrong.'

'So now you're back to flying kites – Jeez, man, that's child's play,' said DiDi.

'W-We like it,' he said, a slight hesitation in the first word because he was feeling anxious.

'Why don't you build another?' she asked.

Jannie's startled glance flew to Esther. It was exactly what he was doing. He'd discovered where he'd gone wrong on the first glider and had decided to build another. He wondered how DiDi had known. He hadn't told anyone, not even Albert. But when he saw her guileless expression, he knew that she didn't know about his new project.

'D-d-don't tell anyone about it,' he said. 'No one knows.'

Esther caught Jannie's eye and wondered what he and DiDi were talking about so secretively.

'Not even Esther,' he said.

'Don't worry, your secret's safe with me,' DiDi assured him. 'But let me help you, I know about hang-gliders. I flew

231

one off a mountain top in Whistler once. I went with my buddies. We had a great time. James came in too close to the cliff and broke a leg. He could've been killed.'

'Y-y-you know about hang-gliders?' he asked, surprised. He felt comfortable talking to DiDi and the words seemed to come a lot easier now.

'Yep. There's nothing like the wind in your face.'

'I have another design that I got from the Internet. Better than the first one.'

'Where you planning to fly it?' she asked.

'Here,' he said, glancing up at the ridge. 'Where I crashed the first one.'

'That's child's play, Jannie. Child's play,' she said. 'You need lift. You've got to push off from a much higher altitude. Table Mountain in Cape Town should be okay.'

'Not with those winds,' Jannie said.

'But you need a mountain like that – to like push off from . . .'

'What are you talking about?' Esther asked suspiciously as she walked towards them.

'I was telling Jannie about Whistler. It's a ski resort outside Vancouver,' she said.

'Do you ski?' Esther asked, eyes as big as saucers.

'A little, but my buddies are good skiers.'

Esther sat next to Jannie, squeezing up to him. Although she liked DiDi, she couldn't help being a bit jealous of her. No fool, DiDi noticed and, with a knowing grin, went to sit with Sissie.

'So what's up, Sissie?' DiDi asked.

Sissie was unusually quiet. On a few occasions she'd felt so guilty and so desperate to talk to someone about what was troubling her that she'd even considered confiding in DiDi. But when she saw DiDi with the others, heard her laughing raucously, she'd change her mind – she didn't want to be ridiculed. She would even have liked to talk to Leah, but the opportunity never seemed to present itself. There were always people around, always interruptions.

Once again, on that day, like other days, there was no opportunity to speak to either of them.

23

For a while the town bustled with visitors, mostly people who wanted to benefit from what was happening, or about to happen, in Vlenterhoek. They'd heard about the proposed development project and came to explore opportunities. 'Vultures after easy pickings' was the way one of the residents referred to them. Some stayed at the Imperial Hotel, others at various B&B establishments that had suddenly mushroomed all over town. The Imperial Hotel began placing flower arrangements in the rooms and chocolates on the pillows – just like the five star hotels in the big cities. Unfortunately the Imperial Hotel was riddled with ants and if the chocolates were not eaten immediately, the ants marched in long black lines across the white pillowcases.

Although many of the residents retained the attitudes inherent in the old apartheid regime, much of the disappointment about Vlenterhoek's failed attempt to bring in tourists was placed squarely on Mrs Potgieter's shoulders. She was still blamed for the way she handled the Vusi Incident. When Danie reiterated that the failure of the tourism industry in Vlenterhoek had a lot to do with narrow-minded and mean-spirited attitudes, everyone seemed to know who he was referring to.

It was time to wake up and see the real picture, he told them.

Danie, of course, had seen the real picture and the potential for business opportunities that others were too blind to see.

Rebecca arrived in town but before checking in at Nora's B&B, she took a little detour to Tweeriviere.

She needed to think – needed time to sort out her priorities, and perhaps time to reclaim her life. She'd spent so much time and energy on politics – thankless job that it was. But politics was all she knew and without it, she'd be wandering around in an emotional wilderness. Ease off, her friends counselled, there are other things in life apart from work.

The morning before she left Cape Town her assistant had taken her files from her. 'You're not taking this work with you,' she'd said firmly. 'It can wait until you get back. Go and have a rest, Rebecca.'

But rest was an alien concept for Rebecca.

Vlenterhoek and her father had stirred up all the old ghosts. She had to stay focused on her work. It was the only thing that kept her sane.

'If you had a husband and a family, you wouldn't be going on like this,' her assistant had told her. Rebecca sighed as she recalled the other woman's lecture. For now, though, there was just Vlenterhoek and the problems it presented. She was determined not to give up until the whole nasty situation had been satisfactorily concluded.

Rebecca enjoyed the drive out into the veld. She drove past the Joubert lands, recognised her father on the tractor and stopped along the fence to observe him. He was so involved in what he was doing, that he didn't see her parked alongside the fence. She sat in the car for a long time, watching as the tractor stalled and he struggled to start it. Getting down off the tractor, he opened the engine flap and worked under the bonnet for a while. The tractor started again with a sputter, spewing black smoke, and then it jerked and shuddered along for about two hundred metres before it died. She watched her father, an old man in indigo overalls, climb down to get the engine started once again. There was something about him, something in his posture, in the beaten-down look about him that drew her sympathy. Her eyes filled, and with the tears came the unravelling of her life. It felt as though every stitch in her fabric was slowly being tugged at – drawn out, pulled apart. Damn, she cursed, and started the car, gunned the engine and drove away in a cloud of dust.

Her father looked up and recognised her car. He watched until the cloud of dust disappeared, then he got back on to the tractor, started the engine and slowly chugged back to the paddock.

Danie was on his way back to the office, trying to figure out what kind of price the Hopkins sisters could realistically expect for their one hundred and twelve hectares, when he spotted Rebecca Fortuin's car turning into the street where Nora's B&B was.

Rebecca was becoming a regular at Nora's. She was still not comfortable under the same roof as her father and knew it would take a long time before she could deal with being close to him again.

She felt comfortable at the B&B and Nora was always happy to fill her in about the latest happenings in Vlenter-hoek. Later, she'd drive out to Hopkins Landing to report on her progress about the land.

Albert and Sissie came to see Rebecca shortly after she arrived. They had seen her drive into town. Albert didn't stay long. Rebecca offered to drive him home, but he had his bicycle with him. Sissie stayed a while longer, chatting to Rebecca. She told Rebecca about school and the hard time they had with some of the kids, how they tormented Albert because he was different. Rebecca sighed. Prejudice in all its strange manifestations was still a problem in many schools.

'It's because we're coloured,' Sissie started by way of explanation, but Rebecca stopped her.

'Don't use that word, Sissie,' Rebecca said. 'We're people of mixed race.'

Sissie looked a bit confused. 'But we are coloured,' she said.

Rebecca shook her head wearily. She was too tired to debate the issue or to explain her views on it. 'It's the word "coloured" that gets me,' she said. 'You know they used that same word with the same negative connotations in the Deep South in America and they probably still do. I want to break the cycle here.' She sighed. 'It would be so nice just to be plain old South African, with no one to care whether you're black or white or green. Nice thought, *nè*?' Rebecca said.

Sissie didn't answer.

'You've got to stand up for yourself Sissie. You're too soft. People will take advantage of you,' Rebecca continued.

Sissie lowered head and studied her hands clasped in her lap.

'What are you going to do when you finish school?' Rebecca asked.

'I don't know yet.' Sissie fell silent, her eyes fixed on her hands. She found a loose thread of wicker on the chair and picked at it. Then, becoming aware of Rebecca's eyes on her, she stopped and sat up straight. 'I'll just stay here,' she said. 'I can't leave Noelle.'

'Did you hear any more about how your brother died?'

Sissie shook her head.

'Did the police not say anything?'

'*Ja*. The sergeant said he died in the veld.'

'But surely they know *how* he died,' Rebecca said.

Sissie shook her head again. 'They couldn't tell. They said he'd been lying out there for a long time. Too long for them to be able to tell. He had a hole in the head. They think it might have been from a wild animal because they say his body was dug up by a wild animal.'

'But how did he get buried?' Rebecca asked.

Sissie found the thread of wicker and tugged at it again. She shrugged her shoulders. She wanted to tell Rebecca about her dream, but changed her mind.

'Don't you think it's strange, Sissie?'

Sissie shrugged. 'I don't know.'

'And they're sure it was Ivan?'

Sissie nodded her head vigorously. 'I found his ID book and then they did some tests.'

Rebecca had forgotten about the DNA tests. 'I see,' she said, wondering how accurate such tests would be on a body that had been lying in the open for who knows how long.

She'd heard that the investigation had been quite rigorous because at first it was thought the body was that of a white man. When it was discovered that the victim was non-white, interest had waned. That was what she'd heard. Rumour or not, the thought that something like that was still happening in the 'new' South Africa made her furious. But then it was happening in many of the rural areas. Black labourers who had spent generations working for farmers were still being evicted from the land in increasing numbers.

She did not express any of these thoughts to Sissie, who sat with her head back, eyes gazing into the distance as if studying something that others could not see.

Two weeks later, Rebecca heard from her office that a provisional deed for the one hundred and twelve hectares had been issued in the name of the Hopkins sisters. It was obviously going to take some time to get the official paperwork done, but the note was authenticated and it was clear that the legal requirements had been satisfied. There had been two witnesses to verify Frans Bosman's signature – they were deceased now, of course, but the document was legally valid.

Another town meeting was called. Rebecca was pleased

because she wanted to gauge how much support there was for the project.

People started gathering in mid-afternoon. They milled around at the town hall entrance and on the lawns surrounding it. Some of them squatted beneath the blanked out apartheid signs. A handful of people from the other side of the sloot gathered across the street. Rebecca had sent Albert out with pamphlets encouraging people from the location to attend the meeting.

The meeting came to order at around five o'clock that afternoon. Danie was at the lectern to open the meeting and to introduce Frikkie, who everyone knew anyway, and one of the engineers from IRH. The small group of non-whites removed their hats, wiped their scuffed shoes on the doormat and stood close to the doorway, looking a little anxious, not quite sure why they were there.

Danie was still giving his introductory speech when some hands were raised. He paused. 'There'll be time for questions later,' he said and continued.

Heckling started and hands were raised again. Again Danie paused, scanning the hall for the hecklers.

'Let me finish the introductions and then we'll get to the questions,' he repeated.

'What about the Springs?' someone called.

'We'll talk about that later,' Danie said loudly into the microphone, which immediately emitted an ear-splitting screech. Startled, he stepped back.

'What about the Springs?' the persistent voice called again.

'Construction will not affect the Springs,' Frikkie said, taking the microphone from Danie.

'How do you know?'

'Because the developers have assured us that it won't,' Danie interrupted.

'They're lying!' a gruff voice responded in Afrikaans. 'The water will be contaminated.'

Rebecca looked around to see who had made this remark.

It was Gert le Roux.

'I'm not selling my land to that son of a bitch!' he added, glaring at Frikkie.

'The development will be good for everyone, Gert. Don't cut your nose to spite your face.' Danie tried to sound reasonable.

'You can all go to hell. You're not getting my land.'

'The development will bring business into town. The town is dying. Can't you people see that? In a few years it'll be a ghost town. All we have left now is a bunch of old people. When they die . . . what then?'

Rebecca listened to the arguments. These were old issues and old debates about the benefits of progress. Often the only ones to benefit were the rich. But she had to concede that Frikkie was right about one thing. Something had to be done to save the town. There were no industries to sustain it. Most of the people in the district were farmers and pensioners. Others worked as labourers or domestics. It was a pitiful situation. But although Frikkie had a good argument, Rebecca thought there had to be another way to achieve this goal. She'd also come to the conclusion that the only satisfactory outcome would be to have all the residents become stakeholders. But to accomplish this seemed almost impossible.

After the meeting Frikkie walked to the rugby field and sat on the bleachers. Alone at dusk, his mind went back to the days when he was playing for his school team. He could almost hear the cheering and feel the heady excitement as girls crowded around after the game. He was eighteen years old then, with stars in his eyes. National pride still lay ahead of him. All that success – then one day his whole world had come crashing down around him.

Despite all that had happened, though, nothing and no one could take away his accomplishments. They were his – something he would cherish for the rest of his life.

He was bitterly disappointed at the way the town was

split on the issue of the development. The more liberal elements viewed the development as an improvement, a way of injecting vigour into a dying town, of providing work for unemployed residents and keeping their young people at home. The more conservative residents believed that the project would destroy the environment. They were afraid the development would siphon the water away from the Springs, to the detriment of the town. They were determined to block the project, fearing that the town would become like other cities, beset with crime, the young people led astray, their quiet, enviable lifestyle destroyed.

Like Frikkie, Rebecca found herself caught between these two positions.

Rebecca spent much of her time at Hopkins Landing where she was able to bounce ideas off the two sisters. She was particularly drawn to Leah. There was gentleness about her, a sense of wisdom and a depth of understanding that went way beyond what she had encountered from the locals.

Much as she wanted to dismiss her exchange with Frikkie, some of what he'd said made a great deal of sense – the rest, of course, was merely Frikkie-bluster. He was right – there was no one else competent to run the town. Mr Makalima, the principal of the black school, was someone she might have considered. He was a good administrator, but had no experience in running a town . . . Oh God, she sighed, what a problem. She decided to have a chat with Mr Makalima to see whether he'd be interested in running for council.

Preoccupied with all these thoughts and with the image of her father as she'd seen him in the Tweeriviere fields, her mind seemed to be too cluttered to think clearly.

'What's up?' Leah asked when Rebecca stopped in later the following morning. 'You look as if you're carrying the burden of the world on your shoulders.'

'It feels that way,' Rebecca said with a wry smile. 'I've been thinking about what to do about this town. Most of all, though, there's the problem of my father . . .'

'What about him?' Leah asked.

The image of her father was so pressing that Rebecca eventually broke down and confided in Leah, pausing often to wipe her eyes and blow her nose.

One of Leah's most appealing qualities was her ability to listen.

'I can't seem to forgive him,' Rebecca said quietly.

Leah took Rebecca's hand in hers. 'I'm the last person to advise you about forgiveness, Rebecca,' she said. 'I have still not forgiven my husband for what he did to me. I've tried to put him out of my mind. He's dead. What more harm can he do? I often think that if I can forgive him, I can bury my pain. But, believe me, I've tried and it's difficult.'

Rebecca nodded. 'What I feel for my father has been building up for years,' she said. 'I used to stuff it away somewhere in the back of my mind, hoping I could bury it. I've filled my life with work, as you know, but now and then all that garbage surfaces and I have to deal with it.' She paused for a moment. 'It's so painful,' she muttered.

'I know,' Leah said. 'But sometimes it's best to tackle it head on.' She gazed away, thinking of her own life and how it had threatened to drag her down into the gutters, but she'd risen out of it, changed her life. 'Have you thought of doing something else?'

'Like what?' Rebecca said. 'This is all I know. Politics is my life.'

'It will also be the end of your life,' Leah remarked.

'I really don't know what else I can do.'

'It'll come to you. Be patient.'

The two women fell silent as Rebecca fidgeted with her car keys. 'To tell you the truth,' she said quietly, 'I've been thinking along those lines myself. But I have to finish what I started here. God alone knows what I'm going to do, but I'm so tired of politics. I really – foolishly – believed I could make a difference. Everything I believed in – truth, justice and the pursuit of happiness . . .' She shook her head and sighed. 'It's still not for us. I think we have a brilliant constitution, but are we ready to apply it wisely? It's hard, for example, for the average, honest, hardworking sections of the population who put their faith in the judicial system, to understand why criminals are allowed back into their communities, their cases dismissed because of a breakdown somewhere along the chain of police procedure. Sometimes judicial decisions are so hard to accept. I found it that way when I saw some of the familiar faces convicted of gross human rights abuses walking the streets as free men. My blood just boils when I witness such poor judgement on the part of our courts. There are times when it seems to me that each judge has his own rather unique interpretation of the constitution. But you don't even have to go back to the Truth and Reconciliation trials, right now, every day, innocent babies are raped, children sodomised and killed, old women murdered, innocent hardworking people are victimised and the horror of it all is that the perpetrators are often sent back into the community to await trial, which could take anything from six months to a year. And why? Because, they say, our jails are full. Well, my solution would be labour camps. Let those people put in a full day's hard work and they'll be less inclined to repeat their offences.'

Leah chuckled. 'That would be an abuse of their human rights.'

'What about the victim's human rights?'

They were silent for a moment.

'Do you know how lucky a victim is to find a judge willing to hand down a courageous sentence?' Rebecca asked. 'It's pathetic, Leah. Really it is. I've always thought that punishment has to be harsh enough to discourage crime.'

'Why didn't you join the ruling party?' Leah asked curiously. 'It seems that's where you ought to be, Rebecca. You would probably have been a lot more effective working for a party in power rather than with the opposition.'

Rebecca thought for a moment.

'My problem, Leah, is that I've never been a lapdog. I'm more of a bulldog. I chose to be in opposition because I could see where this government was headed. Complacency creates rot.' She paused and examined her hands, as though weighing her words carefully before she spoke again. 'I know we have problems. Our police force is overrun with corrupt officials and officers. They lack education. Some of them who have been on the force since the old days are illiterate, poorly trained and many of them lack experience. They fail to prepare cases before going to court, dockets go missing, evidence goes astray – all issues that are of great concern to my constituents, problems that I'm sure can easily be corrected. Why have we not done so yet? Who do we blame for our inadequacy now? Can we still blame it on the apartheid system? It's time we got things done right. What's that expression . . . it's time we walk the talk. You know, we constantly talk about the new, free South Africa and yet there are so many segments of our population that are still not free. After almost a decade of democracy, we're still shackled by crime, poverty and disease. Take a look around you.'

She shook her head. Then, with a wry smile she said: 'I suppose I'm beginning to bore you. But this is what I hear from my constituents every day. They're not concerned about high finance and summit meetings, or impressed with all the luminaries arriving to visit this country. It seems that no matter what huge deals are sealed at these summits, the benefits seldom filter down to the poor. The people who slog for a living don't care about the window dressing. Their concern is about bread and butter issues. Women want to feel safe. They want to know that their children are safe and that if they do need help, response from the police will be immediate and that something will be done about the problem! Damn, I get so frustrated. What my constituents see is the elite – the presidency and the government – basking in glory and luxury, reaping the benefits of prosperity, while

244

they have to eke out a living on the rubbish dumps. They're on the outside looking in at the people who are safe behind their electric fences, protected by their security guards and don't have a clue what goes on in the real South Africa. People like us are part of the real South Africa, the average working person, the women in the townships and the children in the streets. Do these people not count?' She paused again. 'I'm boring you, right?'

'No, you're not,' Leah assured her.

Rebecca looked tired. 'I guess I'm just being maudlin. But I get so mad about the way things are going. I love this country. I would gladly have sacrificed my life for it.'

'I know,' Leah said. 'It is obvious that you care very deeply, but you can't let it eat away at you. What happens here happens elsewhere too. It's a sign of the times, Rebecca.'

'For crying out aloud, Leah – what kind of world do we live in? You tell me. What is the point of being law abiding when criminals are coddled and protected and victims are penalised? Do victims not deserve the court's protection? I think it's horribly ironic that criminals have no fear of the justice system because they know *their* rights are protected.'

'You have a lot of passion, Rebecca. I can see why you are so good at what you do. I'm sure that you *have* made a difference, even though you don't realise it.'

'Maybe. Sometimes I'm not so sure.'

'I still think you're on the wrong side of the fence . . .'

'I'm tired,' Rebecca said. 'Bone weary of this uphill struggle. I don't have any strength left. It's all drained away.'

'Something's bound to happen, Rebecca. I know it. It will come when you least expect it. I wish it for you.'

Rebecca was silent and after a while she asked 'What about you, Leah?'

Leah shrugged 'Who knows? I have options now that I never had before.'

'My biggest problem,' Rebecca said, 'is my father. I have to purge myself of him. I have to deal with him and the

245

things he did to us so I can get on with my life. This rage, trapped in here', she pointed to her chest, 'is paralysing me.'

Leah nodded. 'One has to be ready to forgive. Carrying all those feelings around, locked up inside of you, is what burns you up. You're right. That's what causes the paralysis. I had the miracle of DiDi coming into my life. Without her I don't know what I would have done. She's brought me so much joy and has helped me to make sense out of my life. Of course, I've never told her this. Maybe I should. It might do her the world of good to know how special she is to me. She's closer to me than my own daughter ever was.' Leah sighed. 'There's always the risk of the situation changing. I've often felt her being drawn back to her old life on the streets. I think she's beginning to feel fettered.'

Rebecca listened quietly to what Leah said about forgiveness. Much as she wanted to, she knew that deep down she wasn't ready to take that last step – wasn't ready to cross that final boundary.

'I've thought a lot about forgiveness,' Rebecca said. 'I sat through some of the Truth and Reconciliation Hearings – they were about forgiveness – and I realised then how difficult it was to forgive.'

'But victims did forgive the perpetrators, didn't they?'

'Did they? Do you really think that it was as easy as simply saying "I forgive you"? What about the scars that remain? How are these healed? But even more importantly, *can* they be healed?'

Leah was silent. She didn't have answers.

Rebecca stayed for a while longer. They talked of other things – the town, the weather, and the future of the town now that there was so much interest in it.

Late that afternoon while Rebecca was having tea on the stoep at Nora's B&B, thinking about her conversation with Leah and still trying to make sense of her life, she looked up and saw her father, cap in hand, standing at the gate. Startled, she put her cup down. He was the last person on earth she'd expected to see. She got up and went to the gate.

'Hello, Pa,' she said in a questioning tone.

'*Ja*, hello, Beckie,' he said.

Rebecca was struck by his humility. The way he called her 'Beckie'. Her mother and Suzette were the only ones who ever called her Beckie. He'd never called her anything. She'd always been nothing to him.

She waited for him to speak. He stood at the gate, awkwardly twirling his cap.

'Come inside,' she said.

He shook his head.

'Come and have some tea,' she said.

'*Ja nee*,' he muttered. 'I was just passing the house when I saw you here.'

She knew it was a lie. Nora's place was not on his way to anywhere. She guessed that he had walked all the way from the farm into town to see her.

'Was there something you wanted?' she asked.

'Beckie,' he started again. 'I don't know what to say to you.' He glanced at her and then averted his eyes. He clutched his cap, holding on to it as if it would somehow give him the strength to continue. 'I don't know what came into me all those years ago. I think it was the drink.'

She didn't say anything as she watched him struggle.

He shook his head. 'Most of the time I didn't know what I was doing,' he said bitterly.

The gate was between them. Rebecca's knees felt weak and she held on to it for support. 'You ruined our lives, Pa.'

'I know and I'm very sorry for what I did. I know you can never forgive me, but I have to say these things.'

'So you can feel better?'

'No. So you can feel better,' he said. 'For me it's too late. My life is almost over. You and Albert still have a long way to go.'

She stood quite still, her knees slightly bent, feet apart. It

247

was an aggressive stance and her father felt it. 'I think it is time for us to put aside the past,' he said.

It was the most talking she'd ever heard her father do and she could see that it had taken him weeks to put the words together. 'I stopped drinking six years ago. It's been six years and three months exactly. I'm sorry I made those last years of your mother's life so miserable. I hope that, wherever she is, she can forgive me. I know now that she was a very good woman – more than I deserved.'

He looked into her eyes. 'Beckie . . .' and then words failed him and he fell silent, only his eyes pleading.

'Pa, I have to think about this. Why don't we walk together?' This was something Rebecca would never have done a few years ago, even a few months or weeks ago. But the dynamics in their relationship had shifted. She felt less resentful. He seemed so repentant.

She opened the gate and the two of them walked down the street, turned the block into the main street and then walked past the church, past the stores, past the Glory Café where a few people had gathered and were talking. They fell silent when they saw Rebecca and her father and curious eyes followed them. They walked all the way to the end of the main street with neither of them saying a word. Finally, with dusk fast approaching, her father stopped as if he was about to say something, but changed his mind.

'Do you want a ride back?' Rebecca asked.

'No, it's nice out. I want to walk,' he said.

'Goodnight Pa,' Rebecca said.

'*Nag*, Beckie,' he responded. He put his cap back on and walked away from her.

Rebecca watched him go. She could see how stooped his back was and how his legs were bowed. Most of it, she thought, was from hard work.

Sissie and Esther came by the following afternoon to see her, but Rebecca had already left for Hopkins Landing. The two young girls stayed for a while and chatted to Nora. It was a while since Nora had seen Esther. She didn't come by as often as she used to. She sensed a change in the girl – she seemed more reflective, more mature. And all she could talk about was Jannie

She and Sissie left together and Nora thought about Esther for a long while afterwards. It was as if the young girl had made a momentous decision about her life. No longer did she have those vague dreams about the future, about a mansion in Cape Town. The sparkle seemed to have left her eyes and it seemed almost as if she was willing to settle for what she had in her life.

That same afternoon Leah and Rebecca were sitting on the stoep at Hopkins Landing discussing the proposed IRH development. Rebecca was articulating some of her thoughts and in response to one of her concerns, Leah said, 'I think the people in this town should have a stake in the project, don't you?'

'That's exactly the way I feel,' Rebecca replied, leaning forward in her chair, her hands resting on her knees, her brows tightly knitted. But how? That was the question. Her ideas were still just vague puffs of steam rising out of a cauldron of possibilities.

Leah remembered the Strip Bond she'd found in their house when Charlie died.

'Why don't you sell shares?' she asked.

'How many of the poor people here have money to buy shares? Those who can afford to will buy up everything and nothing would have changed. And are shares actually worth anything?'

'Let those who have money pay for those who don't,' Leah said. Then realising how idiotic her idea sounded, she blushed with embarrassment.

'Shares in a company like IRH are a risk. What if they pull out, the project falls through or, worse still, the CEO bails out with the company assets? It happens all the time, you know.' Rebecca sighed. 'I wouldn't want to be responsible for the townspeople losing their money. There's got to be a better plan.' She chewed on the nail of her right index finger, a habit she'd developed recently. 'In the meantime I'm going to apply to the courts for an injunction to delay the development until we can figure out what to do. I've already spoken to the lawyers. We feel we have just cause in slowing things down. There has been some evidence of corruption, of course – anyway, we'll have to wait to see what happens.'

DiDi brought out a tray of tea. Eventually Rebecca rose, slowly stretching her back. 'You've helped me to sort through a lot of problems today, Leah,' she said. 'Let me see what I can do now.'

'If you need help organising a protest, let me know,' DiDi said. 'I can get things moving in a jiffy.'

'What do you know about protests?' Rebecca laughed.

'I know a lot more than you think. On Vancouver Island I protested to save the forests.'

'How come you never tell me these things?' Leah teased.

'You never ask. But let me just say that they hauled our asses off to jail. End of story.'

'But you must've been very young, DiDi,' Rebecca remarked.

'Yeah,' was all she said.

'You're exactly the person I might need to help,' Rebecca said, chuckling at DiDi's audacity.

'Look,' DiDi said, 'if the water's so good, why don't you guys sell it? Put it in bottles. In Canada they melt glaciers and bottle the water. The water tastes pretty good.'

'That's a great idea, DiDi,' Leah said. 'I know they export a lot of bottled water to the States.'

'It *is* a good idea,' Rebecca said thoughtfully. 'Let me think about it and talk to some people in Cape Town.'

Rebecca left Hopkins Landing with a half-baked plan. It

wasn't all there yet, but somehow she'd have to pull her ideas together. The urgency to find a good plan had intensified. It had to be a watertight plan – something the developers would not be able to wriggle out of. Pretty soon, she thought, the small town would be overrun by investors and fast-talking lawyers. She hoped there was enough time to sift through her ideas because it looked as if Frikkie and his group already had the architect's rendition of the project ready to present to the town.

The one thing in their favour was that many of the residents had been alienated by the overbearing attitudes of IRH. They felt that the company was being too heavy-handed in their dealings with them, and took exception to being treated like country bumpkins.

They were being torn apart by opposing forces: the appeal of money, and the affront to their dignity. IRH was dictating to them and they didn't appreciate having city slickers come to the town and behave as if they already owned it. It was an issue that created conflict in town – even amongst those who might have been swayed by talk of the huge profits to be made in the deal.

Rebecca was pleasantly surprised by the mixed responses. She had initially expected the community to embrace the IRH project without question. It just goes to show, she told Leah. One should never take anything for granted.

The only problem was that the residents had put their faith in *her*. She'd come to talk about the unfairness of the deal, of how things would change for some, but not for others. She'd opened their eyes to many of the pitfalls, and now they expected her to rectify the situation.

She was the politician and she was expected to know what to do and how to do it. For many, especially those living on the other side of the sloot, she was their only salvation.

Others, however, refused to listen to her appeals to reject the idea of the development, at least until such time as she could come up with a plan that would benefit all of them.

24

With DiDi anxious to get back to Vancouver and the registration of the property going ahead, Leah felt it was time for them to return home. She could tell that DiDi was becoming bored and restless and since one was never quite sure what to expect from the young girl, it seemed that now was the appropriate time to decide on a return date.

Leah had hoped to stay another month or so, but she doubted that DiDi would agree. Besides, there were matters that required her attention in Vancouver. And there was also the fact that DiDi needed to settle into a routine and make decisions about her future. They'd already been gone for much longer than expected.

'Are you ready to head back to Vancouver?' Leah asked DiDi.

'Are you kidding!' the young girl exclaimed. 'We can't possibly just up and leave like that now, can we?'

It was clear that DiDi had developed an emotional interest in the outcome of events in Vlenterhoek.

The injunction issued by a Cape Town court to stop heavy equipment from being moved to the development site expired a few days before the equipment arrived. Rebecca was furious.

The residents were disappointed too. Those who had put their faith in Rebecca felt that she had failed them. They stood around in silent protest, no one quite sure how to stop the developers. But those who supported IRH gloated at what they regarded as Rebecca's defeat.

It became a daily ritual for the townspeople to mill around the construction site, pressing up against the chain-link fence, while workers brought in from Cape Town hurried to complete the fence and the hoarding in order to seal off the site.

One morning two opposing placard-carrying groups started hurling insults at each other in the main street. They were obviously gearing up for a confrontation, especially since everyone knew that two leading newspapers had sent their reporters and photographers to the town.

A crowd of undecided residents gathered to watch. Before anyone knew what was happening, verbal abuse turned into fisticuffs. In no time the two placard-bashing groups were at one another's throats, pushing and jostling. The old woman who sold vegetables outside the bank ran for cover as first her cabbages and then the rest of her vegetables were hurled as missiles. When the vendor's inventory of produce was depleted, the two conflicting camps scrambled for stones and rocks.

That day would be remembered for the number of bandaged and bloodied heads in the small town. It took Danie Venter, the sergeant and his constable to calm the situation. Some of participants attempted to vent their ill humour on the black constable, but the sergeant would have none of that and threatened the protesters with jail. The prospect of sitting in jail for a few days and missing out on events in town had a cooling influence on hostilities.

Rebecca was amazed at the amount of passion the project had aroused.

She was also suspicious about the haste with which development permits had been issued and the speed at which

IRH were moving ahead. Corruption seemed the only credible explanation for the one-week injunction on construction rather than the six weeks she'd applied for on behalf of the town's opposition groups.

In the mean time her assistant called from Cape Town to inform her that the Managing Director of IRH was an African-American.

Rebecca immediately asked her to arrange a meeting with him, but Wesley had already returned to the States. They also discovered that IRH was a subsidiary of American Resorts Inc, an international company with vast holdings throughout the world.

Rebecca fretted about her inability to stop them, especially now that it appeared that they had limitless resources.

'It's like an ant trying to stop an elephant,' she told Leah.

'If anyone can do it,' Leah said, 'you can.'

But things were moving too fast. There was hardly enough time to think. Rebecca felt that it was important to slow down the momentum. She needed more time. But more time for what, she asked herself. What could she do? How could she stop them?

'We have to fight,' Gert le Roux told her. 'We'll get nothing out of this project. The townspeople will be as poor as ever. IRH are the only ones who are going to make any money. We absolutely have to stop them.'

Gert was echoing her own sentiments. 'I might have a plan,' Rebecca said.

'What plan?' Gert asked. 'How can we stand up to bull-dozers?'

And there it was. The plan. She didn't really have one, not until Gert's words dropped an idea right into her lap.

Rebecca rallied her supporters. They were all on site the following week when the first convoy of flatbed trucks arrived carrying excavators, caterpillars and cranes.

Leah, DiDi, Rebecca, Sissie, Esther and the boys were

254

amongst the crowd, and so were the IRH supporters. The sergeant and the constable both made their presence known. They had come to keep the peace between the two groups because, as they rightly suspected, conditions were ripe for another confrontation.

A massive caterpillar with huge tracks was unloaded and started moving forward. Crowds had gathered on the periphery of the IRH property, totally disregarding the NO TRESPASSING signs. The caterpillar rolled forward on the dirt road, moving in the direction of the crowd. Leah stepped forward. All those years of anger at Charlie suddenly exploded into a blinding fury directed at the developers. With no thought for her own safety, she stepped out of their midst and, with her jaw firmly set, prostrated herself in the path of the bright yellow caterpillar. Years of accumulated common sense and her basic sense of self-preservation deserted her. The only thought she had was to stop the developers.

Out of the corner of her eye she saw that DiDi had joined her. She tried to send the young girl back, but she refused to go. There was no time for argument. Lying next to her on the roadway, DiDi took Leah's hand and together they braced themselves for the impact as the gargantuan machine hurtled towards them. Leah turned her head and saw that Rebecca had taken her place next to DiDi. The three of them were now directly in the path of the caterpillar.

They were about to be squashed. There was an audible gasp from the bystanders as the caterpillar's tracks rolled forward relentlessly. And then the protest ignited spontaneously. Bystanders and protesters, convinced that the driver had not seen the women, yelled at him to stop. People hopped up and down, waving frantically. Still, the caterpillar rolled towards the three women. The townspeople, holding their collective breath, expected the worst. Some of them closed their eyes and prayed while others, galvanised into action, flung rocks at the caterpillar; some even risked their lives by climbing aboard the moving vehicle. Danie rushed out and stood right in the path of the caterpillar, frantically trying to flag the driver down. The huge tracks ground to a halt just metres from the heads of the prostrate protesters. Danie was incensed. He could not believe that the development company was capable of such ruthless behaviour. He, for one, changed his attitude towards them.

Stunned, Sissie looked around at the shocked faces. She understood then what it was that Leah, DiDi and Rebecca were trying to accomplish and she, too, took her place on the ground next to Rebecca.

Portia and Ephemera were there in hat and gloves. Portia took one look at the bemused expressions of the bystanders and then calmly unpinned her hat, handed it to one of the ladies, and took her place on the ground next to Sissie. Ephemera followed her even though Portia sent her back. One of the other women tried to coax Ephemera away, putting her arm around her shoulders and trying to lead her back to safety, but Ephemera shrugged the woman's arm off and went to lie next to Leah, taking her hand and shuddering with excitement.

Mrs Potgieter, who did not relish the idea of lying down on the bare ground, lowered herself, steadying her shaking knees as she held on to the front end of the caterpillar, and sat bolt upright next to Portia, supporting her back against the monster that had almost run them down. It was a moment to savour. A supreme moment. All those who witnessed it had a sense of the historical significance of that moment. The women were like modern suffragettes.

Apart from Danie, the sergeant and his constable, none of the other men had figured out what was going on. The trouble was that there was too much happening all at once. The sergeant marched over to the supervisor, who had appeared on the scene in his bakkie and threatened to arrest him. With pandemonium all around them, the women lying on the ground looked unbelievably calm and peaceful, almost serene.

It was the most daring thing any of them had ever done in their lives. Mrs Potgieter's heart pounded with a mixture of fear and excitement. She felt as though life was beginning afresh for her.

IRH brought in their security guards to move the protesters off their property. They arrived with guns. One of the guards, brandishing his gun, inadvertently pointed it at Mrs Roussouw, the centenarian. At that precise moment, a photographer clicked his camera, capturing the bizarre scene of a guard pointing his gun at an old woman in a wheelchair.

Mrs Roussouw's niece wheeled her out of the way to the side of the road where she sat defiantly shaking her fist at the armed guard. Someone threw a stone at the guard. A shot rang out, and people scattered in all directions.

The next day, encouraged by DiDi, protesters chained themselves to the equipment. The story travelled fast and soon international journalists were dubbing the confrontation 'the David and Goliath story.'

CNN interviewed Leah. When the story broke overseas the following day there was a huge outcry from Canadian organisations. After all, Leah was a Canadian citizen. The Canadian government protested through official channels and sent a representative from their embassy to investigate what was happening in Vlenterhoek. The conflict had gained a life of its own.

The government was finally forced to intervene. In the meantime the people of Vlenterhoek brought another injunction against the developers to halt construction.

The story caught not only the imagination of the entire country, but of the rest of the world too. It was largely due, they said, to the courage of two women and a young girl. For a few days the usual stories of corruption, hijacking, cash-in-transit robberies, rapes and murders, so abundant throughout the country, were sidelined.

Events of the past few days clearly having been too much for her, Mrs Roussouw tumbled out of her wheelchair a few days later while her niece was elsewhere in the house.

Her niece found her dead on the kitchen floor.

The headlines in the international press read: CEN-TENARIAN DIES FOLLOWING ARMED CONFRON-TATION IN SOUTH AFRICA. The text was accompanied by the now-famous photo of Mrs Roussouw in a wheelchair, looking down the barrel of a gun.

People were outraged, even though the two events were not really connected. Frikkie protested that it was Mrs Roussouw's time. And when one's time was up, it was up.

No one else agreed. The newspaper reports knitted the two events together. In the minds of the residents, the protest had killed Mrs Roussouw. She became a martyr, a rallying point for the protest. Papers around the world carried the story. There were protests in other countries. The directors of American Resorts Inc called a special meeting to discuss the crisis. American Resort Inc share prices on the New York stock exchange fell. The board of directors realised that something drastic had to be done. They were in constant contact with IRH in South Africa, encouraging local executives to find a quick solution to the crisis.

Frikkie's boss, CEO Mr Rosenberg, and his assistant flew into town in the company jet to quell the controversy. Frikkie met them at the airstrip. Mr Rosenberg was tall and lean with small piercing grey eyes. He was a sparse man, both in manner and words, cold, calculating and horribly intimidating. His only passion was Cuban cigars and he was never without one.

Frikkie, who had met the man only once, had never quite recovered from that experience. In his presence, Frikkie had felt like a child, awkward and resentful, and he was dismayed to learn that Rosenberg was flying into Vlenterhoek and that he had to meet him.

Mr Rosenberg's reputation for ruthlessness, especially when it involved the acquisition of property, had preceded him. There was some concern in town about the man's arrival. They'd heard that no one dared question or contradict him. He rarely made an appearance at a site – but because the controversy was getting out of hand, he'd come to sort it out personally. He wanted the issue settled quietly and amicably and as cost-effectively as possible. He was a bottom-line man.

A meeting of the townspeople was called. Mr Rosenberg and his IRH representatives were in attendance. Rebecca was disappointed to find that Wesley was not there. She'd hoped that he'd at least lend a more sympathetic ear to the Vlenterhoek cause. But she took his absence in her stride; her differences, after all, were with those IRH representatives who were present and especially with the CEO. She could see that there was some apprehension amongst the residents. They'd heard via Frikkie what a big shot Mr Rosenberg was. Rebecca, however, was not concerned. She'd encountered much worse than Rosenberg.

The meeting was under way. The residents had given IRH an opportunity to have their say, which was no different from what they'd been saying all along, while Rosenberg quietly observed the proceedings. Finally it was Rebecca's turn to speak.

'You can't just walk in and take over,' she said with a sweeping motion of her hands. 'The Hemelslaagte Springs belong to everyone here. You have to treat the residents fairly.' She paused and looked around the hall, saw the upturned faces watching her, saw the anxiety in their eyes, the trust and the expectation.

'Give them an interest in the project!' she cried. 'Give them a stake in the project and provide them with jobs. Vlenterhoek people must be employed before any outsiders are brought in. Young people will return home if we can guarantee jobs for them.' She paused, gazing around again, trying to gauge the effect of her words. The townspeople were silent. They didn't quite understand that she was demanding empowerment for them, that the residents of Vlenterhoek should be stakeholders in the entire enterprise.

The IRH representatives laughed, shaking their heads at such a preposterous idea. Rosenberg sat in silence; only those cold grey eyes moved, as he sucked on his cigar.

'The people of Vlenterhoek need a break!' Rebecca argued. 'We won't let you come in here and walk all over us! We'll find ways of stopping you. We'll get one injunction after another until you grow roots here and your equipment rusts. And this time,' she glared at the IRH representatives, 'you won't be able to bribe the judges. We're on to you!'

Most of the locals had no idea what an injunction was. They looked bewildered, but trusted that Rebecca knew what she was talking about.

'I already have our lawyers in Cape Town working on another injunction. You will not take one step forward until this issue is resolved!'

The IRH bosses looked at each other. There was a quick flash of irritation and then angry glances at Frikkie while the townspeople tried to sift through Rebecca's words, trying to understand what was happening in front of their eyes.

Mr Rosenberg leaned over and whispered something in the ear of one of the IRH representatives. He nodded.

Leah pushed her chair back and stood up straight so that she could be heard in every corner of the hall. 'We will not sell our land,' she told them in a clear voice, speaking slowly so that everyone could understand her Canadian accent. 'We know how important the land is for the development, but the only way you'll get it, is if you allow everyone in the town to participate.'

She trembled at the sheer impudence of what she'd said. She had no idea where any of this was heading. She and Rebecca had discussed the situation, but had not yet devised a plan.

She'd done her part, though. The rest was up to Rebecca.

Finally the words began to penetrate the befuddled minds

of the townspeople. Words like *shares*, *stakeholders* and *interest* became rocks. Rocks dropped into a pond of their collective conscience. Shock waves splashed to the very fringes of the crowd gathered in the hall.

After a moment of stunned silence, there was a murmur of consternation and then approval. The excitement built. No one could be heard above the din of voices.

Frikkie watched the unfolding events in dismay, but once the idea was put into words, there was no going back. It had to be considered. There was excitement in the town hall and a glorious feeling of satisfaction and exhilaration on the part of Rebecca's supporters. Everyone knew now what she was capable of and was confident that she had their interests at heart. Frikkie they would not trust. Look what he had done to Suzette, they said, and look what his father Hendrik did to the Le Roux family.

After the meeting Rebecca received a note from Mr Rosenberg, asking her to submit a proposal in writing.

Negotiations became more complex, but it all came down to one issue – money, which most people in the town did not have.

A week later, with the assistance of an economist friend, Rebecca submitted a proposal to the government and to IRH.

The proposal was quite daring and unique to the conditions in the small town. She indicated that since the government was encouraging local initiative and black empowerment, IRH should establish a two-million rand Citizens' Heritage Trust Fund, to be managed by the local bank and administered by three persons elected by the residents; that the interest from the heritage fund be equally distributed monthly to each registered resident and that the developers annually contribute ten per cent of gross sales to the fund to take care of periods of low interest rates and to keep up with high inflationary periods; that the developers provide adequate training and employment to at least one member of every registered family; and that they provide quality, subsidised healthcare for employees.

IRH executives baulked. The demands were unreasonable.

'Are you people mad?' Frikkie demanded.

Rebecca stood firm. 'With these conditions, all the residents stand to benefit. You'll have a highly motivated and stable work force. What could be better for business?'

'Two million is outrageous,' IRH countered.

'I'm sorry, but that's what it's going to cost you or else there's no deal.'

For the next two weeks lawyers travelled back and forth with new proposals and amendments, but Rebecca refused to budge from her original conditions.

In the meantime, construction came to a halt as the two sides negotiated.

Hendrik, furious at being locked out of the deal, raged at his son, but there was nothing Frikkie could do. It was out of his hands.

With the interest of the international press and American Resorts Inc's falling prices on the stock market, IRH were obliged to settle. Under pressure, they finally agreed to the terms set out in Rebecca's list of demands. The only clause that still remained a contentious issue was the annual ten per cent contribution of their gross sales. Through continued bargaining this amount was finally whittled down to two per cent. IRH accepted the change. Pressure for a quick settlement had increased, especially in the States, from sections of the public that had supported protests at the World Economic Forum.

Finally, in the interests of goodwill, IRH agreed to pay all legal costs.

When these conditions were accepted, the Hopkins sisters finally agreed to sell their property. The price they were offered was a good one, more than they had expected. Leah, having seen the matter to its conclusion, decided that the time was right to return to Vancouver.

Portia wanted her to stay, but Leah knew that her life was not there in the small town. Besides, she told her sister, she had DiDi to consider and DiDi was as ready as she to go back. They'd been gone for much too long already.

At about two o'clock one morning, a few days after all these decisions had been made, the phone at Hopkins Landing rang. The exchange was now open twenty-four hours a day and it had finally been agreed to lay underground cables to Vlenterhoek.

The phone ringing at that ungodly hour almost gave them all a heart attack. Portia answered. It was Erica calling from Toronto and wanting to speak to her mother.

She had evidently read an account of events taking place in Vlenterhoek in the Canadian newspapers. 'Mom,' she said in a small hesitant voice, 'I'm so proud of you. When are you coming home?'

'Soon, dear. Soon. How are the boys?'

'They're very well, Mom. We're all well.'

They talked for a while. Leah felt more comfortable, more confident talking to her daughter now. She would tell her everything when she got back to Vancouver. A long distance phone call was not the way to do it. She wanted to tell her that there would be a little bit of money now. She could get a bigger place for her and DiDi. It was a thought Leah savoured. At last she had something to look forward to, even though she knew that DiDi might not be around for long. But, whatever happened, there would always be a place for her to come home to. It wouldn't be much, but at least they'd have a roof over their heads.

'I'll phone you when I get back to Vancouver,' Leah said.

'Right. Take care of yourself, Mom. The boys send their love.'

'Thank you, dear.'

Leah went to back to bed, but could not sleep. Her heart was still pounding from being awakened by the jangle of the telephone. She thought of her daughter and her grandsons. She thought of her life in Vancouver. Morning came, the sun filtered through the curtains, lighting up little tracks on the bedcover. Still she could not sleep.

25

On Sunday Rebecca went to see her father. Most of the farm labourers had gone to church and the compound was quiet. Although the front door was wide open, there was no one in the house. Rebecca walked around to the backyard and found her father there. He was sitting under a tree, in one of the upright kitchen chairs, drinking tea from his enamel mug.

'Hello, Pa,' she said.

'Hello, Beckie,' he said. 'Do you want a chair?'

'I'll get it,' she said, and went into the kitchen to fetch one.

'How are things, Pa?' she asked as she placed the chair in the shade and sat down.

Her father didn't answer.

'Where's Albert?' she asked.

'He's on the ridge,' he said.

'I drove by there, but I didn't see them.'

Her father shrugged his bony shoulders. They were silent for a long while.

'I see you've been busy with this other business,' he mumbled.

'Yes.'

He sighed and sat with his hands in his lap, his eyes half-closed. She could tell that he was tired.

After a while he looked at her and said. 'Oubaas Joubert is very cross with you. I heard him say so the other day.'

'I wish you would stop calling him that,' she said.

Her father looked at her questioningly.

'*Baas*,' she said sharply. 'Stop calling him *baas*.'

Her father was silent for a while.

'*Nou ja*,' he said eventually. 'He is very cross with you.'

'Pa, I don't care what Hendrik Joubert thinks.'

'*Ja nee*,' her father muttered. 'But I have to work for him.'

'You can find work elsewhere . . .' she said and then realised what a stupid remark this was.

'Where must I find work? A man of my age – who will give me work?'

Rebecca looked away.

They were silent again, then Rebecca said, 'If things work out, everyone here will have a job.'

'Doing what?' he asked. 'Sweeping floors?'

She didn't say anything.

'Why couldn't you leave well alone?'

'Pa, what I'm doing is for the good of the town.'

'With Hendrik Joubert so angry, I wouldn't be surprised if he fires me because of you.'

'He won't do that. You're a good worker. You've been with him a long time.'

Her father muttered something unintelligible under his breath.

'I'm sorry, Pa, but if I don't do this people like you will lose out.'

'Where will I stay when he puts me off the farm? He'll do that, you know. I can see it coming.'

She shook her head. 'He knows he won't get away with it – not if I'm around.'

Her father sighed, his shoulders slumped, eyes half-closed.

She studied him quietly and after a long silence she said, 'Pa, I have to go now.'

'*Ja nee*,' her father said, sitting up, as if rousing himself from his thoughts.

She got up to go. Her father made an effort to get up as well, but it was too much for him and he slumped back into his chair. She sensed that he had something important to tell her.

She waited, poised to leave and then he said, 'I wish I could turn everything back and start all over again.' He tried to gather his thoughts. 'Beckie,' he said, 'I don't have much time left.'

'What do you mean?' she asked.

'I have this sickness . . . it's killing me . . .' He lapsed into silence.

She didn't say anything.

'I need you to forgive me so I can die . . . in peace. I am tired now, tired of the struggle.' He paused again and lowered his head. 'If anything happens, I want you to make sure that Albert is all right. I promised your mother . . .'

'I'll take care of Albert, Pa . . .'

He waited, but she could not bring herself to say the words he wanted to hear. Instead, she asked, 'What's wrong with you, Pa?'

'Cancer.'

'Who's your doctor?

'Doctor Faurie.'

'When was the last time you saw him?'

'Two weeks ago.'

'Where do you have cancer, Pa?'

'Inside,' he said, vaguely indicating a spot at his midriff.

'In your stomach?' she asked. He shrugged.

'I'll speak to Doctor Faurie. Why are you still working?'

'What else can I do?'

'Pa, look, I think you can take things easy. I'll help out.'

He shook his head. 'I can't sit here waiting to die. I have to keep busy.'

She didn't say anything more. She could feel a dull ache

rising from her neck to her head. One of her stress headaches was coming on. She had to get away from him, had to think about what he'd said and how she could deal with it.

'Pa,' she said, 'I'll come back tomorrow after I've spoken to Doctor Faurie.'

'When will you come and stay here?' he asked.

She hesitated and then she looked into his eyes. 'I'm not quite ready for that yet. Too much has happened between us. Why don't we just take this one step at a time?'

He nodded.

'Tell Albert I was here.'

He nodded again and watched her go.

Rebecca learned that her father had pancreatic cancer. The doctor couldn't tell her how much time he had left. 'It could be any time,' he said. 'It has spread. It's too late. There's nothing anyone can do for him.'

When she left the doctor's office, Rebecca wasn't quite sure what to do. She knew that her father could no longer work. There was no point telling him this because she'd be the last person he'd want to listen to. The only thing she could do was try to ease the financial burden. She spoke to Albert.

Although he had suspected for some time that something was wrong, the news of his father's illness shocked him. 'Will he die soon?' he asked anxiously.

'I don't know, Albert. But I don't want you to worry. I'll take care of everything, see?'

He turned away. He looked so lost and vulnerable that she put her arms around him. 'I want you to do something for me, Albert,' she said.

'What?' he asked, blowing his nose and wiping his tears.

'I have to go back to Cape Town for a short while. I want you to keep an eye on him. Try to get him not to work too hard. If you need me, call me at this number.' She gave Albert her cellphone number. It was all she could do under the circumstances. Albert was too bewildered to take it all in at once and she had to talk to him on several more occasions, to reassure him.

When Rebecca got back to Cape Town she arranged a meeting with Vusi and told him about DiDi's idea of the water bottling venture. She had already instructed her assistant to find someone who knew how to set up a bottling plant. She wanted to understand what was required before discussing it with the residents of Vlenterhoek. If it worked, she thought, it would help to boost morale in the town.

Ian was unable to go to Vlenterhoek for the screening of the film and Vusi volunteered to accompany Josh, who was surprised that Vusi would want to return to Vlenterhoek, in view of his experiences there. The two men brought with them a broadcast-quality video which they planned to show on a big portable screen, which Danie had managed to secure for the occasion.

The town hall was set up for the screening. Hendrik Joubert had offered the hall at the Imperial Hotel, but Danie was afraid that the residents, still quite edgy, might misconstrue the gesture and so he declined.

The screening was a big social event in Vlenterhoek. There was no *bioscope* in this small town, probably one of the few that did not have a cinema. There had been plans to build one a long time ago, but they had been scrapped because of a lack of finance. By the time the cinema project was reconsidered, videos had come along and so had the Imperial Hotel's giant screen. Now, if anyone wanted to see a film in a proper cinema, they'd travel to the next town.

Josh was looking forward to seeing Leah.

He was lonely after his wife's death, and with his kids living in different countries and absorbed in their own lives, there was little else for Josh except his work. A few years ago his son in Canada had invited him to come and live with them, but Josh had always been reluctant to impose himself

269

on his kids.

When he and Vusi arrived in Vlenterhoek, they were surprised to find that there was no accommodation available. IRH engineers and employees had taken up all the available rooms. The rest of the influx consisted of those who had come to reconnoitre developments. There was not a single room to be had at the hotel or at Nora's B&B where Rebecca, having extended her stay, was firmly entrenched.

Fearing another incident similar to the one they had had before with Vusi, Danie asked around, but there was nothing available. He was about to give Josh and Vusi the news that they might have to spend the night elsewhere, when his phone rang. It was Mrs Potgieter. She was talkative and eager to express her opinions on everything now that she had Danie on the phone. But Danie was impatient with her – he thought the Vusi incident was about to resurface. She went on and on about the film show and how everyone was looking forward to it. Danie waited impatiently, tapping his toe and grimacing unpleasantly. Then finally, when he was about to tell her that he was busy, she stunned him with an offer to let the two men stay in her house.

'Look, let's not start that all over again,' he said rudely. 'It's the same man you didn't want in your house before . . .'

'I know,' she said.

There was a long pause.

'I know it's the black man, but I'm offering him a room in my house anyway. Him and the other man.'

'Are you sure? I don't want to get their hopes up.'

'What's wrong with you?' she said. 'Are you deaf? Did I not just tell you . . .'

'Okay. Okay. That's fine. Thank you very much,' he said. 'I'll tell them . . .' He still wasn't sure, not a hundred per cent sure, that the woman wouldn't change her mind. But before he could say another word, Mrs Potgieter put the phone down.

And so Vusi and Josh stayed with Mrs Potgieter. As could

be expected, Vusi was initially very reluctant. But in the end Josh persuaded him to accept the invitation.

'You've got to be bigger than her,' Josh said.

Vusi was characteristically gracious in his acceptance of her hospitality.

All was forgiven. Mrs Potgieter had made amends and, to everyone's surprise, she refused to accept payment for the rooms.

Everyone was invited to the film show. Black and white crowded into the hall, sat shoulder to shoulder. It was the first time in the history of the town that integration had occurred so spontaneously. Everyone was wearing their best clothes. The *première* of 'Ambiance', although unpronounceable for most, was an occasion of importance that everyone seemed to understand.

Local dignitaries and those who had participated in the film occupied the first few rows. The ham-handed mayor and his wife, a diminutive woman with grey hair, sat in the front row, as did Danie and Petronella, radiant as the wife of the town clerk who had made all of this possible. Also in the front row were Rebecca and her father, who looked very pale and shrunken. Albert, Josh and Vusi were also close to the front – Vusi flanked by Rebecca on one side and Leah on the other. Josh sat next to Leah. Ephemera and Portia arrived wearing hats and gloves. Portia had a hard time keeping Ephemera still, but eventually DiDi took charge of her. Jannie, Esther and Sissie sat with DiDi and Ephemera.

The rest of the townspeople took up whatever seats remained. Nora sat a few rows back and so did Rena and Noelle, who had come reluctantly, but Sissie had insisted. She wanted her sister to see the sections in which she appeared. Noelle looked shy and self-conscious. She had never attended an event like this. Her life had consisted of walking a well-trodden path between home and work.

Hendrik was not in the front with the dignitaries; he sat further back with Frikkie and Anna. They had all come out

271

on this splendiferous occasion – DiDi's choice of adjective.

The buzz in the hall sounded like bees swarming. Jannie, Sissie and Esther, who had participated, could hardly wait to see themselves and their names on the list of credits.

Josh had brought a special VCR for the occasion and the film was projected on to the large screen. It looked a bit grainy because the screen was so big. But no one cared, even when the floor shook and the screen wobbled with every burst of laughter and round of applause.

There were exclamations of admiration and hoots of laughter when the audience realised that Esther had taken the part of an Indian maiden. There was more applause when the star dancer performed, and an even larger round of applause when Jannie's kite flew into the sunset. The music, which they had heard before in dribs and drabs, had been edited and was so powerful and moving that some of them felt their chests swell with pride.

The audience sat patiently through a segment of the film shot in Rajastan, which Vusi had deliberately spliced on to the Vlenterhoek film to give the viewers an idea of how Vlenterhoek compared. The consensus was that their segment was much better, although the colour and dancing in the Rajastan segment was something to be admired. Vusi had explained at the beginning that the film was not yet complete. There were two more segments that were still being edited, but he wanted them to see what they had done so far.

There was a list of acknowledgements at the end. It read 'to the people of Vlenterhoek', followed by the individual acknowledgements. Everyone in the hall was touched. They all leaped to their feet to applaud and the screen keeled over, but at that stage no one cared. Vusi came forward and was applauded. Then Josh thanked everyone for their cooperation.

In Ian's absence, Vusi presented a plaque to Danie in acknowledgement of the contribution of the people of the town. Not one person there had any doubt that Vlenterhoek was now on the map.

Afterwards Nora invited Leah and Josh for coffee. Rebecca and Vusi were there too. The two of them got along stunningly, DiDi later observed. 'And you didn't do so badly yourself,' she remarked to Leah. 'What were you guys talking about?'

'My, my,' Leah laughed. 'You are quite nosy, aren't you?'

DiDi tweaked a playful eyebrow, the hoop in her brow doing a little jig of its own. Leah laughed. She hadn't felt so wonderfully relaxed and warm for a long time. She didn't want to admit to herself that it was Josh's presence that had done the warming.

'So, what did he say?' DiDi prodded.

'He'll be coming to Vancouver next year . . .'

'Just to see you?' DiDi asked.

'No, silly!' Leah exclaimed, almost coyly. 'He's coming on business and said he'd look me up.'

'So where will he stay?' DiDi asked. 'We don't even have a home there now. We gave it up, remember.'

'We'll find another place, dear. I've got a little bit of money. Not much – just my share of the proceeds from the sale of the land. I don't think we'll have any problem finding a place to live.'

'Jeez,' DiDi muttered. 'Good thing we came here. Ain't it?'

'Yes,' Leah said.

'Looks like Rebecca and Vusi got along real well too,' DiDi remarked.

'I think so.'

Rebecca did get along well with Vusi. She felt comfortable with him and they'd talked for a long time about things that really mattered to her. It was the first time she had allowed herself to open up to a man in such a way. But that was because she liked him. He was quiet, sensible and a good listener, and the two of them were now sharing ideas about the bottling plant. There were obstacles, of course, to any kind of relationship with him. No matter what she did or who she met, the spectre of her father always interposed. She knew that in order to get on with her life she'd have to do something drastic to get rid of her bad memories.

But each time she saw her father, the delicate membrane of healing was ripped away to reveal the festering wounds.

She thought of the way he'd appeared at Nora's gate to apologise. He'd said what was on his mind. It was more than she had expected. But she was still not willing to let him back into her life.

The time was approaching for Leah and DiDi to return to Canada. They had done everything they could to help their friends and family in Vlenterhoek. Their visit had turned the small town right on its ear – or that's how DiDi saw it.

Many of their friends came to see them off at the station. Some even cried. Mrs Potgieter was there, her resentment forgotten. A lot of old hostilities had been buried by all that had happened in Vlenterhoek. Mrs Potgieter had even forgiven Leah for having held her husband's affections hostage for such a long time. There were many moist eyes as the train pulled out of the station.

'Am I glad that's over with,' DiDi said. 'I can't bear all that crying.'

Leah smiled. She knew that they were both going to miss Vlenterhoek. Who would have thought that their stay would have been so eventful? DiDi was right when she said they had turned the town on its ear. She was sorry to leave Portia just when they were growing closer. She had a feeling, though, that this was not the end. That this was not a final goodbye for her and that, God willing, she'd be back some day.

26

When at last everything seemed to be falling into place, Frikkie went to see Suzette. He was sincere about wanting to make amends. He realised that there was a lot that he had to make up for, so much time lost with his son, but the development project had swallowed him and taken its toll and he wondered whether he would be doing the right thing for Suzette by asking her to marry him.

Frikkie had contemplated pretending that he did not know that Martin was his son, but he knew that sooner or later Rebecca would tell Suzette that she had told him. He didn't want the guilt of neglecting his son hanging over his head. It was time to fix all the things that were wrong. Now that the project seemed to be out of his control, he had time on his hands and he wanted to make a fresh start.

It was a great relief to Suzette when the truth about Martin finally came out. Her only concern was that Martin might hold it against her that she hadn't told him the truth. She wondered if the boy would forgive her for lying to him.

'We'll both tell him,' Frikkie said. He wanted to make it easier for Suzette.

'I don't know how he's going to take it,' she said, trying to hold back her tears. Her son was the focus of her life.

And then there was her father. She didn't know how he was going to take any of this. He was passionately fond of Martin and she was sure that he would not give the boy up to a Joubert.

'Why didn't you tell me when I first came to see you?' Frikkie asked. 'Why did I have to hear it from Rebecca?'

'You ran off. You didn't care, did you?'

He lowered his eyes and was silent for a long time. Then he said, 'I was young and my head was in rugby. I'm sorry.'

Suzette still loved Frikkie. He had been everything to her: he was her life, her dreams, the centre of her universe. She used to pray for this moment. And now that it had arrived, she could remember only the pain and the misery he had brought her. She turned away. He came up behind her and put his hand on her shoulder. She broke down then and wept. He took her in his arms and it was as though the years of separation had never been.

Hendrik was triumphant when Frikkie told them that Martin was his son. He and Anna had suspected it all along.

When Suzette told her father what had happened, Gert le Roux knew that he had lost both his daughter and his grandson, and that there was nothing he could do about it.

A few weeks later, after Suzette's gentle persuasion, Gert sold his land to IRH.

To secure the goodwill of the townspeople, Wesley persuaded Rosenberg to sell them some of the IRH shares so that they would feel that they had a genuine stake in the company. The deal was that IRH would offer ten shares to each household and restrict the number of shares any one person could own. Shares were offered at a nominal price of thirty-six rand each. Notices with this information were posted around town. Hendrik Joubert tried to organise some of the locals to buy shares on his behalf, but this came to Rebecca's notice and he found himself outmanoeuvred by her.

Thrilled at the prospect of ownership in the company,

residents came to invest at the bank that was managing the sale. They came clutching their savings; dirty crumpled notes dragged out from under mattresses, from behind walls, dug up in coffee tins from backyards and pried from under floor boards – each deposit had its own story.

They arrived with socks, bottles, pillowcases, jars and cans filled with their savings. The tellers made snide comments about 'dirty money' and took to wearing latex surgical gloves supplied by the bank for counting it. In the end, buying and paying for shares, which in reality weren't worth much, was what made residents feel that they were truly empowered – more so even than the trust fund. In the larger environment of economics and world finance, the shares represented less than a drop in the ocean, but for the residents of Vlenterhoek it was a huge triumph, a triumph for which they had Rebecca and the Hopkins sisters to thank.

Rebecca discussed the bottling plant with Gert le Roux who was very enthusiastic about the idea.

'It's exactly what we need,' he told her.

Since Gert had time on his hands, she thought he might be the right person to manage the plant on behalf of the town. He was very keen to take on the project.

Construction on the resort started. The once peaceful environment was filled with noise, the landscape permanently scarred by the blasting. Gravel pits were opened a few kilometres away and the heavy traffic to and fro created havoc with the roads. The dust was unbearable and people complained bitterly; many began to regret their decision to develop Vlenterhoek.

Rebecca, who had stayed as long as she could, returned to Cape Town, energised by a mission she had been determined to see through to its conclusion. By the time she left, the contractors had already started excavating.

Locals were employed on the construction site. They were given first consideration before the contractors went outside the town to look for workers. There was enough work for everyone.

But outside workers – both skilled and unskilled – did arrive and the town was beset with new problems that the community had not anticipated.

'I told you so,' the dominee said, as crime became a problem. It was a problem they now had in common with the big cities.

The larger community accepted that this was the price they had to pay for success but, needless to say, they weren't happy about it.

Changes became necessary. The most important was a larger and more effective police force. Security personnel were hired to guard the construction offices. People started locking their doors and putting their garden furniture into their garages at night.

Several accidents marred the development.

Herman's Rock was dislodged from its perch in a blasting operation and the huge boulder went careening down the hill, gathering momentum and taking with it an avalanche of rocks. It cut a swathe of destruction on its way down the mountain, eventually ending up in a pile of rocks on Tweeriviere, where it destroyed one of Hendrik's precious dams. It was fortunate that the rock had stopped where it did. If it had carried on, it would have rolled right through the farmhouse kitchen.

Hendrik demanded compensation and threatened to sue the company. A settlement was reached, but it created new problems for Hendrik because he had difficulty locating another borehole. In the end, the company sent in their specialists and this satisfied Hendrik.

Anna Joubert found she could no longer tolerate Hendrik. He negated everything she believed in and stood for.

One of the things he held against her was that she had put a stone on Ivan's grave.

'Why couldn't you stay out of it,' he raged soon after

Ivan was buried.

The issue swelled between them, sat on their relationship like a huge boil waiting to burst.

'Why did you have to stick your nose into what didn't concern you?' he asked her. 'Do you know what people will say about us?' He just couldn't put the matter to rest.

'And they'll be right,' Anna said.

'Stop interfering in my business!'

She shook her head. 'Hendrik, he was as much your son as Frikkie and Jannie.'

'Are you mad, woman?' he yelled. 'Do you know what you're saying?'

She nodded. She was not going to be intimidated by him – not any more. 'I told you, I've known for a long time.' She was quite calm. Hendrik had exhausted her. 'You treat me like I'm some kind of fool. I'm not and I don't like it when you treat me like one.'

There was something in Anna's voice, in the set of her shoulders, that surprised Hendrik. She turned away from him and he hesitated for a moment, taken aback by her stance. Just as he thought the conversation was over, Anna slowly turned around to face him again. 'Only God will know what happened to Ivan – God and you, Hendrik,' she said quietly. 'And may God forgive you, because I can't.'

The blood drained from Hendrik's face. He did the only thing he could under the circumstances and that was to walk away without comment. She gazed after him, her eyes fixed and sightless and filled with pain.

Life as the residents of Vlenterhoek had known it – for better or worse – was never to be the same again. Their sleepy little town had finally come of age.

There was talk of changing the town's name to something more dignified.

'Vlenterhoek. What kind of a name is that?' an American tourist had asked in the accent that no one understood.

279

Someone suggested a competition to find a suitable name before the official opening of the resort. From the other side of the sloot came suggestions like Madibaburg, Mandela-town, Mbekiville, Yaletown, Newburg. These were quickly rejected. Nothing, it seemed, was as appropriate as Vlenterhoek.

Rebecca was in Cape Town when her father took a turn for the worse. Albert telephoned her from the public phone in town and told her that their father had asked for her.

She came immediately and was at her father's bedside the night he died. He was barely alive when she arrived. It was as if he'd willed himself to live just so that he could see her one more time. His eyes were wide open and followed her around the room as she spoke to Albert.

'Why didn't you send for an ambulance,' she asked him.

'He didn't want to go to hospital,' Albert said. 'He wanted to die here.'

The nearest hospital, she realised, would have been an hour's drive away.

There was so much pain in her father's eyes that she couldn't bear to look at him. She took his hand and squeezed it. She rarely cried, but now she felt the warmth of tears rolling down her cheeks. She swiped at them with her free hand.

Her father seemed to be waiting and she knew what he was waiting for, but she couldn't bring herself to say the words. She squeezed his hand again. That was all she could do. Her brain was telling her that they were only words, words that would comfort an old man in his dying moments. But the words felt like boulders that were too heavy to lift out of her mouth. There was the tiniest movement of his lips, as if he were trying to smile and then he closed his eyes.

'I can't do it,' she whispered. 'I can't.' But the words came involuntarily, as though forced out of her.

'I forgive . . .'

But it was too late.

27

Two years later everyone came to the Grand Opening.

Rebecca Fortuin was back. She'd retired from politics and had gone into business for herself as a consultant.

The bottling plant was up and running. Four of the townspeople sat on the board of Heavenly Waters, as the bottling company had been named. The bottled water was being exported to several European countries. They were now looking at North American markets as well. The label, designed by Nora, was quite eye-catching. The business was doing better than anyone had expected – and it was all thanks to DiDi's inspired suggestion.

Rebecca and Leah, who had come for the opening, were special guests. Josh accompanied Leah, which caused some raised eyebrows.

Old habits die hard, especially among gossips, Leah thought as she smiled at the faces around her. The Town Council, now mostly black and headed by the new mayor, Mr Makalima, were in attendance.

Ephemera held tightly on to Leah's arm, having witnessed Josh's attentiveness. Despite the murmurings of some of the women, Leah was still regarded as the hero of the Vlenter-hoek Saga.

There was never any doubt in the minds of the locals that her arrival, and that of Rebecca, had heralded a new era in Vlenterhoek's history. Everyone wanted news of DiDi, who had sent her regards and small gifts to her friends. She was back at school, studying hard, and hoped to take up flying.

Once Rebecca had been known as the 'coloured Fortuin girl'. Now everyone addressed her as Rebecca or Miss Fortuin. There were a few curious glances in her direction when Vusi made an appearance, sought her out and, with an air of propriety, stood next to her.

Residents, visitors and VIPs came together in celebration. There was not a murmur of dissent to be heard anywhere. The white facade of the huge resort complex with its manicured lawns and pools of spring water shimmered in the morning light. Beyond the complex, the virgin fairways of the new golf course glittered emerald green, cut to perfection. A new variety of fast-growing Canadian grass had been cultivated and laid out like a carpet across the veld. In a year or so, the course designer promised, the immaculate fairways of the new golf course, complete with palm trees and water hazards, would be hosting some of the world's foremost golfers.

Residents of all colours beamed proudly as the President complimented them on their initiative and on providing an example to the rest of the country. He said he was proud to be in their midst and honoured to dedicate the building to Mrs Roussouw, who had died for the Cause.

Rebecca stood in the shade with her brother Albert, tall and lanky and wearing an earring. He now lived in Cape Town with his sister and was studying music at the conservatory. A few metres away Frikkie stood with Suzette and Martin. Suzette was expecting their second child.

Jannie and Esther arrived in his new car. They were married

now and Esther held in her arms their first child, a tousled-haired little boy, almost a year old.

Esther had held on to Jannie and with single-minded determination had proceeded with her plan. Two years after his discharge from hospital, she trapped Jannie into marriage. There was nothing his father could do, not with a child on the way.

It was a disappointment to Nora that Esther had so little ambition, that she had wasted her potential. All that promise, that amazing grace, had come to nothing, she thought, as she observed her. She wondered how long it would be before Jannie tired of being wrapped in her silken cords. It was a mistake. She wished she could tell Esther that trapping a man was stupid and irresponsible and never worked – especially with both of them so young, she nineteen and he twenty. It wouldn't be long before Jannie outgrew her – and then what?

The cleaner from the hotel was there with his family, all dressed in their Sunday best. In fact, just about everyone from the sloot side of town was there, their faces brimming with pride. 'They' were finally recognised as legitimate Vlenterhoek residents, their existence acknowledged and validated.

'You can legislate laws, but you can never change attitudes' was what people used to say to Rebecca, but here was ample proof that money could bridge any gap – no matter how wide the divide. It could do what legislation couldn't. Money had brought black and white together as equal partners, blurring the boundaries between the two groups.

The day after the opening, Josh and Leah left for Cape Town where she was going to spend a week. She was restless about being away from DiDi, and Portia knew that this would probably be her last visit. She wasn't quite sure what part Josh would play in Leah's life. She would miss Leah, but she rationalised that she had managed all those years without her, and when Leah left Portia shrugged back into her old role as caregiver to Ephemera.

The health properties of the water from the Hemelslaagte Springs became a major tourist attraction. People arrived from all directions and all countries. There was talk about eventually having to build a small airport. It was Frikkie's idea, one he was promoting vigorously. But after their experience with one major construction project, the residents declared that another was totally out of the question.

Nora Naude and a few other residents were beginning to have reservations about the resort. The very qualities that had made Vlenterhoek so special were being eroded by the advent of tourism. The advocates of tourism could talk only about the fact that the resort was already booked up for the next two years.

Sissie, Noelle and Rena were offered job opportunities they could only have dreamt of before the changes.

Sissie's appearance in the 'Ambiance' film was noticed by a well-known film producer, who came all the way to Vlenterhoek to offer her a role in one of the popular television soapies. It meant a move to Cape Town

Noelle didn't want her to go, but Nora and Rebecca persuaded her not to hold Sissie back. Opportunities like that did not fall into one's lap every day. It would be a huge achievement for a girl like Sissie to succeed in the big city. Noelle eventually agreed and Rebecca sat Sissie down and pointed out the pitfalls of life in a big city, warning her to be wary of them. She made Sissie promise to send for Noelle as soon as she could because she knew that Noelle would be a steadying influence in Sissie's life. She also thought that it would be an opportunity for Noelle to see the rest of the country and eventually, perhaps, some other part of the world.

Rena, with her computer experience, applied for the job of publicist at the resort. Noelle, who had a natural talent for baking, was offered an opportunity to train with a chef who was being brought in from overseas.

Just about everyone in town – and some of them had never worked before – were given the opportunity of employment.

The cloud of despair that had hovered over the small town and its inhabitants for so long finally lifted. The future looked hopeful.